A KNOT OF SPARROWS

A murder mystery set in the heart of the valleys

CHERYL REES-PRICE

THE BOOK FOLKS

Published by The Book Folks

London, 2021

ISBN 978-1-913516-59-8

www.thebookfolks.com

A Knot of Sparrows is the fourth title in a series of murder mysteries. Details about the other books can be found at the back of this one.

Chapter One

He stood behind the wall of the community centre car park, his eyes fixed to the door of the shop opposite. It was nearly time, any minute she would come out. He'd rehearsed this moment, timed it down to the last second, but this time it was different. This time he would carry out his plan. It would no longer be his imaginings; it would be reality. Every nerve ending tingled, making it difficult to stay still.

A young couple moved along the pavement. He stepped back under the cloak of darkness, he couldn't let himself be seen. Not that people took much notice of him. Most of the time he felt invisible. The couple entered the shop door and the tinkling bell echoed around the deserted car park. He checked the time again. She would be delayed now. How long would it take her to serve the last customers? The first niggles of doubt crept through his mind. Maybe this was a sign that he shouldn't go through with it. Up to now it had been all fantasy, he could walk away, and no one would know what he had been planning. But why should he? He wanted to see the fear in her eyes, the humiliation. She deserved it. These thoughts brought a tightness to his groin and quickened his breath.

He watched the couple leave the shop and a moment later she stepped outside, turning to wave before the door shut. She zipped up her coat and fanned out her long blonde hair. It was a gesture he had seen her do so many times. He hated the way she flicked her hair; it wasn't even real, dyed with extensions, false, like her nails and smile. Always flirting, always wanting to be the centre of attention. She was about to find out the consequences. He watched her plug in her earphones then walk away.

He waited until he saw the outline of the shopkeeper locking up for the night and when he was sure he couldn't be seen, he left the car park. He didn't have to hurry to catch up to her, he knew which way she would go. He pulled his hood up over his baseball cap, adjusted the rucksack on his back and followed, careful to keep a distance.

He heard the clink of the kissing gate as she entered the footpath. He smiled to himself, it was a sign that he was supposed to follow. This was the route she took after work unless someone met her. There was no one tonight. The path led away from the main road, cut across the village and came out near to the entrance of the farm where she lived. He knew exactly how long it took her to get home, knew the path so well he could walk it with his eyes shut. He was confident that no one else would be walking the path tonight.

He entered the gate and closed it gently. The lamp posts were sparse and most of the lights no longer worked. He moved silently in and out of the shadows as he went over his plan in his mind. He thought of the items in the rucksack, he was sure he had packed everything he needed. Gloves? He stopped for a moment. Yes, he had packed them.

She was halfway along the path now and through the second kissing gate where horses grazed in a field that led down to the river. He watched as she stepped off the path and perched on a large stone, resting her handbag on the floor. He crept closer as she bent over to retrieve a small tin from her bag. Opening the tin, she plucked out a joint, lit the end and inhaled. He'd seen her do this most nights. Sometimes she would walk with a group of friends and they would stop at the same place each time. The joint would be passed around and laughter would fill the silent fields. He would make sure there was no more laughter from her lips. Why should she be happy after what she did?

He checked his watch, there wasn't much time left, he had to do it now. He took off his rucksack and pulled out his gloves and put them on before taking out two lengths of twine. He'd already tied the ends to make a slip knot. He placed them in his back pocket. Next he took out a mask, it had been easy to get one as the shops had a variety ready for Halloween. He placed the mask over his face before taking out a gag he'd made from an old sheet and putting it in his other pocket. He was ready.

Sweat gathered under the plastic mask as he approached. She still had her earphones in so would have no warning of what was coming. He was so close now he could smell the marijuana as she blew out a plume of smoke into the night air. This was his last chance to turn back. The doubts started again. This time he was alone. It had been different last time, he'd just watched. She was the reason he'd gone along with it. He understood why the others had to suffer, known the pain they had caused but it wasn't the same, he hadn't needed to see them pay the price for their sins. What he had witnessed still made him feel sick. The visions came to him in the night, invading his dreams until he awoke screaming. If he didn't go through with this it would be for nothing.

He looked at her sitting there, carefree, and thought of what she had done, how many people she had hurt. He felt the anger bubbling in his chest. The sight of her brought it all back. He launched himself at her, knocking her off the stone.

She yelped as she hit the ground and struggled to throw him off. She was stronger than he thought she would be. He fought to turn her onto her stomach. She lashed out and her screams seemed to magnify around them. Her hands scrabbled with his mask and as he fought to keep them away his sleeve rose, and he felt her nails dig into his flesh. He drew back his fist and punched her hard in the face. He felt the pain from the impact travel from his knuckles through the back of his hand to his wrist. She was momentarily stunned so he took advantage and rolled her over before securing her hands and legs with the twine. He turned her onto her back and stuffed the rag in her mouth and secured it with a strip of cloth. He was breathing hard now as he looked down at her and felt satisfaction seeing the terror in her eyes.

He stood for a moment to catch his breath and to enjoy the power he had over her. Then he dragged her back to the path and into the overgrowth. In all his excitement he didn't notice that he was being watched.

Chapter Two

Detective Inspector Winter Meadows stood looking over the outlines of the yurts and caravans that dotted the fields in Peace Valley. Cold air snaked around his body and the dying embers of the bonfire gave off a weak glow. The smell of charred wood lingered on the air and his clothes. He inhaled deeply, the smell reminding him of his childhood and the times he had sat around the fire listening to the singing and laughing of the grown-ups. In his hands he cradled a mug of ginger tea, he blew on the surface before taking a sip. He felt the hot liquid run down his throat and bring warmth to his chest.

'You're off then?'

Meadows turned and saw the commune elder, Jerome, standing behind him. 'Yeah, I thought I'd make an early start. I'll need to go home and scrub up. Can't go to work smelling of bonfire and weed and looking like this.' He rubbed his hand over his beard.

'I don't know,' Jerome said. 'I think it suits you, but I expect clean shaven with a shirt and tie is your armour. Hides your past.'

'I'm not ashamed of where I come from; well, maybe I was as a teenager. Even then I would have been happier staying here than being forced to live another life. Anyway, it was what was best at the time and I guess my life would have been different now.'

'You are what you were meant to be,' Jerome said. 'It's been good to see you. I hope it helped.' Jerome patted him on the shoulder.

'I'm not sure it has, but it's been good to have a break and think things over.'

'It wasn't your fault. You need to let it go.'

'I know, but I could have done things differently and that little girl could still be alive.' Meadows sighed.

'You would have risked your career. You know we are all very proud of you. You're out there making a difference.'

'It doesn't feel like that sometimes. Ryan Phillips walked away. We all know that he was responsible for Ella's death.'

'You know as well as I do that karma has a way of righting the world. If not in this life, then the next. You need to be at peace with yourself.'

'Yeah, I know, and the break has done me good.' Meadows looked at the smoke curling out of a nearby yurt.

'You could stay. At least until the end of the week.'

'No, I best get back.' Meadows drank down the remainder of his tea. 'I left Blackwell in charge.'

'From what you've told me about him, he'll be enjoying himself.'

'That's what I'm afraid of. The team won't be happy.' Meadows laughed.

'I'll let you go.' Jerome held out a small wooden box. 'Something to keep you going.'

'Thank you.' Meadows pocketed the box. 'It's been great to see you. I'll be back up in a few weeks to pick up Mum. Coming here has been a tonic for her. If it weren't for her arthritis I'm sure she would move back permanently.'

'It was her home for so long I expect she misses the life we have here. Don't worry, we'll take good care of her. See you then.' Jerome gave Meadows another pat on the shoulder and walked back to his caravan.

* * *

After a shower and shave, and with the box Jerome had given him safely hidden in his cottage, Meadows drove to Bryn Mawr police station. He was pleased to see only a few cars were parked in the car park as he wanted some time to catch up before the team came in. He felt a flutter in his stomach as he pushed open the door. It was always the same when he had been away from work, he never knew what he would face when he returned. For the past three weeks DS Stefan Blackwell had taken on the responsibility, made the crucial decisions, and probably felt the elation of solving a case or the anguish when things went wrong. Every single case Meadows had worked on had left a mark in some way. He couldn't help the compassion he felt for those who found themselves the victim of a crime. Sometimes that compassion stretched to those who had been driven, fuelled by grief and anger, to commit the crime. Jerome was right, he thought, what he did made a difference to people's lives.

'Good to see you back,' Sergeant Dyfan Folland said as the door closed behind Meadows. 'Edris will be pleased. He's been complaining about Blackwell since you left.'

'Can't leave those two alone for five minutes without a chaperone.' Meadows laughed as he leaned against the desk. 'Did I miss much?'

'Not really. A call came in this morning, missing teenage girl from Gaer Fawr, she didn't come home last night. We'll probably find her with some boy.'

'Let's hope so.'

'And…' Folland shuffled some papers on the desk.

'Why do I get the feeling I'm not going to like this?' Meadows asked.

'Fire in Bryn Coed two nights ago. Jean Phillips' house.'

'Was Ryan Phillips there?'

'Yeah, he and his mother died. Neighbours managed to get out.'

Meadows felt the familiar ache in his chest that came when he thought of the case and the little girl who would never grow up. He thought of the conversation he had had with Jerome only hours earlier. Karma? He was fairly certain that Ryan had been there when Ella Beynon died, and that his mother had lied for him.

'Deliberate?' Meadows asked.

'Looks like it,' Dyfan said.

Revenge, probably one of Ella's family, Meadows thought. 'I heard there had been some trouble there.'

'Yeah, graffiti on the walls, threatening notes put through the door. It would have been better if they'd left the area.'

'Easier said. I doubt they had the means to leave. I better get upstairs before the others come in. See you later.'

Meadows made himself a cup of tea and carried it through to the office where he stood looking at the incident board. There were pictures of the house taken from different angles. The front windows had been blown out and smoke had blackened the paint. He could just make out some of the words that had been painted on the house. 'Child Killer' and 'Murderer' were among them. There were pictures of Jean and Ryan Phillips, and on the opposite side a picture of Ella Beynon. The smiling child brought a wave of sadness over him. Ryan had been Ella's mother's boyfriend. Social services had an order against him having contact with Ella. Whilst there had been no proof of his involvement in her death, it hadn't stopped the judgement within the small community.

'Yay, you're back. I was worried you would decide to stay.'

Meadows turned and saw DC Tristan Edris walking towards him with a smile on his face. The young officer had sandy blond hair, mischievous blue eyes, and a quirky sense of humour.

'Another day of Blackwell, and I would have stuck my head in the oven,' Edris said.

'He's not that bad,' Meadows said with a laugh.

'He's had me doing all the shit jobs. I've been stuck in the office for two weeks. He treats me like his PA.'

'Bitching already?' DS Paskin entered the office, followed by DC Valentine. Paskin, a petite brunette, had a flare of finding information on suspects. 'Give the man a chance to finish his cup of tea.' Paskin took a seat at her desk.

'Good holiday?' Valentine asked. She smiled, showing a set of perfect white teeth. She was the newest to the team and was upbeat and full of energy.

'Yes, thank you.' Meadows felt his mood lift as the usual office banter surrounded him.

Blackwell was the last to enter. Built like a bulldog, he rarely smiled and had a quick temper. 'You've seen that slimy little bastard copped it then.' Blackwell nodded at the incident board.

'Yes and that his mother also died in the fire,' Meadows said. He noticed that Valentine and Edris had scooted to their desks.

'Everyone knows that she lied to give her son an alibi. He supplied the drugs left lying around for the child to take and I'm betting he was there when Ella died. Just because the CPS had insufficient evidence to tie him to Ella's death doesn't mean that he's not responsible, and his mother was as guilty as him,' Blackwell said.

'It still doesn't make what happened to them right,' Meadows said. 'They deserve the same level of investigation as anyone else.'

'I'm giving it my full attention,' Blackwell snapped. 'I'll catch the person responsible and shake their hand before I arrest them. Unless you're planning on taking over.'

'Wouldn't dream of it,' Meadows said with a smile. 'Have you got any suspects?'

'Loads. But no one is talking. All got alibis. No one saw or heard anything,' Blackwell said. 'If they did, they are not going to tell us.'

'Okay, I'll leave you to it. By the way, did the missing doctor turn up?'

'No, why?'

'Folland says there's a report of a teenage girl that didn't come home last night; Gaer Fawr, same as the doctor.'

'She probably stayed out with her boyfriend. As for the doctor, he's run off with his bit on the side. He sent a text to his wife,' Blackwell said.

'I still think it's odd.' Edris stood up. 'He left with no cover for the surgery.'

Blackwell whipped his head around and glared at Edris. 'Are you questioning my judgement?'

Sergeant Folland entered the office with a grim expression on his face before Edris had a chance to answer.

'A body has been found in Gaer Fawr, sounds like it's the missing teenage girl,' Folland said. 'Hanes called it in, he says he'll meet you in the community centre car park.'

'Okay, thanks Folland. Edris, get your coat.' Meadows turned to Blackwell. 'Unless you need him.'

Blackwell looked from Meadows to Edris, seemingly conflicted. Then he huffed. 'He's all yours.'

Chapter Three

Meadows sat in the passenger seat and watched the shoppers milling around Bryn Mawr town centre as Edris drove. After staying in the commune for three weeks the place seemed alien to him, too many people. It was only a small market town with charity and bargain shops, but the scurrying from shop to shop and the cars driving through the centre felt fast-paced in comparison to the calm existence of what he left behind that morning. He wondered now how he had survived London for over ten years.

Edris' chatter brought Meadows out of his thoughts.

'For a moment I thought Blackwell was going to make me stay in the office and do some menial task,' Edris said.

'Nah, he's too clever for that. If he insisted you stay he would be admitting to needing help. Not his style. Besides I'm confident he can manage the investigation. He may be a miserable sod but he's a good detective. You need to cut him some slack. Something in his life is making him unhappy and you have a habit of rubbing him up the wrong way.'

'No, I don't. I only have to breathe to wind him up,' Edris said with a laugh. 'Seriously though, he could have let me look a bit more into the doctor's disappearance.'

'What's troubling you about the doctor? If he sent a text to his wife then I guess Blackwell's right, there's not much we can do. We can't drag him back to his wife.'

'It's not that, it's the way he up and left.'

'He went out on a call and didn't come back that night. I remember, his wife reported him missing the morning I left for my holiday.'

'Yes, but he didn't turn up to see the patient, no cover for his morning surgery and he didn't take anything with him. There was a log of the call late that evening, but the patient, Iris Hawkins, claims she didn't call the doctor out.'

'If he was having an affair then possibly the woman made the call to get the doctor out of the house.'

'Yeah, I guess, but I don't see the point of that. He could have gone at any time. He didn't need the excuse of visiting a patient.'

'Okay, I'll tell you what, if we have some quiet time you can take a look. Follow it up with his wife, see if she's heard anything since the text message, but don't mention it to Blackwell until you have good reason to believe that the doctor didn't leave of his own accord.'

'Thanks.' Edris smiled.

Meadows looked out of the window as they drove past fields and in and out of villages. The Black Mountain range loomed before them as they entered the picturesque village of Gaer Fawr over a humpback bridge. A sign announced it as the winner of the Welsh village of the year award.

'I'm guessing they won't get nominated for that again,' Edris said. 'It'll be the village where people go missing or get murdered.'

'We don't know that it's murder yet,' Meadows said. 'Could be an accidental death.' His gaze fell on a Norman church with a square tower which sat serenely in the centre of the village. Next to the church a yew tree stood proud, its great branches stretching over the headstones that lay beneath.

'Pretty place,' Meadows said.

'If you like that sort of thing. You could die of boredom here. They probably get up to all sorts of things to keep entertained. Did you know half the married couples in Ynys Melyn are swingers? I bet this place could outdo them,' Edris said.

Meadows laughed. 'Swingers? I didn't think that was a thing anymore. Well, if that's all they get up to then good luck to them.'

Edris pulled into the community centre car park where PC Matt Hanes stood waiting.

'Morning, Hanes,' Meadows said as he got out of the car. 'What have you got for us?'

'Body of a teenage girl. I'm fairly certain it's seventeen-year-old Stacey Evans. She was reported missing this morning by her mother. She said she didn't come home last night. Description matches and her parents, Anthony and Cloe, showed me a photo when I responded to the call. Her bag and mobile phone were found close by.'

'Suspicious?' Edris asked.

'Yes,' Hanes said. 'Looks like she was attacked.'

'Okay you better show us,' Meadows said.

'She was working at the shop until half past eight last night.' Hanes pointed to the convenience store across the road. 'It was a regular part-time job.'

The shop window was decorated with garlands of autumn leaves and three carved pumpkins with twinkling eyes. They walked along the pavement then turned off the main road to where an officer stood guarding the gate. Hanes gave the officer a nod and then stepped through the gate and onto a footpath.

'Where does this lead?' Meadows asked.

'It runs for about half a mile then comes back out onto the main road where you can cross over and pick up the footpath that leads to the Iron Age hill fort. The entrance is a few hundred metres from Penlan farm where Stacey lives. We've got both entrances to this path covered.'

'Good,' Meadows said. 'Who found her?'

'That was me,' Hanes said. 'We did all the usual checks – friends, family, anywhere she may have stayed overnight. One of her friends mentioned that she often used the footpath, so I came down to take a look.'

'Why would she come down here alone at night?' Edris asked.

'If she was alone. She could have met up with someone after work or' – Meadows looked around – 'there are very few lights, easy enough for someone to hide in the shadows, but they would need to know that she took this route.'

They reached the second kissing gate and took it in turns to step through. To the right of the path was an open field, on the left gorse bushes and trees. Up ahead, both sides of the path had been cordoned off and SOCO could be seen scouring the ground. As they approached, Hanes pointed to the markers on the ground.

'This is where I found her bag and mobile phone.'

Meadows looked at the area. A large flat-sided rock sat among the markers. The grass around was flattened and clear drag marks could be seen leading back to the path.

'Her earphones were found a few metres away from the phone.'

'Looks like she was sat there with someone,' Edris commented.

'Could have been,' Meadows agreed.

They followed the path laid out by SOCO, through the gorse and trees to a small clearing. Stacey Evans lay on a bed of rotting leaves and mud. She was face down with her blonde hair in a wild tangle. At the nape of her neck a knot secured a gag. Her hands were bound behind her back and she was naked from the waist down. Dirt and scratches covered her lower half, and her legs were tied together at the ankles.

'Her shoes and clothes were found here.' Hanes pointed to the markers on the ground.

Meadows heard the catch in Hanes' voice. 'Thank you, why don't you go off and take a break. I'm sure you could do with a cuppa.'

'Thanks, sir.' Hanes turned away.

Meadows turned his attention back to the girl. Beside her Daisy Moore, the pathologist, was taking her body temperature. Even in this grim situation Meadows felt a tingle at the sight of her.

'Hi.' Daisy gave him a smile.

Meadows returned the smile. 'What can you tell me?'

'Not a lot, I've only just got here myself. From the body temperature and lividity I would say she's been dead for about twelve to thirteen hours.'

'So between nine and ten last night?' Meadows asked.

'Yes, that's my best guess for now.'

Meadows watched as Daisy carefully examined the body. She moved the girl's hair and beckoned Meadows to come closer.

'See the marks here on her neck?'

Meadows crouched down. 'Strangulation?'

'Looks like it, or considerable pressure was put on her neck. Some sort of cloth has also been pushed in her mouth.' Daisy pointed. 'She could have choked. I won't know for sure until I carry out the post-mortem.'

Meadows could see the cloth bulging out of the gag and Stacey's cheeks were puffed out. He could imagine the girl's panic as her breathing and movement was restricted. 'Poor kid.' He stood up. 'Looks like she was sexually assaulted before she was killed.'

'I'll get some photos taken then move her if that's okay with you,' Daisy said.

'That's fine.' He turned to Edris. 'I think it's best we go and see the parents. I don't want them to hear we've found a body through village gossip. We won't be able to move her without being seen.'

They returned to the car park and drove to the outskirts of the village where Stacey's parents' farm could be seen from the main road. Edris turned the car up the track and parked in the yard to the rear of the house. A sheepdog bounded up to them as they got out of the car and several chickens scattered with indignant squawks. Meadows bent down and patted the dog before stepping through the gate that led to the front of the house. A lawn with neat borders was enclosed by a wall, and a wrought-iron table and chair set sat on a slate patio. Meadows knocked the door and stood back.

A woman answered the door. She was dressed in jeans and a woollen jumper with her auburn hair pulled back into a ponytail.

'Mrs Cloe Evans?' Meadows asked.

'Yes.'

'I'm Detective Inspector Meadows and this is Detective Constable Edris.' He showed his ID.

'Have you found her?' Cloe Evans peered around Meadows as if expecting her daughter to be hidden behind. 'I'll ground her until Christmas for going off for the night and not telling us.'

'Shall we go inside,' Meadows suggested. He could feel his stomach twisting with anxiety. He was about to pierce this woman and her family's hearts and no words would be able to soften the blow.

She turned and led them to the kitchen at the back of the house. There a man stood next to an Aga cooker. He was dressed in jeans and wore a green wax jacket with only socks on his feet. He looked like he had just come inside the house. At the kitchen table a girl sat, Meadows guessed her to be about fourteen years old. She had a phone in her hand but looked up as they entered the room.

'Anthony Evans?' Meadows asked.

Anthony nodded.

'The police, love,' Cloe said.

'Perhaps it would be better if you sat down,' Meadows said.

'Oh God, no.' Cloe sank to the nearest chair.

'What is it?' Anthony asked. 'Just tell us.'

'I'm very sorry to have to tell you that we found the body of a teenage girl on the public footpath this morning. We believe that it's Stacey.'

'What do you mean, found?' Anthony's voice rose. 'You mean… you mean dead?'

'I'm afraid so.'

A howl erupted from Cloe that seemed to fill the kitchen and echo around the house. The raw sound of a mother whose child has been cruelly snatched away.

Anthony stepped forward and put his hand on his wife's shoulder. 'It can't be Stacey; she's probably stayed overnight with a friend and knows she's in trouble so is hiding out,' Anthony said. He appeared to be trying to convince himself.

Meadows noticed that the girl had not said a word. She sat wide-eyed, her phone forgotten.

'We found Stacey's handbag and mobile phone. At this stage we are fairly certain that it's her. I'm so sorry.'

'No.' Anthony shook his head and sank down on his knees wrapping his arms around Cloe.

'Perhaps you can help Edris make a cup of tea for your Mum and Dad,' Meadows said to the girl.

The girl nodded and stood, moving silently around the kitchen collecting mugs.

Meadows took a seat and waited until the tea was placed on the table and Anthony and Cloe had composed themselves.

'I appreciate how difficult this is for you all, but I'm going to have to ask you a few questions,' Meadows said. 'I'll try and keep it brief.'

'Oh, Becca, love,' Cloe held her hand out to her daughter. 'Come here.'

Becca took a seat next to her mother and held her hand.

'What happened?' Anthony asked. 'Was it an accident?'

'All I can tell you at the moment is that we're treating Stacey's death as suspicious.'

Anthony put his fist to his mouth to try and stifle a sob.

Edris took a seat next to Meadows and took out his notebook.

'When was the last time you saw Stacey?' Meadows asked.

'After school yesterday.' Cloe picked up a mug of tea, the liquid spilt over the rim as her hand shook. 'She got home at half past three, had something to eat then went out again to work. She works in the shop every Tuesday and Thursday.'

'You didn't report her missing until this morning. Was it usual for Stacey to stay out overnight?'

'No, she's not that type of girl,' Cloe said.

'She sometimes stays over at one of her friends' houses but usually only on a weekend unless one of them has a birthday,' Becca said.

'Can you tell us the name of her friends?' Edris asked.

'Shannon Dugan and Alisha Morgan.'

'Thank you.' Edris wrote down the names.

'What time did you expect Stacey home last night?' Meadows asked.

'She usually gets home about nine. She's always quiet when she comes in as we're in bed.'

'It's a working farm, we're up by four each morning,' Anthony added.

'Are you usually up when your sister comes home, Becca?' Meadows asked.

'I stay in my room out of her way,' Becca said.

'You didn't get on with your sister?'

'Of course she did,' Cloe said. 'They argue sometimes, like all sisters.'

'Did Stacey have a boyfriend?'

'No,' Cloe said.

'I'm going out for some fresh air.' Becca stood up.

Cloe tried to grab her hand, but she moved away.

'Leave her go,' Anthony said.

Meadows watched Becca leave then turned his attention back to Anthony and Cloe. 'How did Stacey seem recently, any problems?'

'No, she was studying for her A-levels and we've been visiting universities. She was really looking forward to going.' Cloe put her hand to her chest as tears spilt from her eyes.

'So nothing out of the ordinary? Did she mention arguing with anyone, or someone bothering her?'

'No, nothing like that,' Anthony said.

'Okay, what about the farm? Have you noticed anyone hanging around, taking an interest?'

'No.'

'Do you have anyone come to help out?'

'Yes, but the same people have worked here for years, seen the girls grow up,' Anthony said.

'Can you think of anyone who would want to harm Stacey or your family?'

'No, I've lived here all my life,' Anthony said. 'This was my parents' farm. I know most of the people that live in the village. Yes, there are a couple of odd characters but no one that would...' Anthony shook his head. 'No, there's no one.'

'What do you mean by odd characters?' Edris asked.

'There's Wayne Weed.'

'I take it "weed" isn't his surname,' Edris said.

'No, it's Lyle. He reckons he was abducted by aliens. I think he probably smokes a bit too much. He just talks a bit of nonsense and spends his evening watching the sky with a telescope. He lives on Rhos farm with his parents. Then there's Bible Bill.'

'Bible Bill?' Edris asked.

'William James. He lives on the farm next door.' Anthony pointed to his left. 'It's a bit run down. He doesn't work the land. Just keeps a few chickens. He sold me the top field a few years ago. He's not quite right, but there's no harm in him.'

'You don't know that,' Cloe said. 'What if he—'

'When you say he's not right, what do you mean?' Meadows asked.

'He's always talking about conspiracy theories and quoting the Bible. He mostly keeps to himself. All the kids around here tease him a bit, call him names, that sort of thing. You know what kids are like. They just want to get a rise out of him.'

'Is he violent?' Edris asked.

'No, he shouts at the kids and they run away laughing. I really don't think he would hurt anyone.'

'Anyone else?'

'No,' Anthony said.

'It would be really helpful if we could take a look at Stacey's room,' Meadows said.

Cloe shook her head. 'She wouldn't like you going in there. She always cleaned her own room, so I didn't have to go in. She liked her private space as all teenagers do. I don't want you going through her things.'

'We will treat all of Stacey's things with respect,' Meadows said as he stood. 'I do understand your concerns, but it is necessary. It would really help us.'

'Let them do their job,' Anthony said. 'What does it matter now?'

Cloe nodded but remained seated.

'Thank you,' Edris said as he closed his notebook and stood.

'I'll show you,' Anthony said.

Meadows and Edris followed Anthony upstairs. It felt cold after the warmth of the kitchen. Stacey's room was the first door on the right and Anthony paused outside with his hand on the handle.

'Perhaps it would be better if we went in alone,' Meadows said. 'We won't take anything with us but it's likely an officer will come to remove Stacey's computer, if she has one, and anything that may be relevant.'

Anthony nodded and let his hand fall away from the handle. 'I'll go back to Cloe then.'

Meadows opened the door and stepped inside. The room was decorated in different shades of grey with purple curtains. A double bed was positioned with the headboard against the wall. The duvet lay crumpled at the bottom of the bed with her nightclothes. A faint smell of perfume lingered in the air. It felt as though Stacey had only just left the room.

Meadows pulled on latex gloves and opened the top drawer in the bedside cabinet. There were packets of condoms and a box of Azithromycin tablets. He picked them up and read the back. 'Treatment for chlamydia.' He handed the box to Edris.

'Dated last week. Looks like she did have a boyfriend.' Edris handed the tablets back.

'Maybe not a regular boyfriend.' Meadows replaced the tablets. 'Or she could have done, and he cheated on her or she cheated on him. One of them passed an STD to the other. That would cause an argument.'

'So she meets the boyfriend after work, they go down the footpath and she tells him to get himself checked and he loses it.'

'No, the bindings and gag means it was planned,' Meadows said as he moved to the desk.

'Yeah I guess, but the boyfriend could have planned it if he was that angry about her cheating, then again it's not a strong motive for killing her. More likely someone random?'

'I think someone who knew her and the area. You wouldn't just hide out on a public footpath and wait for an opportunity.' Meadows picked up a book and flicked through it.

'Maybe someone who was obsessed with her. What about those two odd characters that Anthony mentioned?'

'It's worth looking into, although just because they don't fit some people's norms doesn't make them a suspect. Let's see what we can find out about Stacey's life first. If one of them showed an interest in Stacey then I'm sure she would have mentioned it to her friends or the boyfriend.' Meadows put the books back on the desk. 'Nothing in these. Just notes from classes. We'll get the laptop looked at, maybe we'll find something there.' He opened the desk drawer and plucked out a bag of weed. 'No wonder she didn't want her mother cleaning her room.'

They checked the rest of the bedroom, but it didn't yield anything of interest, so they went back to the kitchen. Anthony and Cloe were sat at the kitchen table. Cloe had her arms around her body and silent tears ran down her face. Anthony sat staring into his mug of tea.

'We've finished upstairs for the moment,' Meadows said. 'A family liaison officer is on the way. Her name is Brianna. She will keep you updated and answer any questions you may have. In the meantime we will need to have a formal identification. We can do this by dental records or a photograph if—'

'No, I want to see her,' Anthony cut in.

'Brianna will make the arrangements. Once again, I'm very sorry for your loss.'

Outside in the yard they found Becca stood by the car.

'Is there something you wanted to talk to us about?' Edris asked.

'Stacey did have a boyfriend. Jack Hopkins.'

'Is Jack the same age as Stacey?' Meadows asked.

'A year older, he's in the upper sixth form. Mum and Dad didn't know about him. She never brought boyfriends home. They always went down the Cwm to drink and smoke.'

'The Cwm?' Edris asked.

'The footpath, that's what we call it.'

'So that's where Stacey and Jack met up?' Meadows asked.

'Yeah, but they split up.'

'Do you know why?'

'They argued about something. Jack was pissed off.'

Meadows had the feeling that Becca knew more about the argument, but he didn't want to push her.

'Thank you for telling us,' he said.

'She could be a real bitch sometimes, but—' Becca's voice broke.

'She was your sister,' Meadows said. 'Why don't you go back inside? You don't want to stay out here alone.'

Becca nodded and walked away.

'So the boyfriend was angry. No doubt about the STD,' Edris said.

'Or maybe she dumped him because he cheated and that's why he's pissed off. Let's wait for the formal identification then we'll go and have a chat with Jack.'

Chapter Four

Jack Hopkins was still dressed in his school uniform. His tie had been discarded and his shirt hung over his black trousers. Meadows could tell that he had been crying by his puffy eyes and blotchy face. He sat on the sofa next to his mother.

'I can't believe she's dead,' Jack said. 'People are saying she was murdered. It's all over Facebook. Becca put up a post.'

Meadows studied Jack as he talked. He was around five ten, slim built with brown hair cut in at the side and teased into a quiff on the top. Could he be strong enough to attack Stacey? Wrestle her to the ground? He glanced at Jack's hands and back to his face. No sign he's been in a struggle, but maybe she was taken by surprise, Meadows thought.

'When was the last time you saw Stacey?' Edris asked.

'On the school bus, yesterday.'

'Did you talk to her?'

'No, she was sat at the back with Shannon.'

'We understand that Stacey was your girlfriend,' Meadows said.

'Was, we split up a couple of weeks ago.'

'Why was that?'

'She was fucking someone else,' Jack said.

Meadows noticed that Jack's mother didn't flinch at his use of bad language. 'Who was the other guy?'

'Dunno,' Jack shrugged his shoulders.

'She had a bit of a reputation,' Jack's mother said.

'Did she tell you she was seeing someone else?' Meadows asked.

'No, I saw it on Facebook.'

'She posted pictures on Facebook?' Edris asked.

'No, there was a video of her and some guy down the Cwm.'

'Having sex?' Meadows asked.

'Yeah, but you couldn't see his face.'

'Who posted the video?' Meadows asked.

'Dunno, it was a fake account. Stacey reported it and it got taken down, but it got posted again. Everyone saw it.'

'Do you have any suspicions about who the other guy was or who posted the video?' Edris asked.

'No, she wouldn't say, and I don't really care. Probably someone on Tinder.'

'You must have been angry,' Meadows said.

'Yeah, I was.'

'You argued with Stacey?'

'Yeah, told her to fuck off. She wasn't even sorry.'

'I'm going to have to ask you where you were last night.'

'You don't think I had anything to do with it.' A look of horror crossed Jack's face. 'That was a couple of weeks ago. It's not like I was in love with her. I'm going out with Lauren now.'

'We still need to know.'

'I was here. Played a few games in my bedroom. My mates were online, you can ask them.'

'He didn't go out,' Jack's mother said.

'Okay, we may need to take your game console to check.'

'Fine,' Jack said.

'Can you think of anyone who would want to hurt Stacey?'

Jack shrugged his shoulders.

'Okay, we'll leave it there for now,' Meadows stood.

'If you do think of anything, let us know.' Edris closed his notebook and they left.

When they were back in the car, Edris said, 'What do you think?'

'The video was posted two weeks ago. I think if he was going to kill her in a jealous rage he would have done so sooner. We need to take a look at the video, see who she was with and find out who was lurking around filming.' Meadows looked at his watch. 'Let's go to the hospital and see if Daisy has anything from the post-mortem.'

* * *

The smell of formaldehyde tickled Meadows nostrils as they entered the mortuary. The smell always reminded him of biology lessons in school.

'I hope Daisy has finished,' Edris said. 'I don't want to go in there unless everything has been put away.'

'Pussy,' Meadows said with a laugh. 'Haven't you ever attended a post-mortem?'

'No, have you?'

'Yes, to be honest I don't blame you for not wanting to see one. Don't worry, we're only here for the results.' He pushed open the door and saw Daisy sitting by her desk.

'Hello, you two,' she said.

'Hi.' Meadows felt a warmth spread through his body. 'How are you?'

'I'm good, thanks.'

'Has your father recovered?' Meadows asked.

'He's on the mend. I think the shock of what happened with my sister was too much for him. He's home from hospital now, so I have a little more time to myself.'

'That's good to hear.' Meadows smiled.

'So you better hurry up and solve this case and take me on that date you promised.'

Meadows was thrilled that she was still interested. Between work and family commitments he thought he had lost his chance. 'I haven't forgotten.'

Edris cleared his throat. 'Right, so are you going to tell us what you've found?'

'I've only just finished. You'll have to wait for the official report.' Daisy stood.

'That's okay,' Meadows said. 'Anything you can tell us will be helpful.'

'I'll take you in and talk you through.' Daisy led them into the post-mortem room.

Meadows' attention was drawn to the gurney in the centre of the room where Stacey lay covered in a sheet up to her chest, with her arms resting at the sides. Her blonde hair was sleeked back, and her eyes were now closed. With the absence of make-up she looked small and childlike. Meadows felt a heavy weight in his stomach, a lead ball of pity and sorrow. He found it difficult to turn off his emotions; he sometimes wished he'd become desensitised to seeing violent death, but it was emotion and the cruelty of life that drove him to find the guilty and to somehow redress the balance.

Daisy moved to the edge of the gurney and lifted the sheet to reveal Stacey's legs. 'As you saw at the scene, she was bound tightly by twine. If you look at the marks and bruising, they indicate a downward pull. It's the same on her wrists. It appears that after her ankles and wrists were bound they were then secured together behind her back. From the wear on the twine I would say the longer end of the binding on the wrists was hooked under the one on her ankles and pulled tightly and knotted.'

'Anything special about the twine?' Edris asked.

'No, looks like standard twine used to bale hay. Easy to come by around here.'

'So it looks like she managed to loosen some of the binding,' Meadows said.

'Or it was removed. I'll come to that in a moment,' Daisy said. 'The marks and scratches on her legs are consistent with being dragged. There is bruising to her thighs and clear signs of sexual assault. Swabs have been taken but there was no seminal fluid, traces of lubricant were found indicating the use of a condom.' Daisy replaced the sheet and moved up the gurney. She gently picked up Stacey's hand.

'You can see that two of her fingernails are broken.'

'So it looks like she put up a fight, maybe scratched her attacker,' Meadows said.

'Yes, scrapings have been taken from under her fingernails.' Daisy returned Stacey's hand to the resting position. 'When we removed the gag we found a ball of material stuffed inside her mouth. Both look like they've been torn from a standard bed sheet. Cause of death: asphyxiation, manual strangulation. See the marks on her neck?' Daisy pointed to them. 'She would have been facing her attacker.'

'So she was killed lying on her back then turned over?' Meadows asked.

'Yes.'

'So, someone killed her then loosened the bindings and positioned her on her stomach,' Edris commented.

'Maybe the killer was ashamed of what he had done,' Meadows said. 'Didn't want to look at her face after he had killed her.'

'I've left the most puzzling aspect until last,' Daisy said. She pulled down the sheet to reveal a Y incision, made during the autopsy, that had been sewn, and the letters and numbers REV17 written in black on her stomach.

'Whoa, what's that about?' Edris asked.

'I don't know,' Daisy said. 'It's written in permanent marker. I took pictures before the post-mortem.'

The writing looked too neat to have been done when Stacey had been alive and probably struggling, Meadows thought. It now appeared ominous under the harsh lights. Black against pale skin. A coldness crept over him, the killer was making a statement.

Chapter Five

He stood on the humpback bridge watching the steady flow of the river. Occasionally twigs and leaves brought down by the winds swirled and danced in the water before disappearing. Sometimes young children would stand on the bridge, throw in sticks, and run to the other side to watch them emerge. One child would always be delighted that their stick won the race. There was no one on the bridge today.

He found the river mesmerising, it put him in a trance and chased away the demons. The cool air on his face eased his headache and he felt peaceful. He had spent the whole day in bed yesterday and most of this morning. He had to force himself to get up. The business with Stacey had left him both emotionally and physically drained. It hadn't been so hard with Ryan and Jean Phillips. One flick of the lighter was all it took. He would have liked to have stayed and watched until the house was raised to the ground but there were innocent people next door. He'd made sure he'd alerted them in time.

He tore his eyes away from the river and made his way into the village. There was still a police presence. They had been knocking on doors asking questions, all along the main road. He was certain no one saw anything. He'd been so careful, had stayed hidden in the shadows of darkness. Still, the police would be talking to everyone and it was only a matter of time before they came to him. It was this thought that was making him feel so ill. Lies didn't come easily.

All he wanted to do was walk down the Cwm and up to the cairns by the old fort on the mountain side, away from the village and people, but the Cwm was still cordoned off. He imagined the police picking at the ground looking for any clues. Nothing to find, he thought.

He was approaching the village shop where a group was stood outside gossiping. A young mother with a child wrapped up in a pram, an old man and two middle-aged women. They're like a bunch of vipers with their fork tongues fizzling behind their teeth, he thought. He forced a smile as he passed them. He was lucky none of them wanted to talk to him today. He walked past the entrance to the Cwm where a policeman stood. A few cars passed him as he continued his walk but other than that, it was quiet.

Another policeman was stood at the exit of the Cwm talking to a man walking his dog. I wonder if they've seen the writing on Stacey yet, he thought. He guessed they would have by now, but would they know the meaning? Probably not and maybe that was a good thing. Then again, the point was to let everyone know what she was.

He had been so deep in thought that he walked past the entrance to the mountain footpath and found himself at the bottom of the track leading to the Evanses' farm. Now he would have to call in to see Stacey's mother. It would look odd if he didn't. You never knew who could be watching. He walked up the track, through the gate and knocked the door. His stomach felt like it was full of maggots, squirming and moving upwards filling his chest and throat.

Cloe Evans opened the door; she looked broken, the pain circling her eyes. He guessed she hadn't slept, probably hadn't eaten.

'Come in,' she said.

He didn't want to go inside. 'I only called around to say...' What did he want to say? His mind went blank. 'I'm so very sorry.'

'Please come in. It helps to have someone to talk to, a distraction.'

He followed Cloe into the kitchen. Covered plates lined the worktops and bouquets of flowers were heaped by the sink. A woman stood trimming flower stems and arranging them into a vase.

Cloe introduced him to the policewoman – the family liaison officer who, she said, had been so helpful. He knew why she was there. She would be watching the family and anyone who visited the house.

'Everyone has been so kind,' Cloe said. 'Bringing food and flowers.'

He let her talk. It just spilt out of her mouth. All he had to do was nod his head, drink tea, and eat a slice of cake. He felt sorry for her, she thought her daughter was a sweet girl, an angel she called her. He finished his tea and stood up to leave. He'd done it, managed to keep it together. Now as long as the doctor stayed hidden there would be no problems.

Chapter Six

Meadows checked the evidence log then gathered the team around the incident board which now displayed a picture of Stacey and the crime scene.

'Are you joining us, Blackwell?' Meadows called across the office.

Blackwell huffed and came to join the team, seating himself next to Valentine and leaning back.

'How is it going with the arson case?' Meadows asked.

'Waiting on forensics but I don't think they'll get much. The house is a shell. Accelerant was poured in through the front door letter box and a rag lit. The glass was already broken in the back door. Someone had thrown a brick through it the night before. I'm guessing to make it easier to pour the accelerant through. Whoever started the fire meant for both Ryan and Jean to die. Both exits were blocked and the fire spread rapidly.'

'Got any suspects?' Paskin asked.

Blackwell shrugged his shoulders. 'It's more a case of who wouldn't have done it. I've interviewed the neighbours, they were pretty shaken. All four had to be hospitalised with smoke inhalation. They were lucky to get out alive. The father says they were woken by someone hammering the door but there was no one there when he got up. He saw the fire and called for help. He then went in to get the family out by which time the fire was pouring smoke into the house.'

'Sounds like the arsonist didn't want the death of the neighbours on their hands, so probably knew them,' Meadows said.

'Yeah, well if they had any suspicions of who started the fire they are not saying. With all the graffiti on the wall you'd think that they would have seen something over the last few weeks,' Blackwell said.

'It was the same with everyone I spoke to,' Valentine said. 'No one in the area seemed particularly bothered by the death of Ryan and Jean.'

'Unless we get some physical evidence or a witness, it's going to be difficult to find the arsonist. Meanwhile it's just a case of speaking to everyone that had it in for Ryan and checking out alibis,' Blackwell said.

'Okay, keep DCI Lester updated.'

Blackwell nodded.

Meadows turned to the incident board. 'Stacey Evans, seventeen years old, found on the footpath in Gaer Fawr. She'd been sexually assaulted and strangled. She left work at the local shop at eight thirty on Tuesday evening and was killed sometime between nine and ten o'clock. If you look at the picture here' – Meadows pointed to the board – 'you'll see that the attacker drew the letters and numbers REV17 across Stacey's stomach. Edris?'

'Yeah, I've run a search of the combination but haven't come up with much. An operating manual for a thermostat, recycling data reference and a nursery provider.'

'Really useful,' Blackwell said.

'You got any better ideas?' Edris asked.

'Maybe it's some sort of social media reference,' Paskin said.

'Could be,' Meadows agreed. 'It is worth looking into.'

'Or it could be initials, with the 17 referring to Stacey's age,' Valentine suggested.

'Can't see many people whose surname starts with a V,' Blackwell said.

'Reena Valentine,' Edris said. 'Have you got a middle name Valentine?'

'Elizabeth.'

They all turned to look at Valentine.

'Only joking. It's Amita.' She smiled.

'I can't see the killer being dumb enough to use his initials,' Blackwell said.

'I agree,' Meadows said. 'As I doubt that Stacey's killing was random, it has to be someone who knows the area well and the footpath. They would also know that Stacey took that route.'

'What about the missing doctor from Gaer Fawr?' Edris asked.

'Not this again,' Blackwell said.

'Well, it could be him: he disappears, then kills Stacey and is hiding out.'

'And the motive?' Blackwell asked.

'Dunno, but it's just a thought.'

'Okay, we're diverging too much,' Meadows said. 'Items found at the scene: Stacey's handbag, phone, and clothing. Several butt ends from joints. We found a bag of weed in Stacey's bedroom; it's likely that she used that area of the footpath so she wouldn't be caught smoking. Fibres and hair were found on the body and scrapings taken from under her nails. There is also the video posted online of Stacey having sex with some unknown off the footpath, the locals refer to it as the Cwm.' He moved to his desk and the team followed and gathered around the computer. 'Tech didn't have too much trouble getting the video, but it will take longer to trace who posted it.' He clicked the icon and a film started playing.

The footage shook at first, with the subject going in and out of focus. It became steady as the person behind the camera stopped moving. Two people could be seen through the leafy frame. Stacey and a man with his back to the camera wearing joggers and a black hoodie. Stacey stood facing him, flicking her hair over her shoulder, and laughing. She then said something to the man, but the sound quality was too poor to make out any words. The man then pulled her towards his body, and they kissed. Stacey's fingers snaked around the man's neck and into his hair. They sank to the floor and the camera angle changed as though whoever was behind the camera had been crouching and now stood. The man fumbled with his clothes until he managed to pull down his joggers.

'Are we supposed to identify him from his arse?' Edris asked.

'That's all we've got,' Meadows said as he paused the film. 'I think you all get the idea. The man's face is obscured the whole time.'

'It looks like an older man,' Valentine said. 'Not someone her own age.'

'I thought so too,' Meadows said. 'So our killer could be the one behind the camera, or the man in the video who doesn't want to be found out. We talked to Stacey's ex-boyfriend, Jack. He claims that she wouldn't tell him who the other man was. The video was posted several times. It seems our camera man wanted to humiliate Stacey but wasn't interested in the other party.'

They moved away from the desk and back to the incident board.

'Valentine, I'd like you to talk to the owner of the shop where Stacey worked. See if there were any problems over the past few weeks. Look at the CCTV footage to see if anyone came into the shop that Stacey was overly friendly with and who else was in the shop the evening she was killed.'

'Paskin, could you check out all the social media. Especially look for any reference to the video.'

'Blackwell, I'll leave you to continue the investigation into the arson attack. Uniform are conducting house-to-house enquires. Edris and I will go to the school and talk to her friends. That's all for now, thank you.'

* * *

Tregib School was situated seven miles from Gaer Fawr and catered for children aged between eleven and eighteen. The building was single storey, tucked away from the main road and surrounded by woodland. Meadows had rung the school before they left so a caretaker was waiting at the gates and waved them through. They were shown to Mrs Hughes' office, headmistress of the school.

'Thank you for seeing us,' Meadows said.

'I'm happy to help in any way I can. We've all been shocked and deeply saddened by the news of Stacey's death. Please, take a seat.' Mrs Hughes sat down behind a desk. She was a tall slim woman with sharp features and a pleasant smile. 'We're organising counselling for any of the pupils that knew Stacey well. We're also talking to the whole school about being extra vigilant. Do you think there is a risk of this happening again?'

'We are treating it as an isolated incident at the moment, but our advice would be to avoid secluded areas for the time being.' Meadows sat and Edris pulled a chair closer to the desk and took out his notebook. 'I don't think you should be overly concerned for the safety of the pupils,' Meadows added.

'That's good to hear. Of course we have very good security at the school.'

'What can you tell us about Stacey?' Meadows asked.

'She was a lovely girl, a good student and popular among her peers.'

'Had there been any problems recently? A drop in grades? Anything that would be cause for concern?'

'No, not recently.' Mrs Hughes straightened her shoulders and adjusted her cardigan. 'About a year ago there was an allegation of bullying.'

'Did Stacey make the allegation?'

'No, the complaint was made against her and a couple of the other girls.'

'Would that be Alisha Morgan and Shannon Dugan?' Edris asked.

Mrs Hughes raised her eyebrows. 'Yes, how did you know?'

'Their names came up in our enquiries,' Edris said.

'So Stacey and her friends were bullying other pupils?' Meadows asked.

'One girl in particular: Erin Kelly. Sadly, Erin took her own life.'

'It must have been a sustained campaign of bullying. Poor girl,' Meadows said.

'We have a very strict policy on bullying here, and I can't say I saw any evidence of bullying, but this was a serious allegation made by Erin's mother, Sarah, after Erin's death. I spoke to the girls along with their parents. The girls were upset by Erin's death. To be fair I don't think they should have been held accountable. There is always a bit of rivalry between teenage girls and – how shall I put it – bitchiness? I think poor Erin must have had some deep-rooted problems to do what she did. It was all very unpleasant at the time. Sarah came to the office on several occasions demanding that there should be some punishment for the girls. I don't blame her, she was distraught. Eventually things calmed down.'

'What about Erin's father?'

'He wasn't around. Sarah raised Erin on her own. I can't see that what happened to Erin would have any bearing on Stacey's death.'

'We're trying to build a picture of Stacey's life and we need to look at anything, no matter how small, that would make someone want to hurt Stacey.'

'I see, well, there's not much more I can tell you. I had a quick chat with all of Stacey's teachers before you arrived. There was nothing out of the ordinary these past weeks and no cause for concern.'

'You've been very helpful, thank you,' Meadows said. 'We would like to talk to Shannon and Alisha if they are in today.'

'Yes, both girls are in. I'll show you to the staffroom. It'll be more comfortable for the girls to talk to you there. My office can be a little intimidating.' Mrs Hughes smiled as she stood.

The staffroom was two doors down from the office and was empty when they entered.

'Please, help yourselves to tea or coffee,' Mrs Hughes said. 'I'll just check the girls' timetables and fetch them; it shouldn't take long.'

'Do you want a cup of tea?' Edris asked.

'No, but you go ahead.' Meadows sat down in one of the padded blue chairs and watched as Edris made himself a cup of coffee from the percolator. 'I think it may be worth a visit to Sarah Kelly. Erin's father would have a motive for killing Stacey.'

'But it doesn't sound like he's in the picture,' Edris said as he stirred the coffee.

'Doesn't mean he isn't in the background somewhere. We need to find out if he had any contact with Erin.'

Edris plonked down on a chair and took a sip of his coffee. 'Erin died over a year ago. If Stacey's murder is for revenge, why wait?'

'I guess grief can eat at you over time. Then there's the man in the video and the one filming. Erin's father could have been stalking Stacey. Waiting for the opportunity.'

'Or the man in the video could have been a teacher, he wouldn't want it getting out that he was sleeping with a pupil.'

'Good point.'

The door to the staffroom opened and Mrs Hughes ushered two girls inside.

'This is Shannon and Alisha, I've explained why you need to talk to them. Sit down, girls. Would you like me to stay?' She turned to Meadows.

'Please, if you wouldn't mind.'

Mrs Hughes took a seat and smoothed down her skirt. Meadows looked at the two girls. Shannon was curvaceous with her school uniform clinging tightly to her figure. Her hair was dyed the same shade of blonde as Stacey's and the skin of her face was concealed beneath foundation. Alisha was petite with olive skin and long dark hair. Both girls were eyeing up Edris with interest.

'We just need to ask you a few questions about Stacey,' Meadows said. 'We understand you were friends with her.'

'We've been friends since nursery school.' Shannon turned her attention to Meadows.

'This must be very difficult for you.' Meadows had expected the girls to be tearful, but they were composed. He wondered if Stacey had been the influencer out of the group.

'I wanted to stay at home,' Alisha said, 'but my mum thought it best I come to school and be with my friends.'

'We're organising a candlelit vigil for Stacey this evening,' Shannon said.

'It will be in the school grounds,' Mrs Hughes said. 'We thought it would be good for the pupils here to have a place to pay their respects in a safe environment.'

'We wanted to do it down the Cwm, but we weren't allowed,' Shannon said.

'How was Stacey these past few weeks?' Meadows asked. 'We understand that she had an argument with her boyfriend, Jack.'

The girls exchanged a look before Alisha spoke. 'Yeah, Jack has been a dick.'

'In what way?'

'Just… you know, not speaking to her, whispering and laughing with his mates every time he passed her.'

'And this was because of the video that was posted on Facebook?'

Shannon looked at Mrs Hughes and bit her lip and Alisha found a thread on her skirt and started pulling at it.

'It's okay, girls, it's best you tell the detectives anything you know. You're not going to get into any trouble,' Mrs Hughes said.

'Yeah,' Shannon said. 'He was pissed when he saw it. Everyone saw it. Jack was really angry, he called her a slut, and his stupid mates were laughing. Stacey went to the nurse's office and went home sick. She didn't come to school for two days. The video kept getting posted and it was being shared.'

'Did she tell you who the guy in the video was?' Meadows asked.

'No, she wouldn't say,' Alisha said. 'We kept on asking her, but she said she didn't want to get him into trouble.'

'So it wasn't someone from school?'

'No. Someone older, married we think,' Shannon said.

'Why do you think that?'

'She said she was bored with the boys from our year and the sex was amazing with this guy. I guess older men know what they are doing.' Shannon glanced at Edris.

Mrs Hughes raised her eyebrows but didn't comment.

'Do you know who took the video?'

'No,' Alisha said. 'It looked like a fake profile. You see them all the time. Just some random pictures and no friends.'

'Did Stacey suspect anyone? Someone from school?'

'Well, we thought it could be fuck-a-duck, he's always hanging around.'

'Shannon!' Mrs Hughes tutted.

'And that is?' Edris asked.

'Donald Hobson. He's in our maths class.'

'Why do you think Donald posted the video?' Meadows asked.

'He's always following and watching us,' Alisha said. 'Not just in school. He turns up everywhere. He probably fancied Stacey.'

'Did you see Stacey on Tuesday night?'

'No, she was on the bus, then she went straight home because she had work,' Shannon said.

'I don't live in Gaer Fawr,' Alisha said. 'We only hang out at school and at weekends.'

'Do you often use the public footpath, the Cwm, in Gaer Fawr?'

'Yeah, there's nothing much else to do. We chill in the field or down by the river,' Shannon said.

'Did Donald ever go with you?'

'Hell no,' Alisha said. 'We've seen him down there creeping around.'

'Now, girls, I don't think you're being fair,' Mrs Hughes said. She turned to Meadows. 'Donald is a little introvert, he doesn't make friends easily. He was good friends with Erin, and he took her death hard. He's been a bit of a lost soul since.'

'A freak,' Shannon said.

'That's enough,' Mrs Hughes said.

'Did Donald blame Stacey for Erin's death?' Edris asked.

'Yeah, he called us all bitches,' Alisha said.

'Did he make any threats?'

'No, well, he said we would all burn in hell,' Shannon said.

'Okay, thank you for talking to us,' Meadows said.

'Right, girls, you can go back to class,' Mrs Hughes said.

Once the girls had left, Mrs Hughes turned to Meadows. 'That was a bit of an eye opener.'

'I can imagine,' Meadows said with a smile.

'Is there anything else I can help you with?'

'Yes, I'd like to talk to Donald.'

'I'm afraid he isn't in school. He hasn't been in since Tuesday.'

Chapter Seven

Donald sat on his bed with his knees pulled up to his chest. He wore a striped dressing gown over his T-shirt and joggers, but he still felt cold. He hadn't been able to eat or sleep since Tuesday. His stomach felt hollow. He wished he could just lie under his duvet and sleep, escape his thoughts for a few hours. It was like a film playing on repeat, he couldn't get rid of the images or quieten his mind. It felt so crammed in his head he thought it would explode. He'd taken a walk hoping the fresh air would make him feel better, it had for a while, but the dark thoughts and feelings soon crept back, and fear covered him like a blanket of lead.

A knock at the front door made him jump. He got up and peered through the curtains. He could see the tops of the heads of two men, he pulled back quickly not wanting to be seen. He crept to his bedroom door and opened it a few inches. Just enough so he could hear. His mother answered the door, and he heard the men introduce themselves.

'We'd like to speak to Donald,' one of them said.

Donald felt his chest constrict, and his heart thumped unnaturally loud, pulsating in his ears. He heard his mother saying that he wasn't well. Maybe they would go away, and he wouldn't have to face them, he thought. But no, she was letting them in, their voices drifting into the sitting room.

'Donald love, can you come downstairs for a minute?'

His mother's words brought with them a wave of panic. He felt heat creep over his body and prickle his skin. He tore off his dressing gown and forced himself to breathe. They must be talking to everyone, he thought. Unless they had spoken to Alisha and Shannon. They would point at him, any reason to make his life hell.

'They don't know anything,' he whispered. He found speaking out loud to himself often made him feel calmer.

'Donald?'

'I'm coming.' He shuffled across the landing then took the stairs slowly. There were no voices coming from the sitting room now. When he entered he saw two men sitting on the sofa, his mother was sat in her usual armchair. All were looking at him.

'Hello Donald, I'm Detective Inspector Meadows, and this is Detective Edris. I'm sorry to have got you up from bed. We just want to ask you a few questions about Stacey.'

'I didn't kill her.' He hadn't meant to say that. He looked from Meadows to Edris then to his mother. 'I didn't.' He could feel the blood rushing to his head, he felt dizzy.

'Of course you didn't,' his mother said. 'Don't get yourself worked up now. Come and sit down.'

Donald perched on the arm of the chair where his mother sat. It wasn't comfortable but there was nowhere else to sit, he looked down at the floor, but he could still feel the detectives' eyes upon him.

'It's okay, Donald, you're not in any trouble. We are talking to everyone who knew Stacey,' Meadows said.

Donald didn't trust himself to speak. The room had too many people in it for his comfort. He didn't like to feel crowded and strangers made him nervous. His mother had lit the gas fire and it felt like the flames were licking his skin.

'Would you rather speak to us on your own?' Meadows asked.

Donald looked at his mother. She didn't look at all worried. He decided he felt safer with her staying. She would know what to say and wouldn't let them bully him.

'No, Mum can stay.' He brushed away the hair that had fallen into his eyes.

'Nasty scratch you've got on your arm,' Meadows said.

Donald looked at the livid red mark that ran up the inside of his forearm and wished he'd kept his dressing gown on.

'It was a cat.'

He forced himself to look at Meadows. He had black curly hair and bright green eyes. A nice face, Donald thought, someone you could confide in. He knew he had to be careful, it would be easy to talk to this man.

'Yours?' Edris asked.

'What?' Donald turned his head to look at the other detective. This one was blond and good looking. He didn't trust him, he'd be like all the good looking boys at school, either ignoring you or laughing at you.

'Cat, was it your cat that scrammed you?' Edris asked.

'We don't have a cat,' his mother said.

'It was outside. I was playing with it,' Donald said. He put his hands on his knees applying pressure to try and stop them jiggling.

'When was the last time you saw Stacey?' Meadows asked.

'Tuesday, she was in the shop.'

'What time was that?' Meadows asked.

Donald shrugged his shoulders, he couldn't remember.

'About six, Donald went to get some milk because we had run out,' his mother said.

'And what did you do after that?' Meadows asked.

Donald felt his shoulders relax a little, he knew what he was supposed to say. 'Came back, had food, then went to the vicarage. I was helping Vicar Daniels set up. We had a film night.'

'Is that a sort of youth club?' Edris asked.

'No, just a church activity,' Donald said.

'Donald does a lot with the church,' his mother said. 'He's been going since Sunday school and he's there every Sunday morning. He's always helping out the vicar.'

'What film did you watch?' Edris asked.

'*The Shack*.'

'What time did the film finish?'

'After ten. I helped clean up and got back about eleven.'

'It was no later than that,' his mother added. 'I was still up when he came in.'

Donald watched the detective write in his notebook. He would have to be careful to remember everything he told them. He knew it was important to stick to the story.

'Do you often walk down the Cwm?' Meadows asked.

The sudden change of question brought on a fresh wave of panic. He could feel the sweat soaking through his T-shirt under his arms and hoped the detective didn't notice. 'Sometimes. I walk down there then up to the cairns.'

'And you saw Stacey there?'

'Yeah, she was always down there with her friends or boys.'

'Any boy in particular?'

'Jack Hopkins, Alex Edwards, some others.' Donald didn't want to say who else he had seen her with.

'Did you see anyone else hanging around down there in the past couple of weeks? Someone you wouldn't expect to see maybe or someone that was watching Stacey?'

'No, not really. I sometimes see Bible Bill, and Mrs Kelly walking the dog but no strangers if that's what you mean.'

'Did you see Bill talking to Stacey or watching her and her friends?'

'No, why would he? She was mean to him. Calling out in a flirty voice, saying things like, "Hey Billy boy, you're looking very sexy today," then laughing.'

'How did he react?'

'Just muttered to himself and carried on walking. I heard him call her a wicked girl once, but it just made her laugh more.'

'Did Stacey ever call you names? Tease you?'

An image of Stacey flicking her blonde hair came to Donald's mind. He could hear her laughter, and her voice full of scorn. See the way she looked at him as if he was shit. There would be none of that anymore.

The detective was looking at him waiting for an answer. His mouth felt dry and his tongue too heavy. He cleared his throat and forced himself to concentrate. 'All the time, but I took no notice. I wasn't the only one. Stacey picked on anyone who wasn't popular.'

'Like Erin Kelly.'

Pain gnawed at Donald's stomach. Erin was never far from his thoughts, all he could do was nod.

'I understand that you were good friends with Erin,' Meadows said.

'Yeah.'

'It must have been very hard for you when she died.'

Donald looked down at his hands. He tried to fight the emotion, but he could feel his throat constricting and tears stinging his eyes.

'He was inconsolable, didn't go to school for weeks,' his mother said. 'She was such a nice girl, always coming around.'

'Donald?' Meadows asked.

Donald looked up. He didn't want to talk about Erin. It hurt too much. 'Yes, I miss her. She was my friend. My only friend.'

'Did you blame Stacey for Erin's death?'

'And the others. They were always picking on her. They wouldn't leave her alone. Calling her names, tripping her up in the canteen so she would fall in front of everyone. It wasn't just in school. She had to stay home after school and the weekends to avoid Stacey. If we were lucky and set off early we could walk up the mountain to get away, but Stacey always found a way to get to her, Facebook and Twitter. Always posting shit.' The words came tumbling out and he couldn't stop them. 'Once Stacey and her friends made a fake Facebook account, pretended to be one of the boys from school and flirt with Erin. They kept it up for weeks. Erin was suspicious at first but then she was really happy thinking someone liked her. A meeting was set up down the Cwm. Erin got dressed up and went down the Cwm thinking it was a date. Stacey and her friends were there, laughing. They filmed it and put it up for the whole school to see. It was really cruel.'

'Did Erin talk much about her father?' Meadows asked.

'No, Erin didn't have a father. It was just her and her mother.'

'She didn't talk about finding him?'

'No, she never mentioned it.'

'Did Erin take drugs?'

'No!' These people didn't know Erin, or what she went through, Donald thought. They think she was some druggy. 'Why are you asking all these questions about Erin?'

'We are trying to find out who killed Stacey and to do that we have to look at her past. Look at people connected to her. In this case you said that Stacey bullied Erin, so we have to consider that someone wanted revenge for what happened to Erin.' Meadows let the statement hang in the air.

Donald was sure the detective could hear his heart beating. The silence stretched on and he wanted to leap from the chair and lock himself in his bedroom.

'Can you think of anyone who would want to hurt Stacey?'

Loads, Donald thought, but he just shrugged his shoulders.

'There was a video posted online of Stacey down the Cwm with a man. Do you know anything about that?'

'No.'

'Did you see it?'

'Everyone saw it.' He felt heat crawling up his neck and spread until his whole face prickled.

'Do you know who posted the video?'

'No.'

'Do you know the man in the video?'

Donald felt bile rise in his throat. 'No.' He stood up. 'I'm not feeling very well.'

'Okay, we'll leave you to get back to bed. Thank you for talking to us,' Meadows said.

Donald bolted from the room, straight upstairs and locked himself in the bathroom. He couldn't go on with this much longer. He'd have to talk to someone.

Chapter Eight

'Are we going to pay Bible Bill a visit?' Edris asked. 'His name keeps cropping up.'

'Yes, but not yet, Sarah Kelly only lives a few doors down. Let's call on her first.'

'So what do you make of Donald?'

'I think he's hiding something.' Meadows looked back at the house. 'He looked scared and that was no cat scratch on his arm.'

'Yeah, I did notice. His reaction was a bit odd when he came downstairs. Most people don't start with "I didn't kill her".'

'No, but then again I don't think Donald comes under the category of most people. The headmistress's description of him, his lack of social interaction and minimum eye contact makes me think he has some social issues. Added to that is the death of his best friend. I'm guessing he also has some emotional problems. Maybe even suffering from anxiety and depression.'

'It doesn't help to be named after a cartoon character. Imagine being called fuck-a-duck on a daily basis. No wonder the poor kid is introverted.'

'It sounds like Stacey and her friends made a habit of bullying people. What else did they get up to?' Meadows knocked on Sarah Kelly's door.

Sarah Kelly didn't look surprised to find two detectives on her doorstep. She stood with a miniature white poodle in her arms and gave them a wry smile.

'I thought you'd make your way to see me,' she said. 'You better come in.'

The layout of the house was the same as Donald's with the stairs directly in front and the sitting room to the right. That was the only similarity. Where the sitting room in Donald's house had been cluttered, Sarah's was minimalistic, light, and airy. There were no ornaments, just a picture of Erin on a shelf with a small vase of flowers and a candle. The smiling teenager had the same red hair and blue eyes as her mother.

'Have a seat.' Sarah indicated the sofa before sitting in an armchair and placing the dog on her lap.

'Thank you.' Meadows sat and waited for Edris to settle and take out his notebook. 'As you probably guessed we're here about Stacey Evans.'

'Because of what happened to Erin you think that I might have had something to do with her death.'

She could have been in on it with Erin's father, Meadows thought. 'We understand that you held Stacey responsible and that you went to the school to make a complaint on more than one occasion.'

'Yes, her and those...' Sarah tucked her hair behind her ear. 'It wasn't just Stacey, but she was the main contributor. If you are expecting me to say that I'm sorry Stacey's dead then you'll be disappointed. I'm not sorry, she made Erin's life hell.'

'I appreciate your honesty,' Meadows said.

'Good, I didn't kill her. There were times late at night when I thought about it, but you can't arrest someone for thoughts. Erin had her whole life ahead of her. I'd messed mine up, but she had a chance. She was going to go to university, leave this place.' Sarah sighed. 'I'd see Stacey sometimes, full of life and laughter. She'd cross the road to avoid me. You'd think I'd feel some sort of relief now she's gone, that the pain would go away. I don't feel anything. I'm just an empty shell, I have been since Erin died.'

'I'm sorry to have to ask but was it a drug overdose?' Meadows said.

'No, she jumped off the top of Herbert's quarry. She walked there. Can you imagine? It took her three hours. I walked in her footsteps. Three hours to think about it, three hours to change her mind. How desperate she must have been to escape this life.' Sarah looked across at the photograph. 'There are many times I thought about joining her. Suicide isn't blameless like an accident or illness. It's preventable, imagine knowing that your child was in so much pain and couldn't turn to you for help. I should have seen the signs, done something more. My pain is my punishment for not being able to protect her.'

Meadows wanted to reach out to her and give her some comfort. He wondered if there was anyone who held this woman in her grief. He wished he didn't have to ask these questions and stir up the pain but there was another mother that was grieving. 'I'm so sorry. Was Erin your only child?'

'Yes, I had Erin when I was seventeen, it was just the two of us.'

'What about Erin's father?'

'He wasn't part of Erin's life.'

'We still need to speak to him,' Edris said.

'You think he killed Stacey for revenge? No, why would he? Like I said, he had no part in Erin's life, no financial help, not even a birthday card. It was what I wanted.'

'Is he local?' Edris asked.

'Yes.'

'Then he knows about what happened to Erin.'

Sarah ran her fingers through the dog's hair then looked at Edris. 'There were no tears, he didn't come to see me. He came to the funeral but so did the whole village. Even Stacey and her friends. I didn't want them there, I thought they would have stayed away out of decency. I caught a glimpse of them standing with their class. If I'd been more myself that day I would have slapped them.'

'We're still going to need his name,' Meadows said.

Sarah shook her head.

'Did Erin know who her father was?'

'Yes, I would never have held back that information. She didn't want anyone to know. I promised her no one would find out. I'm not breaking my promise to her.'

'I understand,' Meadows said. 'I assure you that we only need his name to eliminate him from our enquiries. It won't go any further.'

'You can't make those assurances. If you question him then people are going to wonder why,' Sarah said.

'We'll be as discreet as we can. You know the pain of losing a child, there is another mother who is grieving and needs some answers,' Edris said.

'She knew what her daughter was like. I spoke to her, asked her to get Stacey to leave Erin alone.'

'If Erin is the reason Stacey was killed then I'm sure her mother will regret not intervening for the rest of her life.' Meadows hoped that thought would be enough to persuade Sarah to give him a name.

'Fine, it's Bible Bill. You can understand why Erin didn't want anyone to know. I know what people would say. The gossip and sneering. It doesn't bother me what they say behind my back, but I don't want Erin's name dragged through the mud.'

'We haven't met him yet,' Edris said. 'But we've heard about him.'

'I would imagine that he is quite a bit older than you,' Meadows said. 'May I ask if you had a relationship with him?'

'Are you suggesting he forced himself on me?' Sarah asked. 'No, he didn't. I guess I was a bit like Erin at that age. I didn't have many friends. Bill was always nice to me, so I'd hang out around the farm. His parents didn't mind. I just wanted someone who would love me. Pay me attention. I didn't love him. He offered to marry me when I told him I was pregnant. I don't think he wanted to, he was just trying to do the right thing. When I turned him down he was relieved. I never told anyone he was Erin's father. He was happy to keep the secret.'

'Thank you for telling us. We will need to speak to him,' Meadows said.

'If you're thinking of seeing him now he won't be in. He visits his mother most afternoons. She's in a nursing home. He'll be back in about half an hour. I usually see him when I'm walking the dog.'

Meadows stood. 'We appreciate your time and honesty.'

'There is no point in being anything but honest. When the worst has happened, you find there is nothing to fear.'

Chapter Nine

As they stood next to the car, Meadows had the feeling they were being watched. He looked at the upstairs windows of Donald's house and saw the curtains move.

'Are we going to wait outside Bible Bill's house until he comes home?' Edris asked.

'No, I don't want to scare him off, let's go over to the church, see if the vicar is there. I want to check out Donald's alibi.'

'Can't see he'd make it up,' Edris said as they crossed the road.

'You never know, he may be counting on us not checking. He's got motive and he's at least six foot, solid. Strong enough to overpower Stacey. He is definitely hiding something. At the very least we can rule him out.'

They walked past the wall of the church yard which ran along the perimeter enclosing the graveyard. The headstones spread out past the side of the church and sloped gently behind. When they reached the lychgate they stepped under the wooden roof and Meadows looked at the noticeboard. A quick scan of the information told him the time of services at Saint Herbert's church and the officiating vicar, Reverend Timothy Daniels.

'He probably knows all that goes on in this village,' Edris commented.

'That's what I'm hoping.'

A gravel path led to a porch with an oak door. Meadows gave the door a push and it creaked open, startling a sparrow that had nested in the crevice of the stone wall. He watched it fly out before stepping inside. The church smelled of old wood with a hint of incense. The temperature felt cooler than it had outside. A large stone font stood to the right and a worn crimson carpet ran down the aisle to wooden railings. On each side were rows of long wooden pews. The walls were whitewashed, and all the windows were stained glass depicting scenes from the Bible. Meadows walked slowly down the aisle taking in the atmosphere of the church. It was peaceful and he could imagine the congregation of old filling the church and raising their voices in praise.

At the end of the aisle an ornate pulpit was to the left and two steps led to a pipe organ which stretched up to the ceiling on the right. At the rear of the church, under a magnificent stained glass window, stood the altar behind brass pillars and rope.

'Doesn't look like there is anyone here,' Edris said.

'The vicar could be in the vestry,' Meadows said.

'Should we shout out? I think the vestry is off limits to the public.'

'I think it'll be fine,' Meadows said. 'We'll just knock the door, it's not like it's the middle of the service. I think you'll find it's more of an office.'

'As a child you wouldn't dare go past the railings.'

'You went to church?'

'Yeah, Sunday school.'

'You're full of surprises.'

'My grandmother took me. Don't remember much about it. Just a few stories but I'd always get sweets after if I'd been good.'

Meadows laughed. 'I bet that wasn't often.'

A door could be heard opening and a man appeared from the left of the altar. He wore jeans with a navy knitted jumper, his white dog collar showing at the neck.

'I thought I heard voices,' the man said as he came down the two steps.

'Reverend Timothy Daniels?' Meadows asked.

'Yes, but you can call me Vicar Daniels, Vicar Tim, or just vicar, whichever you prefer. How can I help you?' He smiled.

Despite having a strong square jaw, Vicar Daniel's face had a kindness about it and his soft blue eyes crinkled at the corners. Meadows imagined that he was easy to talk to and someone you could trust with your troubles.

'I'm DI Meadows and this is DC Edris. I hope we're not disturbing you.'

'Not at all. I take it this is about Stacey Evans.'

'Yes.'

'Poor child.' Vicar Daniels shook his head sadly. 'My heart goes out to her family. I was just preparing for the vigil this evening. The headmistress has asked me to speak. I hope to be able to give them some words of comfort.'

'We won't keep you long. Do you know the family well?' Meadows asked.

'It's a small village so you get to know everyone fairly well. I christened both Stacey and Becca. The family doesn't come to church on a regular basis. Easter, Harvest Thanksgiving, and Christmas. Like other families here they work the land and that's a seven-day-a-week job.'

'Have you been here long?' Edris asked.

'I took over the parish some twenty years ago. I was a young man then and terrified of the responsibility, but they welcomed me with open arms. Please take a seat.' He indicated the pews.

Meadows moved some hymn books and sat down.

'Do many attend the services?' Edris asked as he took a seat next to Meadows and turned to face Vicar Daniels who sat on the opposite pew.

'On a good day about thirty-five. More on special occasions. Then there is the elderly and sick to visit so enough to keep me busy. My responsibility is to the whole of the parish here, not just the congregation.'

'So you knew Erin Kelly,' Meadows said.

'Yes, poor soul. Another life taken too soon. Her mother, Sarah, is one of my parishioners, Erin is buried here.'

'I thought that wasn't allowed,' Edris said.

'You mean because she took her own life? Thankfully that's a very archaic view. Although it wasn't that long ago that the church lifted its ban on a full Christian funeral. May I ask why you are interested in Erin?'

'It's just a line of enquiry we're following. We've been told that Stacey didn't get on with Erin and there are some who blamed her for Erin's death.'

'Well, that's putting it kindly,' Vicar Daniels said. 'I do not wish to speak ill of the dead, but Erin suffered greatly from the daily taunts. She was always a delicate child, she had a sort of fragility about her. She also was very kind-hearted. She attended Sunday school and stayed to take her confirmation vows. I dearly wish there was something I could have done to help her.'

Meadows saw the pain in Vicar Daniels' eyes. He understood all too well how it felt not to be able to help someone, not to be able to prevent a death.

'Can you think of anyone who would want to hurt Stacey?' Meadows asked.

'It's not like the catholic church. I don't take confessionals,' Vicar Daniels said with a smile. 'It's also not my place to judge people, point fingers. I'm sorry if I'm not being very helpful.' He looked around the church. 'My calling is to help the souls of this parish.'

'I appreciate your position,' Meadows said. 'I'm grateful for you answering our questions. I understand that Donald Hobson was good friends with Erin.'

'Donald' – Vicar Daniels raised his eyebrows – 'yes, he was. He's also one of my flock. A regular attendee and involves himself in all church activities.'

'We've spoken to Donald and he says he was at the vicarage on Tuesday night.'

'Yes, that's right. We had a film night.'

'*The Shack*?' Edris asked.

'Yes, have you seen it?'

'No.'

'Wonderful film. It did cause a bit of controversy when it first came out, particularly with those who hold a more extreme view of Christianity.'

'What time did Donald leave?' Edris asked.

'About quarter to eleven. I remember thinking it was late for a school night. It wasn't intended but we were late starting. The time we had a cup of tea and a chat.'

'What time did Donald arrive?'

'Around eight. He helped me move around the furniture so we would all have room to sit. He's a good kid.'

'I'm sure he is, but we have to follow up or we wouldn't be doing our job,' Meadows said. 'Who else was at the film evening?'

'Erm, Sarah Kelly, Gemma Lewis, and Tomos John.' Vicar Daniels counted the names on his fingers. 'Oh yes and Mary Beynon, six of us.'

'Mary Beynon?'

'Yes, as you are probably aware she lost her granddaughter, and her daughter is in prison. It's been a very difficult time for her.'

'I can imagine,' Meadows said. 'One last question. What can you tell us about William James?'

'Bill? He attends church regularly. Likes a good theological discussion. He's very well read. He also has strong political views. Not always the best mix. He can come across as narrow-minded and he's not very sociable; partly I think it's to do with a childhood trauma. His older brother was killed in a farming accident and Bill witnessed it. He was never quite the same after that or so I've been told. His father died and his mother is in a nursing home. He was left to run the farm, but he had no interest. Both the house and farm are in a bit of a state. Bill doesn't care for worldly goods, as long as he has books to read and enough food to live on he's content.'

'Well, thank you for your time.' Meadows stood and knocked a hymn book from the pew. He bent down to pick it up and a piece of paper fluttered out. As he replaced the paper, he noticed Eph6:12 written on the top.

'Is this a Bible reference?' Meadows handed it to Vicar Daniels.

'Yes, Ephesians was our *text word* on Sunday. Some of the members like to write down the verse to look up and read the whole chapter later.'

Meadows opened the hymn book and looked at the inside cover. 'There is no name.'

'The hymn books are the property of the church so anyone can use them.'

'Who was sitting here on Sunday?'

'Erm I'm not sure. Some of the older members take the front pews so it's not so far to walk to communion. Mary Beynon and Elsie Jones were there.' Vicar Daniels frowned in concentration. 'I can ask them who else was sat in the front. I tend to look at the congregation as a whole, not at individual people when I serve.'

'If I said REV17 what would come to mind?'

'The Book of Revelation, chapter 17.'

'And what's that about?'

'I'm afraid I don't know the Bible off by heart,' Vicar Daniels said. 'I can check for you if you like.'

'Please,' Meadows said.

Vicar Daniels stepped up to the pulpit, picked up a bible and flicked through the pages. 'Ah, here we are. The whore of Babylon.'

'The what?' Edris said.

'I take it you're not a church goer,' Vicar Daniels said.

'I went to Sunday school but there was certainly no mention of a whore,' Edris said.

'I suppose there wouldn't be.' Vicar Daniels chuckled as he came down from the pulpit carrying the bible. 'The Book of Revelation is quite difficult to interpret. The whore of Babylon, or harlot, is symbolic, a female figure, or a place among some theories.' He looked down at the bible and scanned the words. 'It talks of her judgement and her fornication with the kings on earth.'

Edris' lips twitched. 'So, she's being judged for putting it about a bit.'

Vicar Daniels laughed. 'That wouldn't be my interpretation. Like I said, Revelation is symbolic, it's not talking about some loose woman.'

'But it could be taken literally by some?' Meadows asked.

'Yes, I suppose so if you took the text word out of context. I'm a little curious,' Vicar Daniels said.

'Oh it's just something that came up,' Meadows said.

'Meaning you can't tell me. I understand.'

'You've been a great help, thank you. We'll leave you to get back to your preparations.'

'You're welcome. If there is anything else I can help you with you'll usually find me here or at the vicarage.' Vicar Daniels smiled then turned and walked back towards the altar.

Steel-grey clouds had formed in the sky while they had been inside, casting a dark shadow over the church.

'Do you really think that the writing on Stacey is a Bible verse?' Edris asked.

Meadows stopped at the lychgate and looked back at the church. 'Yes, it fits and it's the best theory we have so far. Stacey was seeing an older man, possibly a married one, while seeing Jack at the same time. Erin by contrast was a quiet girl and attended church regularly. So if this is about Erin we're looking at someone who thinks that

Stacey was sinful and had to be punished. Think of the way the killer left her body. He made no attempt to hide her. The writing has to be a statement, not only meaningful to the killer but also to those who would find her.'

'Makes sense, I suppose. The vicar said Sarah Kelly and Bible Bill are regular attendees of the church. Both would know the Bible reference. Sarah Kelly could have put Bill up to it,' Edris said. 'She was reluctant to give his name. He's got motive and he knows the Bible. He could be easily persuaded to take revenge for his daughter.'

'I agree, when we're on our way you can give Paskin a call, get her to run a check on Bible Bill.'

Meadows drove to the edge of the village, past Stacey's farm and took the next turning. Grass spouted up the centre of the track with overgrown hedges each side which scraped against the side of the car.

The car rocked as the wheels dipped in and out of potholes.

'This isn't doing your suspension much good,' Edris said.

'If I'd known it was this bad I would have parked and walked.'

They reached the yard and the first thing they saw was 'Jesus loves you' painted on the side of the house. Meadows stopped the car, got out and looked around. Old farm machinery stood covered in weeds and rusting. Chickens roamed freely almost filling the yard, they pecked at the ground while keeping their beady eyes on the strangers.

'Ew.' Edris picked his way through the muck and came to stand next to Meadows.

'I don't like the look of this,' Edris said looking at the lettering on the wall. 'What if he has a gun? Most farmers do.'

'Can't see him getting a firearms licence.'

'Yeah but his father could have kept guns,' Edris said.

'The victim wasn't shot. It sounds like he's more likely to hit you with a bible,' Meadows said with a grin. 'We'll just take things gently. Paskin's check came back clear so I don't think you have to worry.'

They walked to the front of the house where brambles snaked their way through the hedge and snagged on their clothes.

'Doesn't looked lived in,' Edris said.

'Probably only uses the back door,' Meadows said as he knocked.

The door opened and a man looked them up and down. He was dressed in orange overalls. The top three poppers were unclasped and revealed a hairy chest. He had wild dark hair peppered with grey and brown serious eyes. There was no hint of a smile.

'What do you want?' the man said.

'William James?'

'Yeah, but I go by Bill.'

'I'm DI Meadows and this is DC Edris. We're investigating the murder of Stacey Evans.'

'Nothing to do with me,' Bill said.

'We are talking to anyone who may have seen Stacey on Tuesday and given that you are the Evanses' neighbour we thought you'd be able to help.'

'Didn't see her,' Bill said.

'Right, is it okay if we ask you a couple of questions?'

'That's how it starts, innit?'

'How what starts?' Edris asked.

'You say you want to ask questions, next thing you arrest me and take away my freedom.'

'We just want to have a chat,' Meadows said. 'Perhaps we could come in for a minute.'

Bill seemed to be wrestling with the decision.

'We won't keep you long,' Edris said. 'If you'd rather talk here that's fine but it's a bit cold and it looks like it's going to rain.'

'A storm is coming.'

'You could be right,' Meadows said.

'I am right. I can smell it in the air. Alright, you better come in then.'

He led them down a gloomy passage which smelled of mould and decay. Meadows noticed the wallpaper was peeling at the corners. The staircase was directly in front of them and as Bill veered through a door on the left a ragged looking cockerel came into view perched on the third step. Meadows came to a stop and Edris who had been looking at a strange painting bumped into him.

Bill turned and followed the detective's gaze. 'That's Frank, I keep it inside as the ladies have been having a go at him. He's just become a father again, come and see.'

Meadows followed Bill into the sitting room and tried not to show his surprise. The walls had been stripped down to the stone. There was no carpet, and the flagstones were covered in dirt, feathers, and dog-ends. The only furniture was an armchair which looked on the point of collapse. Books were piled high in the corner of the room and mould was creeping across the ceiling. A chicken was roaming around, and chirping was coming from a box in the corner.

'That's Greta.' Bill pointed at the chicken then bent over the box and pulled out a fluffy yellow chick. 'There's twelve of them.' Bill stretched his hand towards Meadows. 'Would you like to hold it?'

'He's a vegetarian,' Edris said.

Bill frowned and snatched his hand back. 'It's not for eating. I don't kill any of my chickens, I have named everyone and I can tell them apart. I only sell the eggs.'

'I'm happy to hear that,' Meadows said with a smile.

'It breaks my heart to see the way God's creatures are treated. I don't mind the dairy farms. Taking the milk is fine, but the sheep and pigs.' Bill shook his head. 'Sometimes I let them out before slaughter day. It gives them a chance but don't go telling tales on me.' He gently laid the chick down in the box. 'Do you want a cup of tea?'

Meadows didn't want to think about what the kitchen looked like. 'No, thank you.'

'Okay, do you mind if I get myself a drink?'

'No, you go ahead,' Meadows said.

Edris walked over to the box and peered at the chicks. 'They're kinda cute.'

The sound of the back door slamming made them both jump.

'Shit,' Edris said.

Meadows dashed through the kitchen and out the back door. Bill could be seen sprinting across the field. He took chase with Edris close behind. Parts of the field were sodden and mud flew from his shoes splattering his trousers. A couple of times he lost his footing and slid in the mud. Up ahead Bill had reached the gate and scrambled over. Meadows picked up speed and easily vaulted the gate. He heard a grunt behind him, turned and saw Edris had fallen face down in the mud.

'I'm okay,' Edris panted.

Meadows took off and could see that Bill was slowing.

'There is no point in running,' Meadows shouted.

It wasn't until he had cleared the second gate that Meadows gained enough on Bill to tackle him to the ground.

'Give it up, man,' Meadows said as Bill thrashed around on the ground. He managed to cuff him and haul him to his feet.

'Justice will never be done now,' Bill said.

Chapter Ten

Meadows sat in the interview room opposite Bill and the duty solicitor. He didn't know which of them looked worse: Bill, Edris, or himself. They were each caked in mud and Edris was fidgeting next to him, clearly uncomfortable about not looking his usual groomed self. They had got the worst of the mud off in the station toilets but couldn't do much about their clothes or Blackwell's laughter. Bill sat quietly with his hands folded as if he was praying.

'Why did you run from us, Bill?' Meadows asked.

'I knew this would happen, that you would arrest me.'

'Because of what you did to Stacey?'

'I didn't do anything to Stacey.'

'Then why run? We only wanted to ask you a couple of questions. You must see how it looks from our perspective.'

'I see alright. You decide someone is guilty, choose an easy target and once you've got them inside you don't let them go. You're part of the establishment and it's pointless trying to fight it. Just like the early Christians, they were persecuted. I ran because it was my only chance of escape.'

'You said when you were arrested that justice wouldn't be done. What did you mean by that?'

'Exactly what I just said. You fit me up for killing this girl and the killer goes free. You have to make yourselves look good. Someone has to pay for what happened. It doesn't matter if it's an innocent man. Look at what's happened in the past. How many convictions have been overturned? Those men have lost years of their lives, and what about those on death row?'

This isn't getting us anywhere, Meadows thought. 'I can assure you, I'm only interested in the truth. The longer you take to answer our questions the longer you will be kept here.'

'You can't keep me here.' Bill's face creased with worry. 'Who's going to look after my chickens? They can't be left alone.'

'Your solicitor can make arrangements for you.'

Bill turned to the solicitor. 'You're going to feed them and put them to bed?'

'No, but I can make a call for you,' the solicitor said.

'There is no one to call.' Bill looked at Meadows. 'I'm not saying another word until you guarantee that my chickens will be safe.'

Meadows guessed that Bill cared more about animals than people. Animals weren't a threat to him, didn't judge and call him names. To Bill it would feel like leaving a child to fend for itself, he thought. 'We'll sort something out even if I have to go and take care of them myself,' Meadows said.

'Thank you.' Bill sat back in his chair.

'Right, can you tell me where you were on Tuesday evening?' Edris asked.

'At home.'

'All evening?'

'Yes, looking after the chicks.'

'Did you go out at all?' Edris asked.

'I went to the shop?'

'What time?'

'I dunno. I don't take much notice of the time. I get up when the sun rises and go to bed when I'm tired. It was dark when I went out.'

'How long after it got dark?' Edris asked.

Bill shrugged. 'I put the chickens to bed then went out.'

Meadows sat forward. 'Did you see Stacey?'

'Yes, she was in the shop.'

'What did you do after your shopping?'

'I went home.'

'Through the Cwm?' Meadows asked.

'No, I stayed on the main road. I don't go down that way at night. Sometimes there are kids down there after dark, up to no good.'

'You go that way during the day though,' Meadows said.

'Yes, there's less people.'

'Did you see Stacey there often?'

'Yeah, she was always there with her friends, drinking, smoking, and fornicating.'

'You saw her having intercourse with someone?' Meadows asked.

'More than one but not at the same time.'

'Who?'

'It's not for me to say.'

'It would be really helpful if you told us who Stacey was with,' Edris said.

The solicitor leaned in and whispered something to Bill. Bill shook his head and looked back at Edris. 'The man succumbed to sin. He has to ask for forgiveness from the Lord. She was a temptress; the temptation has now been removed.'

'So, you removed the temptation from this man,' Edris said.

'The Lord works in mysterious ways. None of us know how.'

'It was a human being that killed Stacey Evans, not some deity,' Meadows said.

'Yes, acting on God's instructions.'

'Have you received instructions from God?'

'We've all received instructions from God. The Holy Bible is our manual.'

'And the Bible says you shall not kill,' Edris said.

'I haven't. I will go into eternity with a clean conscience.'

Edris leaned forward and said, 'You'll have an even cleaner conscience if you help us with our enquiries.'

Meadows suddenly felt weary. He longed to go home, take off his dirty clothes and light up a joint. They didn't seem to be making any progress and he'd had enough Bible talk for one day. 'Did you like to watch Stacey?'

Bill frowned. 'No, what sort of man do you think I am?'

'But you admit to watching her having intercourse.'

'I wasn't watching. She went through the trees and I wanted to see what she was up to. I didn't hang around.'

'Did you film Stacey and the man?'

'No.'

'We can check your mobile phone and your laptop.'

'I don't have a phone or a computer.'

'You expect us to believe you don't have a phone,' Edris said. 'Everyone has a phone.'

'I don't. Why would I carry a thing that spies on you? That's what they're for, so they know where you are at all times and listen to you.'

'Who is they?'

'The establishment.'

Edris sighed and sat back in the chair.

The solicitor was looking bemused and Meadows imagined that he thought he drew the short straw with this case.

'Would you be willing to give a DNA sample?' Meadows asked.

Bill shook his head. 'No way, you could use that against me.'

'Only if you killed Stacey Evans. If not, then it would eliminate you from our enquiries and you can go home.'

'I already told you I didn't kill her. Why would I?'

'Because you think that Stacey is responsible for your daughter's death. We know that Erin was your daughter.'

'It's supposed to be a secret. I promised Sarah no one would know.'

'It's okay, Sarah told us.'

'Why would she do that?'

'To help us. We needed to know. You must have been distraught when Erin died, not being able to show how you felt to anyone. Then there was Stacey, alive, laughing and having fun.'

'Forgive them for they know not what they do. That's what Jesus said.'

'Did you really forgive Stacey?' Meadows asked.

'Yes, Erin is okay now. She's happy.'

'And Stacey? Do you think she got what she deserved?'

Bill shrugged his shoulders. 'It's not for me to decide.'

The solicitor made a show of looking at his watch. 'Are you going to charge my client?'

Meadows stood. 'We will hold your client overnight. I suggest you persuade him that it's in his best interests to give a DNA sample.'

'What about my chickens? You promised. Sarah can see to them in the morning, but I'll not send her out in the dark.'

'Your chickens will be taken care of.'

Meadows didn't like the idea of chasing around chickens in the dark, but he didn't want to be responsible for a fox taking a few, particularly when they had lovingly been given names.

* * *

71

The rain was beating against the window and the trees could be seen swaying in the wind when Meadows walked back into the office.

'Well, is he our man?' Blackwell asked.

'I honestly don't know,' Meadows said.

'Between the talk of God and chickens it was difficult to get any straight answers,' Edris added.

'Hopefully his solicitor can persuade him to give a DNA sample. We'll know for sure then. Anything come back from forensics?'

'Yes, they've got a profile from the scrapings taken from under Stacey's nails and from the pubic hair found on her body. It's been run through the system but there was no match,' Paskin said. 'There was also synthetic hair.'

'From a wig?' Meadows asked.

'Looks like it. Short and a mixture of white, grey, and dark brown.'

'So, he didn't want the victim to recognise him,' Valentine said.

'More likely he disguised himself so he wouldn't be recognised by potential witnesses,' Meadows said. 'I'm guessing he planned to kill Stacey so he would have no need for a disguise. It's likely he wanted her to know his identity.'

'Yeah, but he would stand out in the village,' Blackwell said.

'Possibly, but if there were witnesses they would just report a stranger,' Meadows said.

'Maybe it's a vain man who is losing his hair so wears a wig all the time,' Paskin said. The phone rang on her desk, she picked it up and turned away from the group.

'Nah, can't see it,' Blackwell said. 'Men don't wear rugs anymore, they just shave it off.'

'I don't know,' Edris said. 'I wouldn't want to shave mine off. If it starts to thin out I'm having a transplant or a really good wig. You probably can't tell the difference now.'

'Yeah, men spend more time on their hair than women do,' Valentine said. 'You can get some really good wigs online now, Blackwell. I can help you if you like.'

'Bugger off,' Blackwell said. He pushed his fingers through his hair. 'I've got plenty left.'

'For now.' Valentine laughed.

'Okay, so we could be looking at an older man,' Meadows said. 'Or possibly a young man who wants to disguise himself as an older man or woman. I suppose if he put on a wig and a pair of glasses he could get away with it.'

'He could be ill,' Valentine said. 'Lost his hair through chemo and doesn't want anyone to know, or alopecia.'

'It doesn't narrow it down,' Blackwell said. 'Basically, it could be any man from the village or someone that knows the area very well. What about Bible Bill downstairs? Do you reckon he's wearing a wig?'

'No,' Meadows said. 'His hair is too long but I guess he could cover it with a wig, perhaps to stop any of his own hair getting on the victim.'

'That was tech,' Paskin said as she put down the phone. 'They've tracked the IP address that posted the video on Facebook to Donald Hobson's house.'

'That's what he's nervous about. He's been following and filming Stacey so it's likely that he knows who the guy in the video is.'

'Or he's our killer,' Blackwell said.

'He's got an alibi, he was with five people,' Edris said.

'We'll seize his laptop and phone and bring him in for questioning in the morning. While we're at it, I want a search of Bill's house and any surrounding buildings. We're looking for any connection to Stacey or the crime scene. Twine, torn bedsheets, a wig, and a mobile phone. Bill says he doesn't own one, but he could be lying. I think that's it for tonight, go home before this storm gets any worse and I'll see you all in the morning. I'm off to catch some chickens.'

Chapter Eleven

The wind drove the rain into his face and blew off his hood as he battled his way towards the humpback bridge. The water was sloshing around his feet making it difficult to walk. The drains were already full and if the river burst its banks it would flood most of the village.

He didn't want to be out in this weather, he had other things to worry about, but it would look odd if he didn't help. He pulled his hat down over his ears and pulled up his hood. The last thing he needed was a cold.

He managed to battle his way to the bridge where there was already a line of men and women on both sides hauling sandbags along the bank. They were joined by the older generation who looked on with torches held in their hands. He took his position and grabbed a sack, twisted, and handed it over. It was hard work and despite the rain and wind he was soon sweating. A rumble of thunder rolled around them, then the sky lit up with a fork of lightning.

Headlights from an approaching car lit up the working party. He stopped to catch his breath as the car came to a halt at the bridge and wound down the window. He was close enough to see and hear the driver talk to Gwyn Rees, the church caretaker, who was organising sandbags.

'Better turn around, the river is about to burst its banks, you won't be able to get back through this way,' Gwyn Rees shouted above the wind.

'I'll take the mountain road back. I need to sort out Bill James' chickens.'

'I'm not sure Bill will appreciate some stranger hanging around his property. Sorry I can't let you through. Not until I've spoken to Bill.'

'I'm DI Meadows.' The driver held out identification. 'If you're not going to let me through then perhaps you would be good enough to make sure his property and animals are secure.'

'I haven't got time for that now. Fine, go ahead.'

He turned his head away so the detective wouldn't see him as he drove past.

'Bloody idiot,' Gwyn said as he watched Meadows drive over the bridge. 'If he hadn't arrested Bill then he wouldn't have to have come out. Shame we have to deal with this. Would have been a laugh to watch him try and get that lot into a coop.'

He nodded but didn't comment. He didn't like the idea of the police being here. What had Bible Bill told them? Could he have seen something? Bill must have helped the police in some way or why would they bother about the chickens? Maybe they had used it as leverage to get information, he thought. He slowly moved away from the line. No one noticed. They would think he needed a rest. Besides the work was nearly done. This was his opportunity to make sure the police stopped meddling in his work.

He hurried back to his house as he tried to come up with a plan. He knew what needed to be done and God would help him, but how? He could take the car, but the detective would see him coming. Maybe he could wait up on the mountain and flag him down. He shook his head.

That wouldn't work. He quickly changed his hat, put on a pair of gloves, and searched around for a weapon. Then he remembered the shotgun. He was glad he had kept it. He knew it would be useful someday. He made a quick call and hurried out of the house.

There was no one around when he slipped through the kissing gate and ran along the footpath. He'd wrapped the gun in an old coat but now wished he had put it in a holdall or at least something easier to carry. He was out of breath when he reached Bill's farm. He stopped briefly to catch his breath then walked slowly up the dark track. He was grateful for the howling wind, the detective wouldn't hear him coming.

He could see the torch light swinging as the detective waved his arms herding the chickens to the field behind and into the coops. Meadows had secured the two upper coops and was bending down to slide the bolt on the lower ones when he saw his chance. He unwrapped the gun – he could shoot the detective but he didn't trust his aim. He didn't want to kill him, just warn him off. He moved swiftly and brought the barrel of the gun down on the side of Meadows' head. The detective pitched forward so he delivered another blow to the side of his temple. The detective keeled over onto the ground and groaned. He was only stunned but it was enough for him to have time to do what was needed.

When he was finished he picked up the discarded coat and ran.

* * *

Meadows felt the release of pressure on his back, he tried to get up, but a wave of dizziness overcame him. He felt disorientated in the thick darkness. The sound of squawking chickens mixed with the roaring wind echoed through his head and pain ran down his scalp to the base of his neck. He heard a woman's voice call out and fear prickled his skin. Whoever hit him was still here and if he didn't move quickly they would finish the job, he thought. He tried to get up, but a wave of dizziness hit him.

'Are you alright?' A light appeared and he shielded his eyes from the glare.

'Yes, I'm fine.' He tried to stand again, this time using the coop to steady himself.

The light swept across the ground as she came closer. 'You dropped your torch,' she said. He saw a hand grab the torch on the ground. She flicked it on and handed it to him.

'Thanks.' He shone the torch and saw Sarah Kelly, her hair dripping wet and her face ghostly pale in the torchlight.

'You've had a nasty fall,' Sarah said. 'Let me help you.' She held out her hand.

'I didn't fall.' Meadows shone the torch all around him to make sure there were no branches that could have fallen on him. 'There was someone here, they hit me over the head.'

'There's no one here,' Sarah said.

'You must have seen someone.'

'No, I didn't.'

'Were you pulling on my arm?'

'No, I only just got here and was coming to check on the chickens when I saw you.'

She could be lying, he thought, or maybe she was the one to hit me. 'What are you doing here?'

'I had a message from Bill to check on the chickens in the morning. I didn't think anyone would come out tonight, so I thought I better check.'

'It's not safe, whoever hit me could still be here. You better get in my car and I'll call for backup.'

'If someone did hit you then they are long gone. Look, no one can get into the village, the bridge is closed. It's pointless calling anyone out now. I have my own car, let me take you back to my house and clean up that cut on your head.'

Meadows hadn't realised he was bleeding until Sarah pointed it out. She seemed keen to get him away from the farm and to stop him from getting help to search. The village suddenly felt claustrophobic in the darkness, as if the inhabitants were all in on a secret and conspiring against him. *What if she is trying to lure me back to her place and the killer is waiting there?* He thought. He rubbed his hands over his face. The knock on the head was making him feel paranoid.

'I have a first aid kit in my car.' He flicked the torch around as he walked to the car, but with the small beam it was useless trying to pick out someone hiding. He guessed Sarah was right, there was no point calling anyone out. It would be too dangerous to conduct a search in this storm.

He let Sarah help him clean the wound and apply a dressing then he followed her car back to her house, making sure she was safely inside before taking the mountain road home. The rain lashed against the windscreen making visibility poor. The wind rocked the car and the darkness closed around. Meadows hoped that a sheep didn't wander into his path. A few cars had gone over the edge of the mountain in the past and he doubted that, if he got into trouble, there would be anyone along this way soon that would spot him. He kept his speed down even though he was desperate to get off the mountain and home. His clothes were soaked, and his head throbbed.

By the time he reached the narrow track that led to his cottage, it was already struggling to contain the water that ran off the fields. The trees were shredding their smaller branches which bounced off the car, and Meadows was relieved to make a final dash into his home and close the door. He made himself a hot drink then retrieved the box that Jerome had given him. He lifted the lid and inhaled the recently cured cannabis. He rolled a joint and sat back in the armchair and inhaled. With each draw on the joint he felt his muscles relax and he let his mind go over the evening's events.

Who knew he would be at Bill's farm? Bill could have made a call, but that would be easy to check, he thought. Sarah already admitted she had received a message from Bill. There were plenty of men on the bridge and he had identified himself. He was sure he had seen Donald.

The thoughts swirled around, and his head throbbed. He gave up trying to work it out and went upstairs. It was only when he removed his clothes that he saw the letters and numbers PROV1412 written on his arm. He grabbed his phone and typed in the reference and 'bible' in the search engine. The top result was Proverbs 14:12.

> *There is a way that seems right to a man, but its end is the way to death.*

Chapter Twelve

The storm had raged all night, but all was calm as Meadows stood outside his cottage checking the damage to the roof. Slates littered the floor along with twigs but thankfully had missed his car. The roof will have to wait, he thought as he climbed into his car. He had photographed the writing on his arm before trying to scrub it off, but it still remained. Having sent the photo along with one of his head wound to Edris he had received back a shocked-face emoji which had made him smile. He felt a little foolish now getting himself almost knocked out, even more so for allowing his imagination to make him fearful. As he started the engine his phone rang. Folland's name flashed across the screen. He hit accept and Folland's voice filled the car.

'Got a good one for you,' Folland said.

'Great.'

'An unauthorised grave,' Folland said with a hint of amusement.

'What's that supposed to mean?'

'A grave in St Herbert's graveyard that's not supposed to be there. A Vicar Daniels called it in.'

'Okay, I'm on my way.'

Meadows had only got halfway up the lane when he found his way blocked by a fallen tree. He got out of the car and shook his head. It felt like there was some higher force trying to stop him doing his job. It wasn't God that hit me on the head last night, or killed Stacey Evans, he thought. He made a call to the station then walked to the farm to get help. It took over two hours for the farmer, his son, and a tractor to clear away the fallen sycamore tree. When Meadows finally arrived in Gaer Fawr he was pleased to see at least the bridge was passable. He found Valentine outside the church talking to the vicar and another man.

'Morning, sir,' Valentine said. 'This is Gwyn Rees who is responsible for the maintenance of the graveyard and I believe you've met Vicar Daniels.'

'Saw you on the bridge last night,' Gwyn said. 'You managed to get home alright then.'

Meadows noticed that Gwyn was eyeing the cut on the side of his head and wondered if he was the one that had struck him. 'Yes, thank you. When was it that you noticed the suspicious mound of earth?'

'Yeah, like I was telling this young lady. I came early this morning to check for storm damage. We put sandbags around the church last night, but it doesn't always work. If water gets into the church and seeps below, it's a hell of a job to get it cleaned up. After I checked the church with the vicar, I checked the trees for fallen branches then walked the perimeter of the graveyard. The wall of the far left corner has collapsed, nearly taking with it the outer graves. It was while I was checking this that I saw the freshly dug earth.'

'And there's been no recent burials.' Meadows turned to Vicar Daniels.

'No, not in that part of the graveyard. It's very old, most of the graves are over a hundred and fifty years old, some older. Every burial is written in the church register. I checked, there is no recorded burial between the graves that are located there.'

'When was the last time you checked that area?'

Gwyn furrowed his brow. 'Erm, I don't generally clear the older section as often as down here. Probably about a month ago I trimmed the grass and checked for any damage to the stones. Thinking about it, maybe more like six weeks.'

'Okay, thank you. We won't hold you up any longer.'

'I'll stay if that's okay,' Vicar Daniels said.

'Yes, as long as you stay away from that part of the graveyard until we've finished. Right, let's take a look, Valentine.'

'Edris is up there,' Valentine said.

'Where is Blackwell?'

Valentine waited until they were away from Gwyn Rees and Vicar Daniels before replying. 'He's supervising the search on Bill Jones' house. He sent me up here with Edris but said I should go and pick up Donald Hobson as soon as we have a warrant. Paskin's car was hit by a tree last night, so she wasn't in when we left. Blackwell thought this might be a prank for Halloween or someone burying a pet but when we took a look we figured it was too big for either. So, we called in SOCO.'

'I think that was probably wise.'

'There isn't enough room for a digger and the ground is too unstable, so they are having to dig by hand. It's taking ages.'

They walked the path that led through the centre of the graveyard. At first the headstones were black and uniform but as they walked further up different shapes and sizes appeared. Some had statues of angels or crosses, others family plots with obelisks displaying the names of the deceased. As they reached the top of the path they could see a man in a white protective suit approaching.

'Great, you're here.' Edris pulled down his hood and took off his mask. 'They've found a body. Judging by the smell it's been in there a while.' He wrinkled his nose. 'I didn't go close enough to have a look.'

'Looks like we are going to be here awhile,' Meadows said. 'Valentine, you better check up on that warrant and take Hanes with you to pick up Donald. Blackwell can interview him when he gets back from the search. You better sit in and make sure he doesn't scare the kid. Cordon off the lychgate as well; I don't want anyone from the village wandering in.'

'Nasty cut you've got,' Edris said as Meadows followed him to the SOCO van.

'Could have been worse,' Meadows said.

'Worse?' Edris shook his head. 'You could be dead. That Bible verse sounds like a death threat.'

'Nah, they were just trying to warn me off. They could have killed me if they wanted to.'

'Well, it wasn't Bible Bill as he was in custody all night. So, there is a killer wandering around the village attacking people at random.'

'Or he knew I was coming. Then again, there were plenty of people on the bridge last night. Could be anyone.'

They reached the van and were handed protective clothing.

'This place is starting to give me the creeps,' Edris said. 'I reckon there is something wrong with the fertiliser.'

Meadows laughed as he pulled on the overalls and fitted a mask. It was uncomfortable and he could already feel his own breath as they made their way back up the path and across the graveyard. Here the graves were old brown stone with patches of moss. Most of the lettering had eroded over the years, some now were just smooth stone.

A tent had been erected over the site and a pathway marked for entering. A foul smell of rotting meat and sulphur permeated the air and Meadows imagined it would be unbearable without the mask. He braced himself and stepped into the tent. Planks of wood had been laid each side of the hole and against the sides to secure the earth. Mike Fielding, a forensic officer whom Meadows had met on previous cases, was brushing earth off the bloated body. There wasn't much to be seen as the victim lay face down, but it was enough to turn Meadows' stomach.

'We couldn't make the hole any wider.' Mike's voice was muffled by the mask. 'There are graves on each side, and one has already collapsed. It's going to be a bitch to get the body out. Looks like a man to me.'

'Yes,' Meadows said, looking at the back of the head. 'There's not much you can do but photograph each stage and move him. I don't envy you that task.'

'We'll give you a shout when we've got him out.'

'Thanks.' Meadows was grateful to step outside the tent to where Edris was waiting. He walked to the edge where the wall had collapsed. One grave had sunk, another's headstone was leaning. From this position Meadows didn't have a clear view of the road. The graveyard levelled off in this corner before sloping downwards.

'It's far enough away from the church and out of sight of the road,' Meadows said.

'Yeah, but still a hell of a risk. How do you drag a body up here without being seen?'

'Let's go and have a chat with Vicar Daniels. See if the graveyard is locked up at night.'

As they walked back down to the church, they could see a crowd had gathered by the wall. All craning their necks to see what was happening. Meadows ignored the looks as he and Edris disposed of their suits and joined Vicar Daniels outside the church.

'I'm afraid we have found a body,' Meadows said.

Vicar Daniels paled. 'I think I'm in need of a cuppa. Would you like to join me? We could go up to the vicarage.'

'That's very kind, thank you,' Meadows said. 'I'm afraid we are going to be here for some time, and we'll need to keep the entrance cordoned off.'

'What about tomorrow morning's service?'

'We'll do our best to keep the disruption to a minimum. After we've moved the body, I don't see any reason why you couldn't continue with the service. We will need to keep the graveyard off limits. Judging by the crowd, it looks like you will have a full house tomorrow.'

'Yes, it looks that way. Do you know who it is?'

'No, not yet and even if we did we would need to inform the family before we can release a name.'

'Of course. I'll make an announcement before service in the morning if you would be good enough to let me know what I can say.' Vicar Daniels started to walk behind the church. 'There is a shortcut to the vicarage.'

'Handy,' Edris said.

They walked back up the central path, but this time turned left at the top. A narrow pathway led to a wooden gate.

'Much easier than walking around the road way,' Vicar Daniels said. 'Gives me an extra couple of minutes in bed on a Sunday morning.'

They stepped through the gate and into a large garden. In the centre was a round patio area with a hydrangea bush in the middle. A lawn ran around the patio and disappeared into deep borders of shrubs.

'Lovely garden,' Meadows commented.

'Not my work, Gwyn takes care of it.'

Two steps led up to the back door and into a wide hall with a coat stand. As he followed Vicar Daniels, Meadows noticed a stained glass window at the top of the oak staircase. He admired the Vicar's dedication to his vocation. It seemed that the church dominated every aspect of his life, even the home he lived in.

'Come through to the kitchen, I find it is cosier in there,' Vicar Daniels said.

'It's a big house,' Edris said. 'Do you live here alone?'

'Yes, seems a bit of a waste. I expect the vicarage was built to accommodate a large family and to entertain the parishioners.' Vicar Daniels filled the kettle and hit the switch before taking three mugs out of the cupboard.

'You said earlier that there is a register for all burials,' Meadows said. 'Who would have access to that?'

'Anyone is entitled to look at it. It's kept in the church vestry. The register is very old, but we still use handwritten records.'

'It wouldn't be easy to pick a spot that had enough room,' Meadows said. 'Most of the graves are close together.'

'Yes, originally there was plenty of space between the graves and enough land. Later, as the plots filled, the graves were dug closer together. We are running out of room. Most people now choose a church service and cremation but some of the older generation still have plots.'

'You would also need to know that part of the graveyard is not used,' Edris said.

'Not many people go up that far, only Gwyn. Except on Palm Sunday when flowers are laid on nearly all the graves. I guess most people in the village would know the layout.'

'Have you noticed anyone hanging around in the graveyard over the last few weeks?' Meadows asked.

'No, but then I'm mostly indoors. Either here, in the church, or visiting parishioners.' Vicar Daniels poured the water into the teapot. 'Milk and sugar?'

'Just milk,' Meadows said.

'Both for me,' Edris said.

'Are the church gates locked at night?'

'No, they are kept open. There has never been cause to lock them, no vandalism. The church is locked. It's a sad world we live in that forces us to close God's house.'

'Do you keep a digger or equipment on site for digging graves?' Meadows asked.

'No, we use a professional company. There is a shed where Gwyn keeps his gardening tools.'

'It can't be easy to dig a hole to fit in a body,' Edris said. 'How long does it usually take to dig a grave?'

'It depends. They use a digger if the ground is stable otherwise it's by hand. I'm sure I read somewhere it takes about six hours and it is a skilled job,' Vicar Daniels said.

Meadows watched Vicar Daniels pour the tea. He was finding it difficult to figure out how someone could move a man through the graveyard and dig a hole that size without being seen. Probably did it at night, he thought.

'What about noise or light in the night?'

'My bedroom doesn't look over the graveyard so I'm afraid I wouldn't have heard or seen anything.' He handed the tea to Meadows.

'Is there a side entrance here?'

'Yes.'

'Locked?'

'No.' Vicar Daniels sat down. 'Do you think someone came through my garden carrying that poor soul? It doesn't bear thinking about.'

'We have to look at that possibility,' Meadows said and took a sip of his tea. 'It's a more direct route. I'll get some officers to take a look. It would probably be best if you don't use that entrance for the moment.'

'That's fine, I'm happy to help in any way I can.'

'Thank you. I'll have someone get in touch from our press release team. They can help you with any announcement that you make in the morning. I'm sure your parishioners will be wanting to know what's going on.'

'Yes, I think I may just take the phone off the hook.' Vicar Daniels smiled.

They finished their tea and were walking back to the church when Mike beckoned them over.

'Looks like I have an identification for you. It was found with the body.' He held out an evidence bag with a wallet. 'A Dr David Rowlands.'

Chapter Thirteen

Donald woke to the sound of the front door closing. His head was thick with sleep and it took him a moment to remember it was Saturday. He guessed his mum and dad had just come back from the weekly shopping. They always went early. Now his father would plonk himself down in front of the TV and his mother would be in the kitchen trying out some new recipe. She'd been doing that a lot lately and Donald was never sure what was going to be put in front of him to eat. He preferred plain food. Still, she usually brought him back a treat and he was feeling hungry. It was the first night he had slept through without the nightmares and now the police had spoken to him he didn't feel so sick all the time.

He pulled on a pair of jeans and a T-shirt and went down to the kitchen where his mum was unpacking the shopping.

'Put the kettle on, please,' his mum said. 'I picked you up some cakes. We'll have one with a cuppa when I've put this lot away.'

Donald made the tea, took a cup to his father then sat at the kitchen table. His mother placed a box on the table and opened the lid. Chocolate éclairs, his favourite. He plucked one out and took a bite, the cream oozed out of the edges.

'Glad to see you've got your appetite back.' His mother picked up a cake. 'Perhaps you'll feel well enough to go back to school on Monday.'

Donald shrugged his shoulders, finished the cake, and licked his fingers before picking up another.

'The police are at the church,' his mum said. 'They've been there all morning. That detective that was here the other day was just getting out of his car when we passed.'

The cake suddenly felt too heavy and sickly in his mouth. Donald picked up his cup and tried to wash down the mouthful. 'What's going on there?' He placed the remainder of the cake on the table.

'Dunno, but they were dressed up in those white suits, like you see on the TV. Don't look so worried. Vicar Daniels is okay. I saw him standing outside the church. I wonder if someone else has been attacked. Can't see who would have been out last night.'

Anxiety twisted Donald's stomach, he bolted from the kitchen and ran up the stairs. In his bedroom he hopped from foot to foot as he pulled on his trainers. He grabbed a hoodie and hurried down the stairs.

'Where are you going?' his mother called.

'Over to the church.'

'Finish your cake first.'

'I'll eat it when I get back.' Donald slammed the door then forced himself to slow down. He thought it might look odd if he ran towards the church. All along the church wall people stood stretching their necks trying to catch a glimpse of the police. He worked his way among them then stood on tiptoes to try and get a better look. Vicar Daniels was talking to Gwyn Rees but there wasn't anything more to be seen.

'What's going on?' he asked no one in particular.

'Dunno,' Emlyn Harris from the dairy farm said. 'They've been back and forth to the van a few times and another copper just turned up. I reckon there has been another attack.'

'Who?' Donald asked.

'Thought it might be you as no one has seen you for a couple of days.'

'Don't tease the boy,' Mary Beynon said.

Donald hoped that it was another attack, it was better than the alternative.

'Maybe I should go and see Vicar Daniels. Poor soul looks so worried, maybe it was him that found... whatever's been found. He must have had a shock,' Mary said.

'Well, what do you expect? Someone lurking around the graveyard attacking people. I bet he's thinking it could have been him.' Emlyn fell silent as Gwyn Rees left the vicar's side and made his way down the path.

Donald moved with the others towards the lychgate, he wanted to hear what Gwyn would say.

'What's going on, Gwyn?' Emlyn asked.

'I found a grave up the back which shouldn't be there. Looks freshly dug,' Gwyn said.

Donald felt a coldness creep over him. Gwyn Rees continued to talk but he wasn't listening to what he was saying. He knew who lay beneath the earth. He was never supposed to be found. He backed away from the crowd, he didn't want to be there anymore, not now they had dug him up. Images of a body covered in maggots flooded his mind. What would he look like now? The creatures of the earth would have been eating away at him, he thought. The cake curdled in his stomach as he hurried across the road.

'Did you find out what's going on?' his mother asked as soon as he walked in the house.

'No.' Donald went to his bedroom and shut the door.

He paced back and forth, his skin prickling with anxiety. He wanted to crawl back into bed, pull the cover over his head and hide from the world. He felt so scared and alone. His only option was to leave but he didn't know where to go. It would have to be a place that no one would find him. The cave up on the mountain, he thought. No one would think of looking there. He would need food and a blanket to keep warm. He emptied the contents of his school bag onto the floor and began stuffing it with clothes. He'd have to wait until night to take food from the cupboards and sneak out. He found some money laying around, checked his phone was fully charged, put it in his pocket and left the bedroom. He had enough to buy some food and a bottle of water. He'd take it to the cave now and come back. He figured then he wouldn't have so much to carry.

He was halfway down the stairs when he heard a knock on the door. He retreated and listened from the landing.

'It's the police to see you, Donald,' his mother called.

Donald froze. They can't know anything yet, he told himself. They just need to ask some questions. He forced himself to move. He walked into the sitting room and saw a pretty dark-haired woman and a stocky policeman. He looked intimidating with his black vest with a radio clipped to the breast.

'Hello, Donald, I'm Detective Constable Valentine and this is Officer Hanes. We would like you to come to the station with us to answer a few questions. We will also need to take your mobile phone, computer and any other device that is connected to the internet.'

'What? No.' Donald backed away. 'I didn't do anything.' Donald felt the air go out of his lungs and he tried to draw in a breath, but the room was airless. He kept sucking in the air until he felt light-headed.

'It's okay,' Valentine said.

'What's this about?' Donald's father demanded.

'We need to speak to Donald in connection to the murder of Stacey Evans.'

'He doesn't know anything about it. Can't you ask him your questions here? You're scaring the boy.'

'I'm sorry, we have to take him to the station,' Valentine said. 'Your mum and dad can come with you and one of them will be able to stay with you during the interview.'

Donald didn't want his mum or dad listening to what they would ask him. Didn't want them knowing what he had done.

'I don't feel well,' Donald said.

'Come on now,' Hanes said. 'Let's start by getting your computer, shall we?' He took an evidence bag from his pocket and held it open. 'If you'd like to pop your phone in there for me.'

Donald thought about what was on his phone. He should have got rid of it. His mum and dad would see and know what he did. His stomach clenched and without warning he vomited; it hit the floor and splattered Hanes' trousers. He turned and fled, taking the stairs two at a time. He could hear the police behind him. He managed to get into the bathroom and lock the door.

'Donald!' Hanes rapped his knuckles on the door.

They would break the door down if he didn't come out, he thought. Maybe he could get through the window. 'I've had an accident. I need to change my trousers,' he said.

He could hear the police whispering behind the door.

'Okay, Donald, be quick, I'm going to wait outside,' Valentine said.

Donald turned the bath taps on full then opened the window. He managed to squeeze out and land on the extension roof. He was scared of heights but with the threat of the police behind him he didn't stop to think. He jumped off the roof, landing awkwardly. Ignoring the pain, he ran to the bottom of the garden and over the fence. He kept running, his chest hurt, and pain shot through his ankle, but he didn't stop until he reached the open fields. He crept along, keeping close to the hedge then sprinted to the barn. Inside, he climbed the stack of hay. He moved several bales until he had made a hole big enough to climb into then slid the bales above his head. He took out his phone and looked through the numbers. There had to be someone to help him.

Chapter Fourteen

Only Paskin was in the office when Edris and Meadows got back to the station. It had been a long day waiting for the body to be moved and talking to the locals, all of whom hadn't seen any strange activity in the graveyard.

'You managed to get in then,' Edris said. He took off his coat and sat down.

'Yeah, car's a right off,' Paskin said.

'Where are Blackwell and Valentine?' Meadows asked.

'The search didn't turn up anything, so Blackwell let Bill Jones go as he had given a DNA sample. He grunted something and went off. He's in a hell of a mood. Valentine isn't back yet. I think she's avoiding Blackwell.'

'Give her a call and tell her to come in. There is little point continuing to search for Donald in the dark. He can't have got far. Get a picture sent to the local bus depot so they can look out for him. The likelihood is that he's hiding in some outbuilding. We can start again in the morning.'

Meadows took a look at the incident board and saw a picture of his arm with the Bible verse. He turned to Edris. 'Right, you better tell me everything you know about the day Dr Rowlands went missing.'

Edris took out his notebook and flicked through. 'His wife, Linda Rowlands, reported him missing on Tuesday morning the 29th of September after she received a call from the surgery to say he hadn't turned up for work.'

'So, over three weeks ago,' Meadows said.

'Yeah, about that,' Edris said. 'He hadn't arranged any cover for work. We called in to speak to Linda, took some details, asked the usual questions. He had taken a call and left the house about ten thirty on the Monday evening to visit a housebound patient.'

'Linda went to bed and assumed he had come home late, slept in the spare room and gone off to work early. We called in at the surgery. Calls are handled through a call centre after hours. A call out was made for a Mrs Iris Hawkins, an eighty-year-old widow. We checked and Iris claimed she didn't make a call or see the doctor that evening. We then got a message from Linda that afternoon to say the doctor had sent a text saying he was sorry, that he no longer loved her, and he would be in touch about the house and finances.'

'Well, it looks like he didn't send that text,' Meadows said.

At that moment Blackwell sauntered into the room with an aura of discontent.

'You've heard we found the doctor's body,' Edris said.

'You found his wallet with a body,' Blackwell snapped. 'For all you know the doctor could have done someone in then taken off.'

'I don't think that is likely,' Meadows said.

Valentine came through the door looking stressed.

'Well?' Blackwell said.

'Nothing, we've searched everywhere. He doesn't have any friends. We checked with Sarah Kelly and the vicar as well as some of the other church members. No one has heard from him. Other than send out a search and rescue, I don't know what else to do.'

Blackwell huffed. 'What the hell were you thinking?'

'He'd thrown up everywhere and had an upset stomach. I was outside the bathroom the whole time. I didn't know he was going to take off.'

'You should have cuffed the little fucker and brought him in. He could have got changed here.'

'I'm sorry,' Valentine said.

'Yeah, you better hope another body doesn't turn up.'

'Leave her alone,' Edris said. 'You thought the doctor had run off. I told you there was something odd about his disappearance.'

'You can shut the fuck up.' Colour rose in Blackwell's face. 'I acted on the information available. Valentine felt sorry for the kid and it clouded her judgement. Next time, you break the door down; on second thoughts I'll do the bloody job myself.'

'You're being a dick,' Edris said.

'Enough,' Meadows said.

Blackwell snapped his head towards Meadows. He looked like he was about to retort when he grabbed his left arm and the colour drained from his face.

'Blackwell, are you okay?' Meadows asked moving towards him.

Blackwell shook his head as he tried to move to the desk, but he staggered and landed on the floor.

'Call an ambulance,' Meadows said as he knelt next to Blackwell who appeared to be gasping for breath. He loosened Blackwell's tie and collar, then positioned him against the desk. 'Try and take slow breaths, Stefan.' He could see the panic in Blackwell's eyes. 'You're going to be okay. Anyone got any aspirin?' Meadows asked.

Paskin managed to find some in her bag and handed them to Meadows with a glass of water.

'Here, try and swallow this,' Meadows held the glass to Blackwell's lips.

'Call my father,' Blackwell said as he winced with pain.

'I'll do it now,' Paskin said.

'Try and stay quiet,' Meadows said. 'Help is on the way.'

Meadows was relieved when the paramedics arrived and took over.

'I'll go with him,' Valentine said as they put Blackwell onto a stretcher.

'Okay,' Meadows said. 'Keep us updated.'

The office fell silent once Blackwell had left. Meadows turned to Paskin. 'Are you alright?'

'Yes, I'm a bit shocked, that's all. Poor Blackwell. I guess he wasn't feeling well and that's why he was in such a bad mood.'

'You may be right.'

'I shouldn't have had a go at him,' Edris said.

'It's not your fault,' Meadows said. 'It isn't anyone's fault. I'm sure he'll be okay, he was conscious and coherent which is a good sign.'

Chris Harley from Tech came in holding a flash drive in his hand. 'Bad time?'

'No, it's fine,' Meadows said. 'What have you got?'

'I retrieved some files from the laptop that came in this morning. Thought the videos would interest you. They've been uploaded from the phone and deleted, sat in the recycle bin so an easy job.'

'Okay let's take a look,' Meadows said.

They gathered around the computer and a list of files came up.

'Mainly of the same girl and man,' Chris said.

Meadows clicked on a file dated in June and clicked play. It was the same location as the last video, but this time Stacey was wearing a summer dress and the man was dressed in a T-shirt and shorts. Even though his face couldn't be seen, this time a tattoo was visible on his right arm. Meadows paused the video.

'Can you get that tattoo enhanced?'

'Yeah, no problem,' Chris said.

Meadows closed the video and opened a file dated from the previous year. This one showed Erin. It was taken on the mountain and she was aware she was being filmed. Another one showed her up the quarry placing stones on the ground. The next shot was taken from the top of the quarry looking down where the stones formed a picture of a unicorn.

'That's clever,' Paskin said.

'Yes,' Meadows agreed as he paused the video. 'She looks so happy and she was talented. I'm surprised Donald tried to delete these files.'

'He didn't,' Chris said. 'I just put on a sample for you to see. There are loads of them. I'll send up a picture of the tattoo as soon as it's done. I hope Blackwell will be okay.'

'Thanks.'

'It looks like Donald had an unhealthy interest in Stacey,' Edris said.

'Yes, but that doesn't mean that he killed her. He's got a tight alibi, but I think he knows something. He can certainly identify the man in the video. We'll get uniform to pick up the search in the morning. Paskin, can you do a background check on Dr Rowlands. After that, get yourself home. I'll see you on Monday morning.'

'Do you think the doctor's murder is connected to Stacey?' Edris asked.

'It's too much of a coincidence not to be. Two murders in the same village, about four weeks apart. We'll have to wait for the post-mortem. If it's the same killer then he would have left his mark somewhere. Come on, we better go and see the doctor's wife before news gets out.'

* * *

The doctor's house was situated just outside Gaer Fawr. A sprawling lawn with pruned trees led to a stone building with Georgian windows.

'Nice place,' Meadows commented.

'Wait until you see inside. You would swear they were living in Mayfair. Really posh, not a sign of the country in sight.'

'The question is how does a doctor afford all this? A local GP wouldn't earn that much.'

Linda Rowland opened the door and smiled at Edris. 'Hello again. Have you come with news of my wandering husband?'

'This is DI Meadows,' Edris said. 'May we come in?'

'Of course.' Linda stood back.

'We're sorry to call on you so late in the evening,' Meadows said as they followed Linda into the sitting room.

'It's no problem, please take a seat.'

She doesn't seem overly concerned at our presence, Meadows thought as he took a seat on the cream leather sofa. He watched Linda take the armchair. She was dressed smartly, and he noticed a gold watch on her wrist. Her blonde hair was styled into a bob and her make-up pristine. He felt the first twist of anxiety as he prepared to deliver the news.

'You may have heard that we found a body this morning in Gaer Fawr and I'm afraid that we have reason to believe it may be your husband.'

'Oh.'

'There will need to be a formal identification. In this case it will be best if we use dental records, but I think you should be prepared for the worst.'

'I see.'

Meadows waited for an emotional outburst, but none came.

'Mrs Rowlands, is there someone we can call for you?'

'You can call me Linda.' She folded her hands on her lap. 'I have a son in university and one working in Bristol. I'll call them when you are sure.'

'I understand that this must be a shock for you, but we will need to ask you a few questions. Maybe you'd like a friend to be with you.'

'I'm fine. Would you like a cup of tea?'

'No, thank you, but Edris can make one for you if you like.'

She waved her hand. 'Actually, I think I'll have a glass of wine. I would ask you to join me but I'm sure you're not allowed to drink on duty. If you'll excuse me for a moment.'

Linda left the room and Edris raised his eyebrows. Meadows was sure he was thinking the same thoughts. Linda Rowlands didn't appear to be at all upset or shocked by the news.

Linda returned carrying a glass and a bottle of wine. She poured herself a glass, took a sip and settled back on the armchair.

'Does this have anything to do with St Herbert's? I heard there was a lot of police activity there today.'

'Yes,' Meadows said.

A little giggle escaped her mouth. 'Imagine, I've been sitting in church every Sunday morning and he's been there the whole time.'

'We cannot be certain that it is your husband. All I can tell you is that his wallet was found with the body.'

'Well, it seems a more plausible explanation for his disappearance.'

'Than him running off with another woman?' Meadows asked.

'Yes, it's not like he was faithful, the complete opposite. I did mind at first, but the arguments and apologies grew tiresome. We made an agreement that he would be discreet and not cause me embarrassment. It was easier than a divorce. The children were young, and I didn't like the idea of selling the house and ending up struggling in some two-bedroom place in the middle of nowhere while he had a good time. You may find it a strange arrangement, but he didn't question what I spent money on or if I took the boys on holiday.'

'Was there anyone special that you knew about?'

'No.' Linda finished her wine and poured another glass. 'He liked younger women. Didn't matter if they were married or not. It did cause a couple of embarrassing moments a few years ago. I had the odd upset husband turning up at the house.'

'Anyone you knew?' Edris asked.

'Anthony Evans.'

'Stacey Evan's father?'

'Yes, Cloe Evans was one of my husband's conquests. That was a few years back. I think he learned his lesson not to play so close to home.'

'And the other husband?'

'Don't know. I think he was from Llandeilo.'

'What about recently?' Meadows asked.

'I don't know. I'm sure he would have had someone on the go or maybe his charm was starting to wear off.'

'How did he seem before he went missing? Had he been depressed, financial or work worries?'

'No, not that I am aware of. Bank balance is the same and I haven't had any demands for outstanding debts. There wasn't a lot that troubled him. My husband was an arrogant man.'

'Can you think of anyone who would want to harm your husband?'

'Plenty, he was a complete bastard.'

* * *

'Well, she doesn't think much of her husband. She didn't look at all bothered that there's a strong possibility that he's dead,' Edris said when they were back in the car.

'No, but people react differently to shock. Maybe when the news sinks in, it will hit her. Then again if she loved him enough to marry him, that love could have turned to hate rather than indifference.'

'You think she could have killed him?'

'Not without help. I suppose she could have killed him then phoned her sons to help dispose of the body. We'll need to wait until the post-mortem to find out how he died.' Meadows started the engine.

'There is also a connection to Stacey,' Edris said.

'Only that he had an affair with her mother and that sounds like some time ago.'

'What if he turned his attention to Stacey? Linda said he liked his women young.'

'It's possible. We'll have to check if the doctor has a tattoo. But would that be motive for Linda to kill him? She said she knew about his affairs.'

'Maybe Stacey wanted more. What if the doctor was going to leave Linda for Stacey? That would be a scandal, plus she already admitted she didn't want to give up the house and her entitlement to a good life.'

'It's a good theory but why the biblical messages?' Meadows asked.

'Linda does go to church.'

'It's worth checking out the sons. It may just be a domestic and the Bible reference on Stacey was to throw us off the case.'

'Then there's Donald,' Edris said. 'He was following Stacey so he would have known that she was having an affair with the doctor.'

'So, he tells Linda. Maybe he knew about the doctor being killed and that's why he has run. If he is a witness or knows something he could be in danger. I shouldn't have been so quick to call off the search,' Meadows said as they left Gaer Fawr behind.

Chapter Fifteen

The man that sat holding Blackwell's hand let go when Meadows and Edris entered the room.

'Ah, more visitors, Stef.' The man stood. 'I'll get out of your way.' He smiled at Meadows.

'There is no need to leave,' Meadows said.

'It's no problem. I'll go and get myself a coffee. There is only two visitors allowed at a time. Once he gets moved to the wards there'll be more room. See you later.' The man left the room.

Blackwell looked pale, he was hooked up to monitors with a drip in his arm and an oxygen tube clipped at his nose.

'How are you feeling?' Meadows asked as he took a seat.

'Like an idiot,' Blackwell said.

'I'm sorry–' Edris began but Blackwell silenced him by holding up his hand.

'It was a blockage, could have happened any time so you're not taking the credit,' he said with a hint of a smile. 'Have you found Donald Hobson?'

'No work talk,' Meadows said. 'You have to rest.'

'I'm already sick of people pussyfooting around me and I've nothing to do but lie here. The least you can do is entertain me.'

'Okay, no we haven't found him yet.' Meadows filled Blackwell in on their visit to Linda Rowlands.

'I shouldn't have been so hard on Valentine,' Blackwell said. 'I was more pissed off with myself about the doctor turning up dead.'

'You had no reason to believe anything had happened to him,' Meadows said.

'Yeah, he was probably already dead by the time he was reported missing,' Edris added.

'Is that supposed to make me feel better?'

Edris shrugged his shoulders. 'If you'd prefer, I could get a book and read to you.'

'Fuck off.'

Meadows laughed. 'That's more like it. You'll be back with the team before you know it.'

They talked a while longer then left the room as Blackwell began to doze. The man that had been sat with Blackwell was waiting outside the room cradling a paper cup.

'He's just nodded off, so we thought we'd leave him,' Meadows said.

'I think the anaesthetic and the shock has worn him out. I'm Alex.' He held out his hand.

'Winter Meadows.'

'And you must be Edris,' Alex said. 'Stefan talks a lot about you two.'

'I can imagine,' Edris said.

'All good I promise you. He may come across as a bit gruff, but he has a heart of gold and he has a lot of respect for you.' Alex smiled at Meadows.

'How long have you been together?' Meadows asked.

'On and off for about ten years. Stef's father doesn't approve of our relationship and it has made things difficult. I blame myself for this. We'd argued. I didn't find out until late last night what had happened. No one told me.'

'I'm sorry,' Meadows said. 'We only had Stefan's father as next of kin to contact.'

'That's okay, Stefan likes to keep his life private. He'd pitch a fit if he knew I was talking to you. You see, he is one of three boys. His two brothers are in the army and Stefan took a lot of stick growing up. That's why he is always on the defensive. Anyway, I've probably said too much. I'll let you go.'

'It was nice to meet you,' Meadows said. 'Make sure he gets plenty of rest.'

'Well, that's a turn up,' Edris said as they walked down the corridor.

'Not a word to Blackwell. He is entitled to his privacy,' Meadows said.

'My lips are sealed. I actually feel sorry for him. Sad to think his family would make life difficult for him.'

'It happens, there are still bigots in the world. It would be nice if people would bury their archaic opinions, but Blackwell's father is a different generation. Discrimination is taught and handed down. Maybe this will be a good thing and he will consider his son's happiness and break the cycle.'

'I don't know how you manage to find the good in everyone,' Edris said with a laugh. 'I would just say his dad is a dick and leave it at that.'

'You've a lot to learn,' Meadows said. 'Right, while we are here, we may as well call in to see Daisy. Hopefully, she has finished the post-mortem.'

The lift took them to the basement floor, and they followed the corridor through the old section of the hospital to the morgue.

'You're keen,' Daisy said when they entered. 'And have perfect timing. I've just received confirmation that the body in the graveyard is that of Dr David Rowlands.'

'That's a relief,' Meadows said. 'It would have made things a lot more complicated if it wasn't, although I doubt his family would see it that way.'

'I'm not sure his wife would be too bothered,' Edris said.

'Don't be relieved too soon, as there is a lot to go through. I take it you would rather look at the photos,' she said with a hint of a smile.

'Yes please,' Edris said. 'I don't know how you deal with something like that. It's hard enough when it's a fresh body.'

'A fresh body?' Daisy shook her head. 'Honestly, I sometimes wonder if you're safe to be let loose on the general public. You have no sensitivity. Maybe you should sit this one out. The photos are not very pleasant.'

'I can handle it,' Edris said. 'And for your information I am very sensitive.'

'If you say so,' Daisy said with a laugh. 'Grab a seat and I'll talk you through the injuries found on the victim.'

They gathered around the screen and Daisy opened a file. The image showed a close-up of the victim's mouth.

'Death by asphyxiation.' She pointed to the screen. 'Earth found in his mouth, throat, nostrils, and lungs.'

'You mean he was buried alive?' Meadows asked.

'Yes.'

'Poor bugger,' Edris said.

'I think it unlikely that he was conscious at the time. There were no signs that he tried to claw away at the earth. Also, although there are marks from where his hands were bound, there were no bindings when they brought him in. He's been dead between twenty-two and twenty-seven days.'

'That fits with our timeline, although it could be that he was held somewhere before being killed,' Meadows said.

Meadows was so close to Daisy he could smell her perfume. He glanced at her, noticing that wisps of hair had escaped her ponytail and curled down her neck. He forced his attention back to the screen.

'There were also caustic burns to his mouth, throat and stomach. I've sent off a sample for analysis, but my best guess would be bleach. Blood samples show alcohol and morphine.'

'So, he could have been an alcoholic and drug user. I guess he would be able to get his hands on morphine,' Edris said.

'Or the killer could have given it to him to keep him compliant. How much was in his system?' Meadows asked.

'Enough to make him very drowsy and combined with alcohol I doubt he would have been able to put up much of a fight.'

Daisy clicked the mouse and the image changed to a hand with black and swollen flesh. 'Injuries were anti-mortem. All fingers on the right hand were broken, the thumb was left intact.' She changed the photo. 'Small and ring finger broken on the left hand. As you can see the skin has deteriorated so it makes it difficult to determine what weapon was used. They are not snapped. Blunt force has shattered the bone. Possibly a hammer. It's the same with the toes. All toes broken on the right foot.'

Another click and Dr Rowlands' head appeared. Meadows felt his stomach contract and was glad he was only looking at photos. It would have been virtually impossible to identify him from them.

'Damage to the right eye and cheek, again blunt force trauma. A nail had also been hammered into his left temple.'

'Someone really didn't like this guy,' Edris said.

'Finally, we have the writing on the body. Almost missed it given the discolouration.' Daisy changed the picture. 'It's not very clear, but there are the letters LEV and numbers two, four, one, nine, two, and one.'

'I'll look.' Edris pulled out his phone. 'Well, this one is to the point: "And if a man cause a blemish in his neighbour, as he hath done, so shall it be done to him. Breach for breach, eye for eye, tooth for tooth, as he hath caused a blemish in a man so shall it be done to him again.'"

'Is that what the writing on the victims is, Bible quotes?' Daisy asked.

'Yes,' Meadows said. 'I don't like the sound of this one. It could mean our killer is taking exact revenge. The question is, are the victims well known to him and have wronged him personally or is it just anyone he considers has done wrong?'

'If that's the case you'll be looking at a whole lot of victims,' Edris said.

'That's what I'm afraid of.' Meadows stood up. 'By the way, did the doctor have a tattoo on his right arm?'

'No, but what may interest you is the same synthetic hairs that were found on Stacey Evans were also found on Dr Rowlands. Also, there was a bloodstained large flat stone, looks like limestone, that was found with the body. Everything has been sent off for testing.'

'Thank you.'

'Good luck,' Daisy said.

Meadows' phoned bleeped and he took it from his pocket and read the message. 'Vicar Daniels has asked that we go to see him.'

'I hope he hasn't found another body,' Edris said.

'So do I.'

Chapter Sixteen

They found Vicar Daniels in the church kneeling at the altar in prayer. Meadows and Edris stood silently waiting for him to finish. Flower arrangements now decorated the window ledges and tea lights flickered on a metal stand. Vicar Daniels stood and turned around.

'Oh, I didn't hear you come in. I'm sorry to have made you wait.'

'It's no problem,' Meadows said. He noticed the dark circles under the vicar's eyes and thought the recent events must be taking their toll.

'Thank you for coming, I understand that you must be very busy but there is something I need to show you at the vicarage.' He turned to look at the candles. 'I'm sure it will be alright to leave the church open. People have been coming to pray and light candles for Stacey and Dr Rowlands.'

'I understand that Linda Rowlands is a member of your congregation,' Meadows said as they left the church.

'Yes, she attends regularly. She came this morning. I said a prayer with her.'

'How did she seem?'

'Considering what's happened, she was very composed.'

'Did Dr Rowlands attend church?'

'Only on special occasions.' Vicar Daniels stepped onto the path that led through the graveyard. 'Before we get to the vicarage, there is something I want to talk to you about. I've wrestled with my conscience all night. You see I do have a responsibility to keep a confidence but sometimes it is in the individual's best interest for me to break that confidence.'

'I understand,' Meadows said. 'Has someone told you something about Stacey Evans or Dr Rowlands?'

'Not exactly. It's Donald. I'm very worried about him. He called me last night.'

'Did he tell you where he was?'

'No, he told me that the police had come to arrest him. Is that true?'

'We needed to ask him a few questions in connection to the murder of Stacey Evans, but I can't tell you more than that.'

'I see.' Vicar Daniels opened the gate and they stepped through. 'He seemed to think he was in trouble and he would go to prison. He said he had done something.'

'Did he say what he had done?' Edris asked.

'No, he wouldn't tell me. He said he was ashamed and that his parents would disown him. He was very distressed and claimed he could never come home. I told him whatever it was that he had done couldn't be that bad and all he had to do was ask for forgiveness. I tried to persuade him to come to the church and then go to the police. That it would be better for him to come clean. I offered to stay with him.'

'Did he agree?' Meadows asked.

Vicar Daniels stopped at the top of the garden. 'Not at first. He said he was scared and also cold and hungry. He wanted me to take him food and blankets. I thought if I could see him, I could persuade him to come back with me. In the end he agreed to come to the church to talk. I told him once he had something to eat and was warm, we could discuss what to do. I waited in the church until after midnight then took my car and drove around to see if I could find him.'

'Did he call again?'

'No, I tried calling him, but the phone went straight to voicemail. I hate to think of him alone and scared. I was hoping there was something you could do, maybe trace the call.'

'I'm afraid it doesn't work like that. We could trace the signal and see which tower pinged when he made the call, but it won't give us an exact location,' Edris said. 'I expect that he has turned the phone off and even if it was on, I doubt he'd keep on his location settings. Then again his battery could have died.'

'What should I do if he calls again? Should I just go to meet him?'

'Try and reassure him. Things are rarely as bad as we imagine,' Meadows said. 'We can arrange to speak to him at home if that will make him feel better. I'm sure it will only amount to a ticking off and some embarrassment. At the moment we are only interested in finding Stacey's killer and he may have information that could help us.'

'I'll do my best, now about the other thing. Follow me.' Vicar Daniels led them through the side gate and to the front door to where another Bible verse had been written.

'When did you notice it?' Meadows asked.

'This morning, I suppose it could have been there last night, but I generally come up the church path and use the back door. Given that you asked about a Bible verse when we first met at the church I thought it may be of interest. Can I ask if it has anything to do with your investigation or is this something separate?'

'Yes, the verse we spoke about does have a bearing on the case, but I would appreciate it if you didn't mention it to anyone. It's not public knowledge.'

'Of course. Should I be worried?'

'Have you looked up that particular verse?' Meadows indicated the door.

'Yes, it's Deuteronomy. "But the prophet who presumes to speak a word in my name that I have not commanded him to speak or speaks in the name of other gods, that same prophet shall die."'

'It does sound like some sort of warning,' Meadows said. 'What does that reference mean to you?'

'Well, a lot is said about the false prophet in the Bible. One that would speak, and others will follow. But it is not the word of God. I'm assuming someone has taken offence to one of my sermons although as far as I am aware I have never misquoted the Bible.'

'I think perhaps you should be extra vigilant. Meanwhile we can send someone to check the security in your home.'

'I'll put my trust in the Lord.'

'Even so I would be happier if you took some precautions. You said yourself you were at the church until late last night. Perhaps it would be better not to be alone in the church after dark and maybe don't take in visitors. I understand that it is part of your work but it's better for the time being.'

'What about visits to my parishioners?'

'Again, I think you should be cautious. Is there anyone that can accompany you, so you are not alone?'

'I could take one of the church wardens on visits. I'm sure I'll be fine. I'll just have to write my sermons with a little more care.' He smiled. 'I'll pray for you and the parish that this will be over soon.'

'Thank you, I'm happy to take all the help we can get.'

Chapter Seventeen

Meadows gathered the team around the incident board and updated them on the post-mortem and the visit to the vicar. It was strange not to see Blackwell sat in his chair with his legs stretched out. Hanes had joined the group and DCI Lester sat at the back listening intently.

'Do you think that Vicar Daniels is the next intended victim?' Lester asked.

'I think the killer has had plenty of opportunity and it is just a warning. In the same way the killer could have easily killed me the night I went to Bill Jones' farm. That was a warning for me to back off, perhaps Vicar Daniels knows something but is not aware of the relevance, and the warning is not to speak to us.'

'I think it would be prudent to keep a presence in Gaer Fawr for now. We can't have uniform there twenty-four hours but if they are seen to regularly drive around and maybe walk around, talk to people, it will not only reassure the public but may deter the killer,' Lester said.

'I agree,' Meadows said. 'I've asked uniform to call on Vicar Daniels to check the security on the vicarage and the church.'

Lester nodded his approval.

'Okay, Dr Rowlands, our first victim,' Meadows continued.

'That we know of,' Edris said.

'Well, given that no one else is missing from the area. I think it's safe to assume,' Meadows said.

'What if the killer is not from the area,' Paskin said. 'Or they could have killed before. Perhaps we should be looking at any unsolved case or cases that looked accidental, or suicide. What about Erin Kelly?'

'I've looked over the case. The outcome of the inquest was suicide. There was a thorough investigation and no evidence of foul play. I think the killer is a resident of Gaer Fawr. No one knew my plans to go to Bill James' farm the night I was attacked. Bill James' solicitor made one call to Sarah Kelly. She herself told me she had received the message. There were a number of men on the bridge that night dealing with the flood water. I identified myself. No one else would have got access over the bridge as it was blocked.'

'Sarah Kelly could have made a call to someone,' Edris said.

'There is that possibility. So, are we agreed we need to treat Dr Rowlands as the first victim?' Meadows looked around and saw the team's nods of agreement. 'Something must have triggered the killer.'

'So we're looking at a serial killer,' Valentine said.

'I don't think we want to use that label at the moment,' Lester said.

'There are two victims,' Paskin said. 'And for all we know he could be planning his next kill.'

'The connection between Stacey Evans and Dr Rowlands has not been made public,' Lester said. 'We need to keep it that way. There will be speculation given the close proximity of the victims. I'll deal with the press, but we need to move quickly before he strikes again. I'll also make an appeal for information.'

'I agree,' Meadows said. 'I think our best option is to concentrate on Dr Rowlands. The victims were found with biblical references.' He pointed to the board. '"The whore of Babylon" – it seems Stacey Evans was having an affair with a married man. Tech have provided a picture of the tattoo seen on the video. It looks like a baby's hand print in the centre of the design. We need to be on the lookout for anyone with that tattoo. Maybe check local tattoo parlours to see if anyone remembers tattooing that design. It could be our killer or someone the killer wants to protect. Now to the doctor. "An Eye for and Eye" – it was a horrific attack, he was made to suffer. So, what is the doctor guilty of in the killer's eyes? Paskin, what did you manage to find out?'

'He wasn't well liked. There is a Facebook page dedicated to complaints and general gripes about Dr Rowlands. It's called "Doctor Rowlands is a twat." A lots of posts, some examples: "Apparently it's my fault I have underactive thyroid because I'm fat;" "He told me I had gout when I had an infection in my foot." Those are some of the tamer ones.'

'The injuries inflicted on the doctor were quite specific,' Edris said.

'You need to go through all the posts and bear the injuries in mind,' Meadows said.

'There were also three complaints made to the GMC. He was cleared of misconduct on all three cases. I've requested the details.'

'Who made the complaints?'

'Sarah Kelly, Tomos and Ellis John, and Gemma and Rhodri Lewis.'

'As well as Sarah Kelly I've heard those other names before,' Meadows said. 'Edris?'

Edris flicked through his notebook. 'Yes, you're right: Sarah Kelly, Gemma Lewis, and Tomos John were at the movie night last Tuesday evening with Donald Hobson.'

'So, they all have alibis,' Valentine said.

'Not Rhodri Lewis, or Ellis John, only Gemma Lewis and Tomos John were at the vicarage,' Edris said.

'We also have to consider the possibility that the killer isn't working alone,' Meadows said.

'Yeah, I can't see one person digging a grave and moving the doctor,' Paskin said.

'It's not impossible,' Edris said. 'The doctor could have been lured to the graveyard. Easier than moving him afterwards.'

'I can't see it,' Hanes said. It was the first time he had spoken during the briefing and everyone turned to look at him. 'Why would anyone meet up in the back of a graveyard? And the doctor was called out.'

'He's got a point,' Meadows said.

'What if Linda Rowlands made the fake call after she killed the doctor?' Edris said. 'She calls her sons to help her out, then one of them kills Stacey. The doctor was known to be sleeping around.'

'What have we got on the sons?' Meadows asked.

'Both have alibis. I've checked them out,' Paskin said.

'There is also Donald Hobson. Valentine, where are we with the search?'

'All outbuildings on the local farms have been checked. We also searched his home again in case his parents were concealing him. They are very angry and worried. We've managed to get phone records from Donald's network provider. He's made two calls since he went missing. One to Sarah Kelly on Saturday night and one to Vicar Daniels last night.'

'Interesting,' Meadows said. 'We already know he called the vicar but why did he call Sarah Kelly? Valentine and Hanes, look at all the video footage Donald took of Erin and check out their favourite places, particularly anywhere where he could shelter. If he's not involved then I'm sure he knows something.'

'Paskin, go through the Facebook posts and track down the administrator and look for those with complaints that match the doctor's injuries. They will all need to be interviewed, take someone with you. Valentine and Hanes can give you a hand when they've finished with the search. Edris and I will talk to Sarah Kelly again then see the other two on the list that made complaints to the GMC.'

'Do you need extra help?' Lester said. 'I can get a DS transferred from Carmarthen until Blackwell returns.'

Meadows didn't like the idea of having a new face on the team in the middle of an investigation. 'Folland has let me have a few uniforms, they are all up to speed on the case. Perhaps it would be a good idea to have someone take over Blackwell's arson case.'

'Okay, I'll sort it out. I'll let you get on.' Lester left the room.

'That's all, thanks everyone, let's meet back for a briefing after the interviews. Hopefully by then we will have a credible suspect.'

Meadows returned to his desk and picked up his jacket. 'Edris, can you print off a copy of the post-mortem report for Erin Kelly? You can read it on the way. I'll just check through Donald's phone records, see who else he's been calling.'

Chapter Eighteen

'This is pretty grim reading,' Edris said as Meadows drove towards Gaer Fawr. 'Poor kid. She landed on the rocks face down.'

'The doctor was buried face down. Could be significant.'

'There is a fracture to the cheekbone which is consistent with the doctor's facial injury. A lot of fractures but I can't see anything specific to the hands or feet. She didn't die instantly.'

'Was she alive when they found her?'

'No, she was pronounced dead at the scene which means she was lying there alone and dying. She had internal bleeding.'

'Which the killer tried to achieve by pouring some sort of bleach down the doctor's throat, maybe,' Meadows said.

'It's very gruesome. Can you see Sarah Kelly inflicting those injuries on the doctor?' Edris asked.

'Who knows the limits someone can be pushed to. Sarah would have been present at the inquest and heard all the details of the post-mortem. I don't imagine you could ever get over that. All that anger and grief and nowhere to channel it.'

'Yeah, I guess, but she can't have killed Stacey Evans. She has an alibi and also it was a sexual assault,' Edris said.

'No, but she could have involved someone else?'

'Like Bill James?'

'The DNA results came back negative,' Meadows said.

'Okay, someone else then, working with Sarah.'

'Someone who wears a wig.'

As they drove over the humpback bridge, they saw Sarah Kelly walking her dog.

'We'll just wait outside her house, give the village an opportunity to see us. Stir things up,' Meadows said.

They had only been sat a few minutes when there was a knock on the window. Meadows turned his head and saw Mrs Hobson standing on the pavement.

'Have you found Donald yet?' Mrs Hobson asked as soon as Meadows stepped out of the car.

'No, I'm afraid not. We do have officers searching for him.'

'There was a frost this morning. He's been out for two nights in the cold. This is all your fault, coming around and frightening him.'

'I'm sorry if it looks that way to you,' Meadows said. 'We only want to ask him a few questions. If he contacts you, please reassure him that's the case. We can talk to him at home if it makes him feel more comfortable.'

'And you couldn't have done that to start with? He hasn't been in contact. For all you know he could be lying somewhere ill and alone.'

Mrs Hobson started to cry. A couple of people had stopped on the pavement opposite and were watching the exchange. Meadows wanted to give her some reassurance, tell her that Donald had spoken to Vicar Daniels, but he didn't want to break his confidence.

'We are tracking Donald's phone, he made a call and is still in the area. I can't tell you more than that at the moment. But at least you know he hasn't gone far. We'll let you know as soon as we hear anything.' Meadows was relieved when Sarah Kelly joined their group.

'Has something happened?' She touched Mrs Hobson on the arm.

'No, they haven't found him yet. You know what Donald is like. Tell them, he's a good boy. He'd never hurt anyone.'

'I know,' Sarah said. 'Try not to worry. I'm sure he'll turn up.' She gave Mrs Hobson a hug.

'Can we have a word?' Meadows asked.

'Okay.' Sarah took the keys from her bag and opened the door. 'I'll pop over later,' she called to Mrs Hobson before stepping through the door. 'People told me the same thing when I couldn't find Erin, try not to worry.' She shook her head as she walked into the sitting room. 'It's a stupid thing to say. It didn't stop me worrying and it will be the same for Donald's parents. You know when something is wrong. You feel it as a parent.'

Meadows looked around the room. Last time he had been there it was sparsely decorated, now it was stripped bare and several boxes stood in the corner.

'Do you think Donald's parents have cause to worry?' he asked.

Sarah shrugged off her coat. 'I dunno. I hope he'll be okay. He's a nice kid and he was a good friend to Erin. He comes over often to see me. Have a seat if you want.' She sat in the armchair and the dog jumped on her lap.

'How has Donald seemed to you over the past few weeks?' Edris asked.

'Alright, he wasn't well last week but I guess another dead teenager brought it all back. Did you come here to ask me about Donald? Because there isn't much else I can tell you. Like his mother said, he's a good lad. Never been in any trouble.'

'We came to talk to you about Dr Rowlands. I'm sure you've heard by now that his body was found in St Herbert's graveyard,' Meadows said.

'Yeah, the village has been buzzing for the last couple of days.'

'You made a complaint to the GMC about him.'

'Yes, it's common knowledge and you'll probably find I'm not the only one to have done so.'

'Can you tell us the nature of the complaint?' Meadows asked.

'In the weeks leading up to Erin's death, she had become withdrawn. It was more than the bullying, although that was a major factor. She had lost weight, no interest in food, or plans for the future. She used to spend her weekends with Donald but in the end she just stayed in bed. Not bothering to get dressed.

'I took her to see Dr Rowlands about two weeks before she died. He was dismissive, saying that most teenagers go through that stage – moody and staying in their rooms. Things didn't improve so I took her back to see him the day she died. I insisted she needed help. I suggested anti-depressants or some sort of counselling. He basically told me I was being an overprotective mother. He went off on a tangent about the problem with kids these days. Schools stopping competitive sports not to hurt children's feelings. Their every whim being met. He said Erin was oversensitive and she needed to toughen up. Go out more, buy some new clothes and put on some make-up, then she might feel a little better. That night she walked up to the quarry.'

'Do you think Dr Rowlands could have prevented Erin's death?' Meadows asked.

'Yes, he could have helped her when I first took her to see him. She was clearly suffering from depression. That point was made in the inquest. He could have referred her to a mental health team. He made her feel worse. He could have given her an option, a little hope that she would get better. She was in a dark pit with no way out and he took away her last chance.'

'The GMC cleared him of any misconduct, that must have been very difficult for you,' Edris said.

Sarah turned her attention to Edris. 'Well, they only had his word against mine. He was the one to write up the medical notes, he would be unlikely to have written anything that would make him look bad. He probably changed it to look like there was no indication of Erin's depression.'

'And now he's dead,' Edris said.

'I won't pretend to be shocked or upset. I freely admit I detested the man. It seems my prayers have been answered. It won't bring Erin back or do anything to diminish the pain I feel, but at least there has been some sort of justice.'

Meadows thought of the Bible quote and wondered if Sarah was referring to some Old Testament justice. She seems to think that the doctor got what he deserved, he thought.

'I'm going to have to ask you where you were on the evening of the 28th of September. It was a Monday,' Meadows said.

Sarah sat back in her chair and smiled. 'You expect me to remember?'

'You must have some idea.'

'You think I killed Dr Rowlands and Stacey Evans?' Sarah laughed.

'You blamed both of them for Erin's death.'

'I was at the vicarage watching a movie the night Stacey was murdered.'

'That doesn't mean that you didn't help plan to kill her,' Edris said.

'Oh, so you think I have someone who would avenge my daughter's death? In case you haven't noticed, I am completely alone, and I don't have money to pay someone to do my bidding.'

'You still haven't told us where you were the night Doctor Rowland was murdered,' Meadows said.

'If it was a Monday night then I guess I would have been in work.'

'Where do you work?' Edris asked.

'Parc Wern care home. I do the night shift. Four nights on four nights off.'

'What time do you start?'

'Eight and I finish at eight. You don't think I killed the doctor, dug a grave and pushed him in, do you?'

'Not alone, no,' Meadows said. 'There were certain injuries to Dr Rowlands that were consistent with Erin's injuries. Also, a large piece of limestone was found with the doctor.'

'Limestone is very common around here.'

'Yes, but you can see how it looks. Both cases appear to be connected to Erin. If you are not involved then it is likely to be someone close to you or who was close to Erin.'

'I've told you there is no one.' Sarah stroked the dog.

'There's Bill James.'

'Whom you arrested and let go because he's innocent.'

'What were you doing at Bill's farm the night I got attacked?' Meadows asked.

'I told you I was checking on the chickens.'

'Yet you had a message to go the next morning. You knew I would be there. In fact, only you and Bill knew I would be there that night. Who else did you tell?'

'No one. I didn't think you would come in the storm, so I went to check. I didn't see anyone on my way down.'

'Did you phone anyone? We can check your phone records.'

'Go ahead if you can't take my word. I have nothing to hide.'

'You haven't exactly been helpful,' Meadows said.

'I have answered all your questions.'

'You didn't tell us that Donald had contacted you on Saturday night.'

'You didn't ask. Why would you expect me to volunteer that information?'

'You know we are looking for him and his mother is worried.'

'But Donald hasn't done anything wrong. While your questions and implications don't bother me, Donald is sensitive. It's no wonder he's run off.'

'Where is he?'

'I don't know.'

'I think you do and you're not telling us. What was the call about?'

'That's between Donald and me. He needed someone to talk to.'

Meadows could feel his patience slipping. 'Are you moving house?' He indicated the boxes stacked in the corner of the room.

'I thought it was about time I had a clear out. I haven't touched Erin's things since she died. It's time to move on, maybe I will sell up and move out of the area. Too many bad memories here. So, are you going to arrest me?'

'Not today, but if I find that you have withheld information that could help catch the person responsible for the murders then I will arrest and charge you.'

'Well, if that's the case there isn't any more I can tell you.' Sarah stood and the dog jumped down. 'I'll see you out.'

* * *

'Well, she didn't seem bothered,' Edris said as he clipped on his seat belt. 'Most people would be a bit nervous being questioned in relation to a murder.'

'The way she sees it is the worst has already happened in her life. If she is involved, she is very confident that we have nothing to tie her to the murders. She knows where Donald is, and I think it's more than a clear out of Erin's things. She has almost stripped the house.'

'I thought that too. Maybe she's planning on running away.'

Meadows started the engine. 'But with who? Not Bill Jones.'

'The man with the tattoo?'

'Possibly, but if he was with Sarah then why was he sneaking around with Stacey?'

'Unless he was with Stacey first. She threatens to tell his wife. He gets talking to Sarah and they work out a way to solve both their problems,' Edris said.

'Yes, but it would need to be someone very close to Sarah for her to trust him.'

'What about a brother? Everyone here seems to be related.'

'Good point. Ask Paskin to check out Sarah's family history and her work. See if she was working the night the doctor went missing and if it would be easy to leave for a few hours unnoticed.'

'Are we going to see Tomos and Ellis John next?'

'I want to go to Iris Hawkins' house first. See where the doctor was heading the night he went missing.' Meadows pulled the car away from the pavement as Edris called Paskin.

Bill Jones was out in the field mending a fence close to the road when they passed. He held up his hand in greeting and Meadows returned the gesture.

'Looks like you made a friend,' Edris said.

Meadows laughed. 'Well, I need at least one in this village seeing as someone here was happy to knock me over the head.'

Just before the cattle grid that led onto the mountain, Meadows stopped the car at the entrance to the track that led to Iris Hawkins' house and got out. He walked part way down the track and looked around.

'You can't see much over these hedges and the house is quite a way down.'

'Good place to grab the doctor without being seen,' Edris said.

'If Iris Hawkins claims she didn't see the doctor that night then he would have been intercepted on his way down the track. So, I'm guessing the killer parked somewhere along here and waited so the doctor would have had to get out.'

'So, where's the doctor's car?' Edris asked.

'That's a good question. The killer could have knocked the doctor out, put him in the boot and driven him to the church then come back later for his car.'

'Bit of a walk,' Edris said. 'Also risky for the doctor's car to be seen at the church. Then he would have had to get rid of the car.'

'So, we are back to two of them. Easier to tackle the doctor. It would have to be someone the doctor recognised and didn't feel any threat from, or he wouldn't have got out of the car.'

'Could be Sarah Kelly. He would have got out for a woman. He wouldn't have felt threatened. The killer hides and as soon as the doctor is out of the car he creeps up behind and hits the doctor over the head.'

'One drives the doctor to the graveyard. The other drives the doctor's car and disposes of it. They arrange a pick-up place. It's late and dark so no one sees,' Meadows said.

'Do you want to call on Iris Hawkins, see if she heard any cars that night?'

'No, she's elderly and I don't want to worry her. Even if she heard the cars it won't make any difference. You spoke to her when the doctor was reported missing?'

'Yes, I believed her when she said she didn't call out the doctor,' Edris said.

'We'll need to trace the call.'

'I already put in a request.'

'Great. Okay, let's go and see Tomos and Ellis John. See why he made a complaint about the doctor.'

Chapter Nineteen

J&J animal food stores was made up of three large, corrugated iron storage sheds plonked down in a field with a gravel track and parking area. Meadows and Edris entered the first one where a section had been boarded for a makeshift office. They were greeted by a man in his sixties sitting next to a mobile gas fire warming his hands. He had short cropped grey hair and friendly blue eyes. Meadows quickly scrutinised his hair and wondered if it could possibly be a wig. A very good one if it is, he thought.

'Tomos John?' Meadows asked.

'No, that's my son. Is something wrong?'

'No.' Meadows smiled. 'You must be Ellis.'

The man nodded.

'We just need to ask you both a couple of questions.'

'This to do with that quack?'

'Dr Rowlands? Yes.'

'I see, I heard you'd been around talking to people. I hope you're not going to drag us off to the police station like you did with Bible Bill.' He smiled. 'Anyway, I can't really tell you anything and neither can Tomos. We haven't been to Gaer Fawr surgery since... well, not for a long time.'

'Why is that?' Edris asked.

'Bloody useless doctor, that's why.'

'You and your son made a complaint to the GMC about the doctor,' Meadows said.

Ellis looked down and rubbed his hands down his thighs, then sighed. 'Yeah, you best talk to him about that.'

Meadows got the impression that the subject was upsetting Ellis. 'Okay, can you tell us where we can find your son?'

'End unit.'

'Thank you.'

They left the warmth of the office and saw Anthony Evans pulling up in a Land Rover. He jumped out and approached them. 'Have you got any news?'

'No, I'm sorry. As soon as we do have news I promise we will let you know. I'm sure Brianna has been keeping you informed,' Meadows said.

'Not really. I don't see the point of her hanging around when she could be out looking for Stacey's killer, or is she there to spy on us?'

'Brianna is a family liaison officer and is there to help you in any way she can,' Edris said.

'She's been very good to us, it's just I don't know what to do. I feel helpless.'

Meadows felt sorry for Anthony and understood that to him it looked like they were making little progress. 'Just be there for your family.'

'That's just it, I can't bear to be around them all day, watching my wife sit there like a zombie. She doesn't eat and hardly sleeps. She's lost all interest in life. I have to work. The farm won't look after itself, but it just gives me more time to think. I look at everyone in a different light now. Always thinking it could be one of them that killed Stacey.' Anthony looked over at the three storage units. 'What are you doing here?'

'We're just following a line of enquiry,' Edris said.

'For Stacey? Or are you now concentrating your efforts on finding out who killed Dr Rowlands?'

'There are certain aspects of the case we can't discuss but I assure you we are doing everything in our power to find Stacey's killer.'

'As long as you're not putting him first. Dr Rowlands was a waste of space. I doubt you'll find many that have a good word to say about him.'

'I understand you had a problem with him?' Edris said.

'You've been listening to gossip about Cloe and him. That was years ago. I forgave my wife. I was working all hours and that slimy bastard knew how to play on a woman's emotions.'

'Were you patients of Dr Rowlands?'

'Yeah, I wanted to move to another doctor, but it was more fun to watch his embarrassment every time I went in to see him. I never let Cloe go alone.'

'What about Stacey? Did she see Dr Rowlands alone?' Edris asked.

Anthony's eyes narrowed. 'Do you think he came on to my daughter?'

'We're just checking for any connection,' Meadows said.

'She wouldn't have had anything to do with him. She knew I didn't like him, but she didn't know about the affair. I guess someone could have told her but that would be all the more reason to stay away from him.' Anthony's eyes widened. 'You think it's the same person? The same man that killed the doctor attacked my daughter? I know what he did to her, he–' Anthony's voice broke.

'We don't know that for certain,' Meadows said. 'As I explained there are certain aspects of the case we can't discuss with you, but we are looking into any connection between the two cases. You will be informed of our progress.'

'Just catch the bastard.' Anthony walked away.

'I wish I had some news for him,' Meadows said as they walked towards the end building.

As they entered the unit they saw a man dressed in jeans and a hoodie. He was around six foot with a solid build and shaven head. He was picking up sacks of animal feed two at a time and stacking them.

Looks strong enough to dig a grave and move a body, and he could disguise himself with a wig, Meadows thought.

'Tomos John?' Meadows asked.

The man threw down a sack and turned to face Meadows. 'Yeah.'

'DI Meadows and DC Edris. Is there some place we can talk?'

'We can talk here. There's no one around,' Tomos said. He picked up a bottle of water and took a sip. 'I can move some sacks for you to sit on if you like.'

'No, thanks. We're alright standing,' Meadows said. 'Looks like heavy work.'

'It's okay. I'm used to it. Dad has had me working here since I left school.' Tomos smiled. 'I like working outdoors and you get to chat to the customers when they come in. So, what can I do for you?'

'We're investigating the murder of Dr Rowlands and we understand that you made a complaint to the GMC.'

'Yes, I did.'

Meadows saw the same sadness in Tomos' eyes as his father's when he mentioned the complaint. 'Can you tell us what that complaint was about?'

'He killed my mother,' Tomos said.

'What do you mean by that?' Edris asked.

'She was ill. She'd been complaining about a bad stomach and being sick for days and went to see Dr Rowlands. He told her she had a stomach bug, and it would clear up in a few days. The next day she was in terrible pain. She wasn't one to complain so I knew she must have been bad to agree to call out the doctor. He came out that evening. He seemed pissed off that he had to come out. He prescribed some stronger painkillers and told her to rest and go to the surgery in a couple of days if she wasn't any better. That night I was woken by my mother's screams of pain. I called an ambulance. She made it to hospital, but it was too late. She had an infected gallbladder and the infection had spread. She died of sepsis.'

'That must have been very distressing for you,' Meadows said.

'Distressing? You've no idea. Watching my mother in agony and my father holding her hand, not being able to do anything for her. He hasn't been the same since. She should have been sent to hospital when she first saw the doctor. She would have lived if she had got help then.'

'The GMC cleared Dr Rowlands of negligence. You must have felt like there was no justice for what happened to your mother,' Edris said.

'They all stick together. The coroner was on the doctor's side.'

'Did you speak to Dr Rowlands about it?' Meadows asked.

'Yeah, I went to the surgery. I told everyone there what he was like. When he came out of his office I told him straight. He as good as killed her himself.'

'What did he say?'

'Nothing, no apology. Said he would call the police if I didn't leave. I was banned from the surgery along with my father. Now if we need a doctor we have to go to Llandeilo.'

'When was the last time you saw Dr Rowlands?' Edris asked.

Tomos shrugged his shoulders. 'I dunno. I haven't spoken to him since that day in the surgery. He was in church at Easter, I think.'

'Can you tell us where you were on Monday evening, the 28th of September?'

'I couldn't tell you where I was three days ago let alone three weeks.' Tomos laughed. 'One day is pretty much like the next except Sundays.'

'Do you work here every day?' Meadows asked.

'Six days a week.'

'What do you do in the evenings?'

'Sometimes Dad and me stop off for a pint. I usually cook dinner, Dad's not so good in the kitchen. Then we watch TV.'

'You're not married? Or have a girlfriend?'

'No, I tried a few dating apps. Went on a couple of dates but nothing came of it. It's just Dad and me.'

'Last Tuesday you were out.'

'Yeah, film night at the vicarage.'

'Did your dad go with you?'

'No, he stayed at home.'

'What time did you get there?'

'About half eight and left at half ten.'

'Do you know Stacey Evans?' Meadows asked.

'She used to come here sometimes with her father.' Tomos picked up the bottle of water and took another drink. 'Is that it? I should really get back to work.'

'One more thing. Do you have a tattoo?'

'Yes.'

'Can you show us?'

Tomos took off his hoodie and pulled up the sleeve of his T-shirt. A lily was engraved on his arm.

'It was my mother's favourite flower,' Tomos said.

'Thank you for your time,' Meadows said. 'We may need to speak to you again.'

'Fine.' Tomos pulled back on his hoodie then moved to pick up a sack.

Meadows and Edris left the building and walked back to the car.

'Funny how he claims not to remember one day to the next, yet he remembers what time he went to the vicarage and what time he left,' Meadows said as he started the engine. 'It's almost as if he knew he would need an alibi.'

'His father wasn't at the vicarage. He could have attacked Stacey. Tied her up and waited for his son to come. There has to be a margin on the time of Stacey's death. He wouldn't have to have kept her tied up for very long before his son turned up,' Edris said.

'I suppose if he left the vicarage a little earlier than he claimed. They both have motive to kill Dr Rowlands but what's the motive for killing Stacey?'

'Stacey pissed off a lot of people. Maybe Tomos met her on Tinder and she teased him about it.'

'It's not much of a motive,' Meadows said. 'We've still got Gemma and Rhodri Lewis to interview. Maybe something will come of that.'

The phone rang as Meadows pulled out onto the main road. He accepted the call and Valentine's voice filled the car.

'We've found Donald.'

Chapter Twenty

He felt exhausted and all he wanted to do was to curl up under the duvet, go to sleep, and never wake up. The problem was when he slept he had the most vivid nightmares. It was getting difficult to tell what reality was. He was having doubts if he was following the right path. He had moments of clarity when he felt himself and went about his daily business, until he would hear talk in the village – a reminder of what had happened, that it was real. Then he would remember what he had been chosen to do; no matter how hard, he had to see it through.

He pulled on his coat and put a hat on. He noticed some hair had fallen onto his shoulders. He brushed it off. He should get a new wig, he thought, but there was no point now. He left his house and breathed in the crisp air. He used to love the smell of the coming winter, now he couldn't smell anything. He felt like the world had lost its flavour, become bland, grey, and lacking true feelings. As he walked through the village, he noticed a man was taking photos of the church and a woman was scribbling notes. He knew at once that they were from the newspaper. It was too late to try and avoid them.

'Good evening,' he said.

'Hello,' the woman said. 'Would you mind answering a few questions?'

'Not at all.' He smiled. 'Though I doubt there is much I can tell you.'

The woman proceeded to ask him a series of questions while people came past and walked into the church. Most of them only stayed a few minutes. He guessed they were lighting a candle, making a show of paying their respects. Hypocrites, he thought. Most of them hadn't stepped foot in the church other than for a wedding or funeral.

'Are you afraid?'

'What?' His mind had wandered while the woman had been talking to him.

'Are you afraid living in the village where already two people have been murdered?' the woman asked.

'Not at all. This is my home and I'm sure the police will catch the culprit soon.' What he really wanted to say was that he had no reason to be afraid. He hadn't done anything wrong. He'd led a good life, kept the commandments.

'Thank you for talking to us,' the woman said. 'Do you mind if we take your photo?'

'No, that's fine.' He forced a smile as several shots were taken. Then he left the two of them and headed to the river.

Thankfully, there was no one on the bridge or footpath that followed the river. The light was fading, and he guessed no one wanted to be in an isolated spot in the darkness. They were all too afraid. Shame they didn't have the same fear of God, he thought. It was like Sodom and Gomorrah in these valleys at times. Sex and money were what occupied their minds. They gave no thought to God until they needed him. Then they went flocking to the church praying for those who had been taken and praying for their own safety. Others were quick to blame a God they claimed they didn't believe in. God's fault when the storm flooded the village, God's fault when there was an accident, or someone got sick and died. They didn't see it was their own doing.

He felt now like the weight of the world was upon him and there was not enough time to put things right. He'd done these things for the good of those who lived here, tried to show them the way. He'd even left clear messages, only the police had chosen not to share the word of God. People wouldn't know why Stacey and the doctor had to die, or Jean and Ryan Phillips. Did it matter, he thought. Would it make a difference to the way people behaved? Two of them had been marked forever and he had left a message for the other two. He wondered if the police had seen it and made the connection. Ryan and Jean would have seen it before they died although he doubted they would have understood the meaning – Godless people, the pair of them.

He thought of the police now, how they were scurrying around trying to find answers. A police car had driven through the village and would no doubt be back again later this evening to keep a watchful eye. He wasn't afraid of getting caught but there were things he needed to do before that time. Then there was Donald. Would the police have found him? If only he hadn't let him down. He'd trusted him, thought his faith was strong but he'd become afraid. Fear driving him to make the wrong choice. He had to stop him. There had been no other option. He sat down by the bank and put his head in his hands. Poor Donald. If the doctor hadn't been found all this wouldn't be necessary. There would have been no connection to make. He shook his head to try and clear his thoughts. He needed to find the strength to do this last thing. Then it would be finally over.

Chapter Twenty-one

Meadows took the Black Mountain pass that snaked its way through the rough grass, past rocks and streams that trickled down into the river below. The road rose higher then levelled off before they came to a gravelled car park. From here they would have to walk.

The quarry, once accessible to vehicles, was now blocked by a large iron barrier. Too many accidents with young drivers meeting up on a Friday evening to blast music and drink had forced action to be taken, so now only those wishing to walk and take in the views frequented the quarry.

Meadows felt the wind bite at his face and whip his hair around as they climbed higher. The track to the quarry led upwards until the valley below rolled out at one side while a path cut into the grass was visible on the other side. The narrow path led up the mountain side and to the top of the quarry, while the track continued to wind its way around at a lower level.

Meadows stomach was churning by the time they rounded the bend of the track and saw what was left of the old workers' cottages in the distance. He didn't like to think about what they would see when they reached the cliff face, but his imagination got the better of him. His thoughts turned to Erin and how she must have felt as she left the track and took the higher path. He wondered if Donald had followed her footsteps, alone and frightened.

As they came level with the empty shells of the cottages, they met with Valentine and Hanes. Valentine's shoulders were hunched against the cold and a deep sadness could be seen in her eyes. Hanes was rubbing his hands together.

'I've called SOCO and also requested that the barrier be taken down so we can get the vehicles up,' Valentine said.

'Good, are you okay?'

Valentine nodded. 'It's just, if I'd—'

'It's not your fault,' Meadows said. He knew the weight of guilt and didn't want her to carry that burden. 'Donald ran away of his own accord, if not then he probably would have run away after we spoke to him. I doubt you could have changed the outcome. The only person responsible is the killer.'

Valentine nodded. 'He was probably so afraid he thought this was his only way out. Poor kid.'

'That's assuming that it was his choice. Why don't you go back to the station? Get yourself warmed up and take a break. You too, Hanes.'

'I think I would rather stay,' Valentine said.

'I'll wait for SOCO,' Hanes said. 'I can also keep an eye out in case anyone happens to come walking this way.'

'Okay.' Meadows nodded. 'Right, let's take a look.'

Meadows and Edris followed Valentine around the final bend to a clearing and a semi-circular cliff face of jagged limestone. Donald lay on his back with his left leg twisted grotesquely outward.

Meadows stepped closer and looked down.

Donald's hair was wet, and the blood had been washed away from his face. A deep gash down his right temple over his eye and cheek made Meadows feel nauseous. A few yards from Donald lay a bunch of dying flowers. Meadows stood back and looked up.

'No chance of surviving a fall from up there,' Edris said.

'No,' Meadows agreed. 'You would need to choose the right spot. A bit further over and you could land on one of the ledges. You saw the pictures from Erin Kelly's file. Does it look like the same spot?'

Edris walked back and surveyed the area. 'I would say yes or near as.'

'I'm guessing the flowers are for Erin's death anniversary,' Meadows said.

'You think Donald brought them up?' Valentine asked.

'They look like they have been there a while,' Meadows said. 'Donald wasn't wearing a coat when he left the house, was he?'

'No,' Valentine said. 'Unless he had one ready in the bathroom, but I can't see that being the case.'

'No,' Meadows agreed. 'So where did he get this coat?' Meadows pointed to the navy parka Donald was wearing.

'Looks a bit small for him,' Edris said.

'That could be why it isn't zipped up. Have you taken a look up top?'

'No, we thought we'd wait for you,' Valentine said.

'Okay, we'll take a look. Edris do you want to stay and give Hanes a hand? Better start cordoning off the area. We'll also need a point of reference when we get up there.'

'Yeah, no problem,' Edris said.

Meadows and Valentine picked their way up the grassy path that wound around the side of the mountain and up to the top of the quarry. They passed the danger warning sign instructing walkers to stay away from the area. Meadows could sense Valentine's unease.

'You afraid of heights?'

'Yes,' Valentine said. 'Especially when there are no safety precautions in place. You'd think some sort of fence would be put up.'

'You better hang back,' Meadows said. He left Valentine and approached the top of the quarry. Down below he could see Edris and Hanes. He waved and Edris moved to indicate the place where Donald lay below. Meadows moved towards the spot, careful not to get too close to the edge. The wind was stronger at this height and, although heights didn't bother him, he could feel a weakness in his legs. A loose rock or the wet grass could easily cause him to lose his footing. His eyes scanned the ledge until he saw the scuff marks. Bits of stone had been disturbed and an indent in the ground looked as though someone had tried to dig in their heels.

Meadows felt a fizzle of anger as he thought of Donald being thrown over the edge, his screams unheard. He walked back to Valentine.

'Looks like there was a struggle and what's worse it's likely someone he trusted. I can't see the killer managing to drag him all the way up here. He was a big lad, and we would have seen some evidence of a struggle before the edge.'

'It doesn't bear thinking about,' Valentine said. 'Unless someone was with him and tried to stop him jumping and now is too frightened to come forward.'

'I guess that's a possibility, but I doubt that's the case. The other question is what was he doing up here? Is this where he has been hiding for the last two nights? Or did someone bring him up here? Come on, let's take a look to see if we can find somewhere he could have been sheltering.'

They walked back down the mountain side and picked up the quarry track. Meadows could see down below a park ranger was removing the barrier and a SOCO van was waiting by the entrance.

'I saw some old lime kilns as we walked into the quarry, maybe worth a look.'

They checked the first one which was secured by iron bars. The second one was open with the iron bars pushed in. Meadows switched the torch on his phone and shone it over the ground. There were a few broken bottles and cigarette ends on the floor but there was no evidence that someone had been sheltering recently.

'Doesn't look like he was hiding up here,' Valentine said.

They joined Edris at the clearing and as Meadows filled Edris in on what they had discovered at the top of the cliff, his eyes scanned the surrounding area.

'Is that an opening in the rock?' Meadows pointed to a gap that was around fifteen foot up from the ground.

'Could be,' Edris said.

'Come on, let's take a look.'

They scrambled up the cliff face with Meadows taking the lead. Several times his foot slipped, sending down a scurry of stones.

'Looks like a cave up here,' Meadows said over his shoulder. He pulled himself up over the overhanging rock and then held out his hand to Edris to help him up.

With the torches of both their phones they lit up the entrance to the cave. Inside was a blanket, an empty plastic carton, bottles of water, and chocolate wrappers.

'Looks like Donald was laying low here,' Edris said.

'Yeah, but who brought up the blanket and food? He didn't have anything on him when he left the house unless he went back home to get some things, but his mother looked genuinely worried when we saw her. I'm thinking Sarah Kelly. He phoned her on Saturday night. And she was unwilling to give us the information. He also called Vicar Daniels, but he did tell us.'

'Do you think Sarah would be able to kill Donald?' Edris asked as they picked their way back down.

'She could have taken him by surprise. Easy enough to get him to walk to the top with her. Maybe she told him she wanted to go to the place where Erin jumped.'

SOCO had already made a start erecting a tent over Donald, and Daisy arrived shortly after. Meadows could feel the cold penetrating his coat and he shoved his hands in his pockets to try and warm them. Edris was talking to Hanes, and Valentine stood with her back to the wind watching the activity.

'Are you sure you don't want to go back to the station and warm up?' Meadows asked.

'No, I'm okay,' Valentine said.

'I suggest when you've finished up here you go straight home. You've had a rough day.'

'It's been a rough week.' Valentine gave him a weak smile.

'All the more reason to go home and forget work for a few hours. Get your boyfriend to spoil you for the evening.'

'He's gone,' Valentine said.

'I'm sorry to hear that,' Meadows said.

'Yeah, he was a bit of a dick in the end. He left last week. I'm not so bothered about that; it's just now he's gone I'm left to pay the rent on the flat. It's too much with just me so it looks like I will have to move back in with my parents for a while.'

'I'll move in with you,' Edris said.

'I'm not that desperate!' Valentine laughed.

'I meant as flatmates,' Edris said.

'Yeah, and I would have to put up with a different girl coming out of the bathroom every morning.'

'I'm not that bad,' Edris said.

'How many girls have you dated in the last month?' Valentine asked.

'I don't think I want to hear the answer to that,' Meadows said. 'Right, I think Daisy has had enough time for the initial assessment. I'll go and see if she can tell us any more.'

'I'm coming with you,' Edris said and followed him to the tent.

Inside the tent Daisy was crouched next to Donald. Under the lights that had been erected, Donald's face was a stark contrast to the blushing boy Meadows had interviewed a few days earlier.

'He's been dead for no more than twenty-four hours,' Daisy said.

'The question is, did he jump of his own accord?' Meadows asked.

'There is nothing that stands out,' Daisy said. 'Injuries are consistent with a fall. The gash to his head is likely to have been caused by being struck against the rock as he came down, particularly if he pitched forward when he went over. I'm afraid it will be down to forensics to look at the trajectory of the fall.'

'Of course,' Meadows said. 'There is also an incline towards the bottom of the cliff so he could have rolled. It wouldn't be easy to tell if he was moved, say, to check if he was dead.'

'No,' Daisy agreed, 'but if he was moved then it would have been soon after death.'

'Can you quickly check the body for any signs of writing?'

Daisy pulled up Donald's sleeves and checked his forearms before lifting his jumper. As she moved it up his chest, Meadows saw the letters and numbers MAT26:14 in black ink.

'I think that answers your question as to whether he jumped of his own accord,' Daisy said.

Edris had taken out his phone and was reading from the screen. '"Then one of the twelve, the one called Judas Iscariot, went to the chief priest and asked, 'What are you willing to give me if I deliver him to you?' So they counted out for him thirty pieces of silver."'

'Sounds like Donald was going to tell us what he knew, and the killer saw it as a betrayal.' Meadows felt anger flush through his body. 'Poor kid never stood a chance. The killer was never going to let him live and he probably reached out to them for help. Thank you, Daisy.' Meadows stepped outside the tent.

'I think I should be the one to tell Donald's parents,' Valentine said.

'Let me go and see his mother,' Meadows said. He didn't want Valentine to go through the ordeal of dealing with Anwen Hobson's anguish and anger.

'Perhaps you can go with Hanes and pick up Donald's father. After that, I want Sarah Kelly picked up and find out anything we can about her, even if it's a parking ticket. That woman knows something.'

Chapter Twenty-two

Meadows stood holding Anwen Hobson's wrists as she screamed and tried to hit him. Edris was in the kitchen making a cup of tea and trying to find some brandy to put in it. While Meadows had expected an outburst, he wasn't prepared for the hysterical state that Anwen had got herself into. He hoped that Valentine and Hanes would turn up soon and wouldn't experience the same problems.

Edris came into the room and placed a cup of tea on the table. 'I've called the local doctor, he says it's best to let the grief take its course,' he said above the screams.

'Mrs Hobson. Anwen, please,' Meadows said. 'Your husband is on his way. If you don't calm down, I'm going to have to restrain you. I really don't want to do that.' He let go of her wrists and although she continued to sob she no longer tried to strike him. 'Come and sit down.'

Anwen allowed herself to be guided to the sofa where Edris placed the cup of tea in her hand. 'I've put a bit of brandy in it, for the shock,' he said. 'Try and drink a little.'

The cup shook as Anwen brought it to her lips, but she did manage to take a few sips. The front door crashed open and a moment later Cerith Hobson hurried into the room and threw his arms around his wife. Meadows left them and met Valentine and Hanes by the front door.

'Do you want us to pick up Sarah Kelly now?' Valentine asked.

'Yes and call her work. See if she was working last night.'

'What should we tell her?'

'Nothing. I want to see her reaction when I tell her we found Donald. I'll be there as soon as I can.'

Meadows went back into the sitting room and found Cerith and Anwen sitting side by side on the sofa, silent tears ran from their eyes and both had a stunned look.

'I'm so very sorry for your loss,' Meadows said as he sat in the armchair. 'I understand how difficult this is for the two of you, but I need to ask you some questions and then take a look at Donald's room.'

'You've already taken his laptop,' Anwen said. 'You scared him, made him run away. If you hadn't have come here he would still be with us.'

'I don't understand how this could have happened,' Cerith said. 'Donald has never been in trouble, if he was, he would have told us. What made you think that he had anything to do with what happened to that girl? I'll be making a complaint. This is your fault.'

'We did have cause to speak to Donald and there were a number of other people we have spoken to in relation to the case. Right now we need to find out Donald's movements and build up a picture of his life over the past few weeks,' Meadows said.

'What happened?' Anwen asked. 'You said you found him up the quarry. Did he… did he—'

'Don't do this,' Cerith said.

'I need to know,' Anwen sobbed.

'We are treating Donald's death as suspicious,' Meadows said.

'What? No,' Cerith said. 'Donald's a quiet boy, he isn't into drugs or anything like that. Why would anyone want to hurt him? Unless, are you saying that it's the same person that killed Stacey Lane and Dr Rowlands? That someone is out there killing people at random? You knew there was a danger, and you did nothing about it.' Cerith stood up, his nostrils flaring, and his fist clenched at his sides. 'There have been no warnings, you could have stopped this. Why didn't you warn people?'

'We had no reason to believe that Donald or anyone else was in danger,' Edris said.

'Please Cerith, sit down,' Meadows said. 'We have to look into the possibility that Donald knew something about one or both of the murders. It's possible that he knew the killer and that's the reason he ran away.'

'He ran away because he was afraid of going to the police station. You treated him like he was guilty of doing something to that girl,' Anwen said.

'There are certain things about the Stacey Evans' case that I cannot discuss with you at the moment, but we do believe that Donald had information that could help.'

'No,' Cerith said. 'If he knew something he would have told us.'

'Can you tell us how Donald has been lately? In particular the last three weeks?'

'He hadn't been feeling well,' Anwen said. 'He had a stomach bug or something. You know that he was sick when your lot came to take him. I think this business with Stacey upset him. Flowers left by the entrance of the Cwm and the atmosphere in the village. I think it brought it all back. He hid away for a month after Erin died. We thought he would never get over it, but he was doing alright until about a month ago.'

'What happened?'

Anwen wiped her eyes. 'I don't know, he became withdrawn again. I don't know exactly when he changed. First he seemed on edge, it was like he was expecting something to happen. Then he was sick, he came home one night, and I heard him being sick in the bathroom.

The next few days he stayed home from school. He didn't come out of his room, didn't want to eat or see anyone. Usually, we would sit down as a family on the weekend and watch a film, but he didn't want to, didn't even go to church that weekend. Then he seemed to perk up, going out for walks, back to school and church.'

'Did he give you any indication of what was bothering him?'

'No, his grades were good at school, he was predicted to get As. He was going to go to university to study psychology.' Cerith's voice broke.

'Was Donald your only child?'

'Yes,' Anwen said. 'We had Donald later in life than most couples. But we were happy just the three of us.'

'Did Donald speak about Dr Rowlands?'

'No.'

'Was he a patient?'

'Yes, I wanted him to go and see the doctor when he was being sick, but he wouldn't go. In any case, Dr Rowlands was gone by then. It was about the time we all thought he had run off.'

'So Donald's behaviour changed at the same time the doctor went missing.'

'I guess so, why?' Anwen asked. 'Do you think Donald saw something and that's why... but he would have told us.'

'We don't know yet if Donald was a witness to what happened to the doctor, but it would be really helpful if we could see his room now.'

'I don't see how it will help,' Anwen said. 'I don't like the idea of you going through his things. He wouldn't like it.'

'It may help us to find the person responsible,' Edris said. 'We will treat his things with respect and sensitivity.'

'Fine, if it's really necessary,' Cerith said. 'Come on, I'll show you.'

Meadows followed Cerith upstairs with Edris following. The landing was only a small area with three doors. They all stood cramped together. Cerith paused before opening the door to Donald's room and stepping inside where he stood staring at the bed.

'We won't be long,' Meadows said as he snapped on latex gloves.

'Okay,' Cerith said before leaving the room and closing the door behind him.

There was a smell of stale body odour and old socks in the room. The bed was unmade, and a pile of clothes were heaped on the floor. A desk with a screen and games console stood against the wall and was littered with sweet wrappers. There were no posters or any form of memorabilia in the room. Meadows stepped over to the bed and picked up a rucksack that was sat next to the pillow. Inside he found various clothes.

'Looks like he may have been planning on running away before Valentine and Hanes called around.'

They worked silently, looking through drawers and in the wardrobe. Among a pile of school books, Meadows found a notebook with a picture of Erin taped to the front. He flicked through and saw dates and notes on Stacey's movements.

'He was following Stacey for a while,' Meadows said as he handed the book to Edris.

'But why?' Edris said as he scanned the contents.

'Maybe he wanted to find something out about her he could use to cause embarrassment.'

'Well, he certainly did that by posting the video online, but this carries on after that,' Edris said. 'He was stalking her.'

'Which means he could have been aware of who killed her. He would have known everyone she talked to, or if someone else had been watching her. Better bag that up as evidence.' Meadows picked up the bible from the bedside table and opened it up on the marked page. 'He was reading up on forgiveness.'

'Poor kid was really messed up,' Edris said.

They didn't find anything else in the room and when they returned to the living room Cerith and Anwen were sitting silently.

'We've found a notebook which may be of help,' Meadows said. 'It is the only thing that we have taken.'

'Will we be able to see him?' Cerith asked.

'Yes but not just yet. A family liaison officer will be here shortly and will answer any questions you may have. I am so very sorry for your loss. We will do everything in our power to catch the person responsible for this. We'll see ourselves out.'

* * *

Only Paskin was in the office when Meadows and Edris walked in.

'Valentine's gone to visit Blackwell. I told her to get off home after that. Hope that's okay,' Paskin said.

'Yeah, that's fine. You should get off too, it's been a long day,' Meadows said. 'Find anything interesting on Sarah Kelly?'

'No, not even a parking ticket. One sister who lives in Kent. Both parents alive and living in Gaer Fawr. She doesn't use social media. Here's a copy of her phone records.' Paskin handed Meadows the sheet.

Meadows looked down the columns and noted the names Paskin had written next to the numbers. 'Interesting.'

'I also contacted her work. She wasn't working the night Dr Rowlands went missing, or last night. They were very complimentary about her. Said they would be sorry to see her go. Apparently she handed in her notice last Saturday.'

'After the doctor's body was discovered,' Edris said.

'Yes, that and the packed cases – it looks like she is planning on leaving,' Meadows said. 'Good work, Paskin. I'll see you in the morning. We better get on and interview Sarah Kelly.'

'She's in interview room one and not very happy,' Paskin said.

'I don't expect she is,' Meadows said with a smile.

Sarah was sat with her arms folded across her chest. She glared at Meadows when he entered the room.

'Do you know how long I've been waiting here? You better have a good reason for dragging me away from home.'

'I'm sorry we kept you waiting, we were delayed.' Meadows turned on the recording device and noted the time, date, and those present. 'Did DC Valentine explain this will be a formal interview and that you are entitled to legal representation?'

'Yes, just get on with it. I can't be bothered to wait for you to get someone who has never met me to sit here and give advice. I think enough time has been wasted.'

'Good, if you're happy to proceed and understand you can change your mind.' Meadows opened the file on the desk and waited a moment. 'When we spoke at your house earlier today you said that you had received a call from Donald Hobson on Saturday evening.'

'Yes.'

'Will you tell us what that phone call was about?'

'I told you he just wanted someone to talk to.'

'I would like you to tell us exactly what that phone call was about.'

Sarah huffed. 'And I told you that is between Donald and me.'

'Did he ask you to meet him?'

Sarah looked down at the desk and didn't comment.

'He called you because he was worried,' Edris said.

Sarah looked up. 'Yes.'

'About talking to the police?'

'Yes, he's just a kid, of course he would be worried. I think anyone would be concerned about being questioned about a murder.'

Meadows noted that she talked about Donald in the present tense. He wondered if she was just being clever or it was the case that she really didn't know.

'You went to see him up the quarry.'

Sarah looked surprised at the mention of the location but didn't say anything.

'You took him a coat, a blanket, and some food. We know someone did. It would be easy to test the blanket and the containers. I'm pretty sure any fingerprints found would show that they belong to you.'

'Okay, fine,' Sarah said. 'He was cold and hungry, so I took him some things. If you've found Donald why are you bothering to ask me? You can tell Donald it's fine, that I won't get into trouble. What are you going to do? Charge me with stopping the kid freezing to death.' Sarah sat back and folded her arms.

Meadows glanced at Edris and could tell he was thinking the same: Sarah was acting very cool if she had killed Donald, but then again, she had time to prepare.

'You phoned Tomos John after you had spoken to Donald.' He pushed a piece of paper towards Sarah and indicated the number.

'Yes, so?'

'What is your relationship with Tomos?'

'We're friends.'

'Why did you call him?'

'Because I was worried about Donald.'

'Why not call his parents?' Meadows asked.

'Because Donald asked me not to.'

'Did Tomos go with you to the quarry?'

'No, I went alone.'

'But you told Tomos that is where Donald was hiding.'

'No, I didn't tell anyone.'

'Are you sure about that?'

'Yes.'

'So Donald calls you, you talk to Tomos and then you go up alone.'

'Yeah, why would I take Tomos with me?'

'And you went back the next night.'

'No.'

'Really?' Meadows raised his eyebrows.

'What did you talk about on Saturday night?' Edris asked.

'Not much. I told him he was better off going to the police.'

'What did he say?'

'He didn't want to go home.'

'Did he tell you why?'

'No, I guess because he knew your lot would come.'

'You didn't think it odd that he was hiding away if he had done nothing wrong?'

'Like I said, he's just a kid. He is frightened of getting arrested by the police.'

'But we didn't arrest him,' Edris said, then looked at Meadows.

'Perhaps he was frightened for another reason,' Meadows said.

Sarah shrugged her shoulders.

'How long did you stay with him?'

'About half an hour.'

'And you just left him there in that small cave. Frightened and alone.'

'I didn't go up to the cave with him.'

'There were flowers up the quarry. Did you leave them?'

'Yes, I took them up on Friday morning for Erin.'

'You called Donald on Sunday afternoon,' Meadows said.

'Yes, to check on him.'

'Then you went up again Sunday night.'

'No, I told you I only saw him on Saturday.'

'I think you went up on Sunday. Did you walk to the top of the quarry with Donald?'

'No, I told you I saw him on Saturday and that was it. I didn't want to go again in case I was seen and gave him away.'

'Someone went to the top of the quarry with Donald. By your own admission you didn't tell anyone else where he was hiding.'

'Why don't you ask Donald? I don't know who else he saw.'

'That's the thing, we can't. We found Donald at the foot of the quarry this afternoon, in exactly the same place Erin was found. But you know that, don't you?'

'What! No, he wouldn't have.' The colour drained from Sarah's face.

'Who wouldn't have done what?' Meadows asked.

Sarah opened her mouth then closed it again and shook her head. 'I mean Donald wouldn't go up the top of the quarry. He wouldn't jump. Is he going to be okay?'

'No, I'm sorry, Donald died sometime yesterday.'

'No, it can't be.'

Meadows watched as Sarah became more and more distressed. Edris left the room and came back with a glass of water and handed it to her. She took a sip and set the glass down.

'Are you okay to continue?' Meadows asked.

'Yes. It's just a shock. I don't understand. Why would he do it? He knew the pain I went through with Erin. He wouldn't do that to his parents.'

'Oh, he didn't jump of his own accord. It looks like someone persuaded him to go to the top of the quarry then pushed him off. You must see how this looks. First you omit to tell us that Donald phoned you. Then you claim that you didn't know where he was.'

'I didn't want to give him away.'

'But you knew how worried his parents were. You of all people should have known what they were going through, yet you didn't tell them that he was up the quarry or even that he was safe.'

'His father would have gone up to get him. Donald would never have trusted me again. Oh God, this is my fault.'

'Why do you say that?'

'Because if I had told his parents he would still be alive.'

'Who did you tell?'

'No one.'

'Sarah, if no one knew he was up the quarry, that just leaves you.'

'I would never hurt Donald.'

'Who else did he call?'

'I don't know. I told him to call Vicar Daniels. I thought he might persuade Donald to come back.'

'Who else?'

'There is no one else.'

'We think Donald knew Stacey's killer. He may have been a witness. I think that is why he was afraid. If you know what Donald was hiding or who he was protecting, you need to tell us. If you are afraid we can offer you protection.'

'I don't know anything.'

'Why have you packed up your house?'

'I told you I'm having a clear out.'

'It looks like more than a clear out. You also handed in your notice at work.'

'I'm fed up with doing the night shift.'

'You could have asked them to move you to day shift. They are very complimentary of your work, I'm sure it wouldn't have been a problem. Do you have a new job?'

'No, not yet.'

'So you leave your job with no other form of income.'

'I have savings. I just wanted a bit of space to have time to think about what I want to do with my life.'

'You told us you were working the night Dr Rowlands went missing. We checked with your employer. You weren't on duty that night.'

'So? I told you I couldn't be sure.'

'Where were you?'

'If I wasn't at work then I would be home. Alone. It's not like I have a great social life. I have answered all your questions so unless you are going to charge me, I'd like to go.'

Meadows closed the folder on the desk. 'You are free to go but I would advise you to stay in the area. Aiding and abetting murder is as serious as if you committed the crime yourself. Secondary liability carries a lengthy sentence. If you know anything it would be in your best interests to tell us now.'

'I have nothing to say.' Sarah stood. 'I'll find my own way out.'

The door shut behind Sarah and Meadows leaned back and rubbed his hands over his face.

'Do you really think she is involved? She looked devastated when you told her about Donald,' Edris said.

'She knows something. If she didn't kill Donald then I'm sure she knows who did.'

'But why keep quiet? She must know the danger she is in.'

'Maybe she doesn't think she is in any danger. If she is protecting someone then she trusts them. That could change now. I think she would have happily stayed quiet about Stacey and the doctor's murder. By her own admission, she wasn't sorry that they were dead. It's different with Donald. He was Erin's friend, and he also visited her to make sure she was okay. When I told her about Donald she said, "he wouldn't have". I don't think she meant that Donald wouldn't have jumped. I think she meant that the killer wouldn't have murdered Donald. That wasn't part of the plan.'

'So what now?'

'We find out who Sarah is protecting and hope that she doesn't turn up as the next victim.'

Chapter Twenty-three

Meadows was sat at his desk looking through statements before the briefing. The rest of the team had gone to get a morning coffee. Mike from forensics came into the office carrying a file.

'Morning, Mike,' Meadows said. 'What can I do for you?'

'Got the results on the limestone found with the doctor. Thought I'd come up and go through it. Get out of the lab and stretch my legs.'

'I hope it's something interesting. So far it's a bit of a mess with nothing solid to tie any of the suspects to the crime scenes.'

'Not sure it will help but we do have a partial thumb print and we got a match.'

Meadows felt a fizzle of excitement. 'You got a name?'

'No, I'm afraid not. The partial matches a print that came off the brick from Ryan Phillips' house.'

'What brick?'

At that moment, Edris, Paskin, and Valentine came in followed by Hanes.

'What did we miss?' Edris asked.

'We're about to find out,' Meadows said. 'Go on Mike.'

'Uniform attended a call from Jean Phillips the night before the fire. She said that a brick had been thrown through the back door window. To be honest it wasn't top priority. After the fire I got one of the interns to run the test, we were snowed under with the fire and then Stacey Evans. The results went to Blackwell. Then of course he was taken ill, so I guess it was passed on. It was only when we ran the test on the limestone that we hit a match for the prints taken from the brick, so I took another look.' Mike pulled a photo from the file and handed it to Meadows. 'I'm sorry this wasn't brought to your attention earlier.'

'Shit,' Edris said as he peered at the photo.

A coldness crept over Meadows as he stared at the letters and numbers. 'Thanks Mike, and don't worry. There is no error on your part. It's a good job you picked this up now, otherwise we wouldn't have had a clue.'

'I'll leave you to it. I'll move quickly on the evidence from Donald Hobson. I should have the initial reports by this afternoon,' Mike said then left the office.

'Right.' Meadows walked over to the incident board and picked up a marker. 'Edris, what have you got?'

Edris read from his phone. 'EX23, Exodus. It's one of the ten commandments. "Do not lie, bear false witness." It goes into different forms of lying. The first one, "Put not your hand with the wicked to be an unrighteous witness."'

'Jean Phillips covered for her son saying he was home the day Ella died,' Meadows said. 'I think it's safe to say that one was meant for her.' He wrote on the board.

'The next one is Romans 12:19. "Vengeance is mine,"' Edris said. 'Oh this doesn't sound good. He thinks he's some sort of avenging angel. Do you think he's going to kill again?'

'I think it likely,' Meadows said. He finished writing and turned to the team. 'This adds a complication. We now have Ryan and Jean Phillips to add to the victims. There was also the verse left on the vicar's door and the one written on my arm. Although I feel these are warnings, I don't think the killer will hesitate if they think we are interfering, so you all need to be careful.'

'So, are we dealing with a serial killer?' Valentine asked.

'I don't really want to use that label,' Meadows said, 'but we now have five victims. Something must have triggered the killer. As far as we know, the doctor was the first victim. Paskin, how did you get on with social media?'

'Most of it was just gripes about the doctor. Nothing serious or that would indicate a threat. I tracked down the administrator of the page. Jessica Watkins, mother of two boys. I had a chat to her, she was unhappy about the doctor's treatment of her "woman's problems" as she put it. She agreed to take the page down. She didn't think she was inciting hatred and said that the page was for the community to air their concerns.'

'We still have the three complaints with the GMC,' Valentine said.

'Yes, Edris and I talked to Tomos John and Sarah Kelly yesterday. We still have Gemma and Rhodri Lewis to talk to.'

'Do you still think that Sarah Kelly is involved?' Edris asked.

'Yes, she has good reason to harm both Stacey Evans and Dr Rowlands, also to kill Donald if he knew something. She has quit her job and packed up her house. If she isn't involved, she knows who is, I'm sure.'

'What about Ryan and Jean Phillips?' Valentine asked.

'Good question,' Meadows said. 'Erin Kelly was depressed, maybe she was taking drugs and Ryan was supplying her.'

'Sarah called Tomos John after she had spoken to Donald,' Hanes said. 'Maybe he murdered Stacey. If Sarah Kelly is involved then she is acting with someone close to her.'

'Tomos John was at the vicarage the night Stacey was murdered,' Edris said.

'Well, someone else from the church then,' Hanes said. 'It has to be, with all these biblical quotes.'

'Not necessarily,' Meadows said. 'Not everyone that believes in God goes to church. In this case we are dealing with someone with extreme views. Someone who is taking the words in the Old Testament literally. Churches tend to preach love and forgiveness.'

'Yeah but look at the biblical reference found on the vicar's door. The killer obviously disagrees with what the vicar preaches so it has to be one of the parishioners,' Edris said.

'How many did the vicar say attended regularly?'

'About thirty-five, then there are those who come on special occasions.'

'Too many to bring in for questioning,' Meadows said. 'We need to concentrate on those with a motive.'

'So far that's Ellis John, the rest have an alibi. Do we bring him in for a formal interview?'

'We still have to find the man with the tattoo,' Meadows said. 'It's our only firm lead. Have we got anywhere with the local tattoo parlours?'

'No,' Paskin said. 'I sent a copy to all the local parlours as far as Swansea. I'll extend the search.'

'Good, I still think we should concentrate our efforts on the doctor. Something happened to set the killer off. Edris, do you want to fill everyone in on the phone call made to the doctor the night he went missing?'

'The call came in at 9.30 p.m. A call centre picked up the call as it was after surgery hours. Details were given for Iris Hawkins. Her name and address, date of birth and her medical condition. The call handler then checked the details and called Dr Rowlands as he was on duty. The caller was then called back and given the name of the doctor and the time he would attend. The number was traced to an unregistered pay as you go mobile phone. Two previous calls had been made from this number, two weeks apart. Each time for different patients and found to be a false call when the doctor arrived.'

'From this it looks like our killer planned the attack in advance. I would imagine to check out when Dr Rowlands was on duty and maybe to watch him. Valentine, as you were working on the Ryan and Jean Phillips case with Blackwell, can you go over all the statements? See if there is a connection to Gaer Fawr and Dr Rowlands. Also, it may be worth speaking to Mary Beynon.'

'I've already taken her statement. We talked to all the family,' Valentine said.

'May be worth talking to her again. She's Ella's grandmother and lives in Gaer Fawr. She's a member of the church and is likely to have some good friends. There may be something there. Find out how well she knew Stacey Evans and Dr Rowlands. Paskin and Hanes, talk to everyone we've interviewed in connection with Stacey Evans and Dr Rowlands, see if there is a connection to Ryan and Jean Phillips. Edris and I will talk to Gemma and Rhodri Lewis. We need to move fast. The killer or killers are out for vengeance and could already be planning their next move.'

Chapter Twenty-four

Meadows drove to the bottom of the cul-de-sac in Gaer Fawr and looked at the neat row of bungalows.

'Looks like council buildings for elderly residents,' Edris said. 'We'll be lucky to find a killer living here.'

As Meadows parked the car, a door to one of the bungalows opened and a lady stepped out. She was wrapped up in a coat with a scarf around her mouth and a woollen hat pulled down to her eyes.

'Mary Beynon,' Meadows said. 'Interesting that she lives next door to the Lewises.'

Mary Beynon locked her door and as she turned to walk onto the pavement her eyes met with Meadows'. She stopped for a moment and a look of worry flitted across her face. Meadows stepped out of the car.

'Hello Mary, how are you?'

'I can't complain,' Mary said. 'If you wanted to see me, you'll have to come back. I have an appointment with the doctor.'

'That's okay, we were just here to see your neighbours, but Detective Valentine will call you later. We need to ask you a few more questions.'

'I've already given her a statement. She came around with that other detective. I have nothing more to say. I'll tell you the same as I told them. I can go to my grave in peace now.'

'There have been some developments since then,' Meadows said.

'You mean the things that have been going on in the village? I can't really help you there. Things happen for a reason and I put my trust in God. His wheel turns slowly but it does turn.'

'That may be the case but it's not for people to take the law into their own hands. If you know anything about the arson attack on Ryan and Jean Phillips' house, you should tell us. You're a mother yourself. Jean Ryan was protecting her son as most mothers would. Do you really think she deserved to die?'

'My granddaughter didn't get the chance to grow up, she didn't deserve to die. She was just a baby.'

'I know, and I am so sorry for what happened but if you want peace then there has to be an end to it. Ryan and Jean had a family. Would you think it right if they then took revenge for what happened to their kin? You could stop it now before anyone else dies. Jean and Ryan dying can't bring Ella back.'

Meadows could see the pain in Mary's watery blue eyes, and she seemed to be wrestling with her conscience. She shook her head sadly.

'I put my trust in the law once and look what happened, besides there is nothing I can tell you that would help. I don't blame you for what happened. You did your best and what you thought was right at the time.' She touched Meadows' arm. 'You shouldn't blame yourself.' She turned and walked away.

'Should we just let her go?' Edris asked. 'She knows something.'

'I'm sure she does but what good is it going to do to drag her to the police station? If she does know who the killer is, she isn't going to tell us, and we have nothing solid to tie her to the murders. She's not a well woman and I doubt she would have the strength to kill. Come on, let's get on with interviewing the Lewises.'

Gemma Lewis answered the door. She looked to Meadows to be in her mid-twenties. She had long dark hair, and her chocolate eyes were puffy as though she had been crying for some time. Balanced on her hip was a boy of around four years old. He had a crop of dark hair and was snuggled against his mother's chest. A hearing aid was tucked behind his ear.

Meadows made the introductions and showed his identification. 'I'm sorry to disturb you but we'd like to have a chat with you and your husband.'

'Rhodri is in work. Is this about Donald?' Fresh tears pooled in her eyes.

'Yes, and also Doctor Rowland.'

'I can't believe Donald is gone.' Gemma wiped away a tear. 'He was a lovely boy. You better come in.'

Meadows followed Gemma into the sitting room. There were two sofas positioned in an L shape but no other furniture. Gemma settled the child on the floor with a few toys and took a seat. It was then that Meadows realised why the room had been set up in such a way. The little boy wore no shoes, and all his toes and part of his right foot was missing. Meadows eyes travelled to the child's hands. He had only a thumb on his right hand and the little finger and ring finger was missing from his left hand.

'It's quite a shock when you first see him,' Gemma said.

Meadows looked away from the child and caught Edris' eye, he knew he would be thinking the same. The child's missing digits matched the injuries they had seen in the post-mortem photos of the doctor.

Meadows took a seat next to Edris. 'How old is he?'

'He'll be four next month.'

'He seems to manage very well,' Meadows said as he watched the child pick up a toy between the palms of his hand.

'He's very bright, aren't you, Harry,' Gemma said and signed with her hands. 'He's also deaf but is picking up sign language quicker than me. It's just a little more complicated without fingers. So how can I help you?'

'You and your husband made a complaint to the GMC about Dr Rowlands.'

'Yes.'

'Was that about Harry?'

'Yes it was. Harry was born a normal baby. When he was fourteen months old he became unwell. We thought it was just a cold at first. When his temperature became high I took him to see Dr Rowlands. He examined Harry and told me it was just a virus and to give him paracetamol. I asked about antibiotics, but he said they would be no good. Then he went on one of his rants about how antibiotics have been abused.

'Harry became worse as the day went on. Rhodri came home from work and called the surgery. Dr Rowlands wasn't concerned, he tried to tell us that first-time parents were usually anxious. We ended up taking Harry to hospital. He was diagnosed with meningitis. You can see for yourself what that meant for Harry. He will never lead a normal life. He needs constant care and suffers with fits. It hasn't been easy for us as a family. We decided it wouldn't be fair on Harry to have another child. Anything we do has to be carefully planned.'

'What was the outcome of the tribunal?' Edris asked.

'Dr Rowlands was cleared of negligence. It was decided that he couldn't have known it was meningitis when I first took Harry to the surgery. He didn't take our concerns seriously. If we hadn't taken Harry to hospital he would have died. Precious time was wasted and if Dr Rowlands had prescribed antibiotics it could have made a difference.'

'When was this?' Meadows asked.

'Two and a half years ago,' Gemma said.

Harry made a noise and motioned with his hands. Gemma stood up, picked up a beaker from a shelf, and knelt down next to the child. Harry positioned the beaker between his hands and took a sip. He smiled then lifted the beaker again, but it slipped. Gemma made to grab it, but it tipped, and the liquid soaked through her sleeve.

'Never mind,' Gemma said and signed to Harry as she pulled up her sleeve.

Meadows saw the tattoo on her forearm and leaned forward. 'Nice tattoo,' he said. 'Unusual pattern.'

'It's Harry's hand print from when he was a baby, the symbols around it are Celtic. Of course, we didn't know then what would happen. I'm so glad we had it done.'

'Does your husband have the same one?'

'Yes, he does. We had them done together in Cardiff, why?'

'It looks like one I've seen before.' Meadows saw Edris raise his eyebrows.

'Where does your husband work?' Edris asked.

'Penlan farm.'

'With Anthony Evans?'

'That's right.'

Meadows felt a tinge of excitement. This could be the first real break they had had in the case so far. 'So you knew Stacey Evans,' he said.

'Yes, so sad. Poor Cloe and Anthony. Stacey used to babysit for us now and again. We don't get out very often. My mother helps but sometimes it's a bit too much for her. She gets herself into a state if Harry has a fit. Stacey was good with Harry.'

'Had she babysat for you recently?'

'Yes, a few weeks ago.'

'And how did she seem?'

'Fine, her usual self. Full of school gossip and the latest boyfriend.'

'Did Rhodri get along with Stacey?'

Gemma frowned. 'What do you mean?'

'Well, were they friendly?'

'She spoke more to me. Rhodri would drop her home after she babysat but he would be back in a few minutes. If that's what you are getting at.'

'I'm sorry, we have to ask these questions,' Meadows said. 'You spoke about Donald earlier. Did you and your husband know him well?'

'I knew him from church.'

'You attend regularly?'

'Yes, unless Harry has had a bad night.'

'And your husband?'

'Yes, he goes unless he has to work on a Sunday morning. If it's lambing season or hay cutting then he works all week.'

'We won't keep you any longer. Thank you for your time,' Meadows stood. 'You've been very helpful.'

He gave a wave to Harry who waved back. Could a killer be living in this house, he thought as he left the room. And if so, was he unstable enough to hurt his own family?

Chapter Twenty-five

Meadows started the engine and pulled away from the pavement, his mind was racing. Could it be this simple, he thought, that they just stumble on the killer? If that was the case Rhodri Lewis hadn't done much to cover his tracks.

'I think this is our man,' Edris said. 'We now know he was the one having an affair with Stacey.'

'Yes and he has motive for killing the doctor. Injuries to the doctor are identical to the child's amputations. I'm not sure where Ryan and Jean Phillips fit in.'

'I'm sure we'll find out,' Edris said.

'We have to tread carefully. Things could get unpleasant if we arrest Rhodri at the farm in front of the Evanses. If it turns out for some reason Rhodri is not our man, he won't stand a chance in this village.'

'It's got to be him.'

'If it is him, did he act alone? He's young and probably fit working on the farm. He could easily have overpowered Stacey but what about the doctor?'

'I suppose if he caught the doctor by surprise...'

'He'd still need to get the doctor to the church, kill him and bury him, then get rid of the car. That would take some time and I'm sure his wife would have noticed his absence.'

'Unless she was in on it,' Edris said.

'Or he could have had help from someone else and by arresting Rhodri we could trigger his accomplice into acting.'

'Well, that depends on who it is. If it's Sarah Kelly, then she's more likely to run. He was sleeping with Stacey so he could well have been sleeping with Sarah.'

'Good point. There is also Donald, Rhodri wouldn't have known that he was hiding up the quarry. There was no phone call from Donald to Rhodri, only a call made to Sarah and the vicar. I can't see the vicar telling his parishioners where Donald was hiding, so it has to be Sarah. She could have told Rhodri. Better get uniform to keep an eye on her,' Meadows said.

Edris made the call as Meadows drove to Penlan farm. He was hoping that they would find Rhodri on his own and that he would come quietly.

Cloe Evans answered the door. She looked worse than the last time Meadows had seen her. She had a pasty complexion with dark circles under her eyes and didn't look like she had washed her hair in a while.

'Do you have news?' she asked.

'No, I'm sorry. We are following up on some leads. We would like to talk to Rhodri Lewis. I understand that he is working here today.'

'Why do you want to talk to Rhodri?'

'It's in connection to another case. We're hoping he may have some information for us.'

'He's up in the second field helping Ants with the fencing. Just follow the track.'

Meadows was pleased that Cloe didn't want to go with them. They walked around the back of the house and onto the muddy track. Meadows did his best to stay out of the puddles, but he could still feel water seeping through his shoes and soaking his socks.

'Ew.' Edris' foot sank into the mud and squelched over his shoes.

Meadows laughed. 'It will come out in the wash.'

'These are my best work shoes. Do you know how much they cost me?'

'Maybe you should buy yourself a pair of wellies.'

They arrived at the second field where about twenty pigs were grunting and snuffling around the ground.

'You got to be kidding me,' Edris said. 'I'm not going in there.'

'They're up there.' Meadows pointed to the far side of the field where the two men were working on the fence. 'Come on, your shoes are already muddy, a bit more won't make a difference.'

Edris looked at the pigs. 'It's not the mud I'm afraid of.'

'Really?' Meadows grinned. 'They won't hurt you.' Meadows opened the gate. 'Quick we don't want to let them out.'

'They bite,' Edris said.

'Only if they are hungry. They can smell carnivores. I'll be alright, but they may want to take revenge on you.'

'You're not helping.' Edris moved through the gate and stayed close to Meadows as they walked across the field, his eyes watchful of the pigs.

A line of new fence posts ran across the top of the field and Rhodri and Anthony were hammering them in with sledgehammers. Both men wore only jeans and T-shirts despite the cold and Meadows could see Rhodri's toned muscles and the tattoo on his arm. He thought Rhodri would easily have the strength to overpower both Dr Rowlands and Donald.

Anthony put down his sledgehammer when he saw Meadows and Edris approach and Rhodri stopped work and moved to join them.

'Have you brought news of an arrest?' Anthony asked as he wiped his brow.

'No, we've come to talk to Rhodri.'

'What about?' Rhodri asked.

'We'd like you to come to the station to answer a few questions,' Meadows said.

'You!' Anthony shouted. He grabbed the sledgehammer and lifted it in the air as he moved towards Rhodri.

Meadows stepped between the two men and caught the sledgehammer as it came down, he felt the impact through his wrist. Anthony tried to pull the weapon back.

'No,' Meadows said. 'Don't be stupid, Anthony. We just want to talk to him.'

'I didn't touch her,' Rhodri said backing away.

'We need to speak to him about Dr Rowlands,' Meadows said as Edris stepped beside Anthony and tried to restrain him.

Anthony was breathing hard, his eyes wide and nostrils flaring but he relaxed his grip. 'What have you done, Rhodri?'

'Nothing,' Rhodri said. 'Tell him.'

'Anthony, please,' Meadows said. 'You need to let us do our job. Rhodri may have some information.'

'If I find out you had anything to do with Stacey's murder there won't be no need for a trial.'

'You know I wouldn't hurt Stacey,' Rhodri said. 'Come on, I've been coming here since I was a kid.'

Anthony allowed Meadows to take the sledgehammer. 'If you know who did this, you better tell them.'

'I don't know anything,' Rhodri said.

'Come on, let's calm things down. Rhodri, you better come with us,' Meadows said.

Rhodri nodded. 'I'll see you later, I'll come back to finish the fence.'

'I don't think that's a good idea,' Anthony said.

'But I–'

'Let's just give Anthony some space, shall we,' Edris said taking Rhodri by the arm and leading him away.

When Meadows felt certain Anthony wasn't going to attack Rhodri again, he moved away.

'Just because we take someone in for questioning it doesn't mean that they are guilty,' Meadows said. 'There is a process that we have to follow, and speculation and rumour doesn't help. I promise you that I will tell you personally when we charge someone with Stacey's murder. Rhodri has a family, you know the situation with his son. It's not fair on his wife if people start coming to their own conclusions. I would ask you to keep this to yourself for the time being.'

'Fine, are you gonna give me back the sledge so I can get back to work?'

Meadows figured Rhodri was far enough away, so he handed back the sledgehammer and followed Edris and Rhodri.

Edris had put Rhodri in the back of the car and was sat next to him when Meadows got in. He turned around in the seat and looked at Rhodri.

'When we get to the station, you will be formally arrested. I didn't want to do it in front of Anthony so I hope you will have the courtesy to behave yourself while I drive.'

'Arrest?' Rhodri paled. 'I don't understand.'

'It will all be explained to you. I suggest you keep quiet now and wait for legal representation.'

Rhodri remained quiet on the journey and when they arrived at the station Meadows formally arrested him and left him with the custody sergeant to explain his rights.

After a cup of tea and something to eat, Meadows ran a background check on Rhodri and put together a file. The incident board was now crowded with information and while lines could be drawn to join Stacey, Donald, and Dr Rowlands, there didn't seem to be anything that linked Ryan and Jean Phillips other than the Bible verses found on the brick.

'Rhodri's solicitor is here,' Edris said. 'He's had a chat with Rhodri, and they are ready now.'

'Good, let's see if he's ready to talk.'

* * *

Meadows entered the room and laid the file on the desk. The duty solicitor that had been assigned to Rhodri was one that he had met on several occasions.

Edris sat down, switched on the recorder, and noted the details of the interview.

'Shall we start with the murder of Dr Rowlands?' Meadows asked.

Rhodri remained silent and Meadows hoped he wasn't going to take the no-comment stand. He looked closely at Rhodri's hair. It was dark brown and cropped short. Easy to fit a wig over the top to disguise himself, he thought.

'We spoke to your wife this morning and she told us what happened to your son, Harry. Following Harry's illness you made a complaint against Dr Rowlands.'

'Yes, it's no secret,' Rhodri said.

'You must have been very angry when he was cleared of negligence by the GMC. It's understandable,' Meadows said.

'Of course I was angry, you've no idea of what it feels like. I'm supposed to protect my family. I had to watch my son fight for his life, make decisions to remove his fingers to stop the spread, and again his feet. Every day I watch him struggle, every time he fits, it could be the one that takes him. I wake up angry every morning. It festers away and feels like there is a hole in my stomach.'

'Did you talk to Dr Rowlands after the tribunal?'

'Yeah, I saw him outside church, the first Easter after Harry was sick. I told him what I thought of him.'

'How did he react?'

'He said he was sorry about Harry, but it wasn't his fault. That I would have to accept that it was a virus and

175

unpreventable and we should move on with our lives. Then he gave me that smug smile of his.'

'You felt he had got away with it?'

'Yeah.'

'So you decided to take matters into your own hands?'

'No, but he had it coming to him. I'm not sorry he's dead.'

'Where were you on the evening of Monday, the 28th of September?' Edris asked.

'I don't know. Probably at home, I am most evenings. Gemma and me did go out for a meal on a Monday night a few weeks ago. I'm not sure if that was the 28th. You'll have to ask Gemma.'

'Well, it would have been late in the evening. After nine, so enough time to have a meal and ambush the doctor,' Edris said. 'Do you know Iris Hawkins?'

'Yes, I've done a little work for her. Repaired a couple of fences and done some odd jobs around the house. She can't manage now.'

'So you know the property and I expect you know Iris pretty well.'

Rhodri shrugged his shoulders. 'I suppose so.'

'I'm guessing she'd make you a cup of tea while you were working. Tell you her troubles.'

'Yeah.'

'So you knew she wasn't well?'

'Where is this going?' the solicitor asked.

'Someone made a call claiming that Iris was ill and needed a doctor. They knew the details of her illness,' Edris said. 'Dr Rowlands was abducted from Iris's property and taken to the church graveyard. You knew Iris well, you had motive for killing the doctor and you're a strong man. I would imagine you would have no problem overpowering him.'

'It's been over two years since Harry was in hospital,' Rhodri said. 'If I was going to kill the doctor I would have done so then.'

The solicitor put his hand on Rhodri's arm as if to calm him. 'My client has told you his whereabouts on the 28th of September and, as you are aware, he comes from a small community where any number of people would know Iris Hawkins and her ailments. Do you have any evidence that links my client to the murder of Dr Rowlands? A complaint against the GMC is hardly strong motive for murder.'

'This isn't just about the murder of Dr Rowlands,' Meadows said. 'It also concerns the murder of Stacey Evans, Donald Hobson, and Jean and Ryan Phillips.'

'What the fuck?' Rhodri's eyes narrowed. 'I didn't kill them. Do you think I'm some sort of psychopath?'

'Let's talk about Stacey Evans,' Meadows said.

'What about her?'

'You knew her quite well.'

'I work for her father, so I've seen her around the farm. She also looked after Harry a couple of times, but I wouldn't say I knew her that well.'

'Really? So that's the only time you saw Stacey? At the farm or babysitting.'

'Yeah, well, and in the shop sometimes.'

'Do you have a tattoo?'

'Yes.' Worry flitted across Rhodri's face.

Meadows took a picture out of the file and slid it towards Rhodri. 'Can you confirm that this is your tattoo?'

Rhodri looked down. 'It looks like it.'

'Would you agree that it's quite unique?'

'Gemma has one.'

'Yes, we saw it: it's of your son's handprint. Were you having an affair with Stacey?'

'No.' Rhodri shifted in his chair.

'The thing is, Rhodri, you were seen with Stacey on more than one occasion in a compromising position. We also have film footage that shows you together.'

'Okay, yeah I had sex with her a few times. I made a mistake.'

'Was she going to tell your wife?'

'No, she wasn't like that.'

'You wouldn't want Gemma finding out, or did she find out?'

'No, she doesn't know. No one knows.'

'Where were you on the evening of Tuesday, the 20th of October?'

'I don't know.'

'It was the night Stacey was murdered. I would have thought you'd remember that night.'

'Erm, yeah. I'm not good with dates. I was at home looking after Harry. Gemma had gone to the vicarage to watch a film.'

'Did you leave the house at all?'

'No, Harry can't be left alone. Unless you are suggesting that I took my son out and murdered Stacey while he watched.'

'I understand your mother-in-law sometimes looks after Harry.'

'Yes.'

'So, did she come over that night to watch him?'

'No, it was just me.'

'We will be checking.'

'Fine.'

'What about Sarah Kelly?'

'What about her?'

'Does Sarah ever look after Harry?'

'No.'

'Did Sarah know about your affair with Stacey?'

'No, no one knew.'

'Someone knew as you were filmed. We know of at least two people who saw you together. You would have a lot to lose if Gemma found out about your affair. Did Stacey threaten to tell her? Maybe she wanted more from you.'

'No, I broke it off months ago.'

'The footage was taken last month.'

'Okay maybe it wasn't that long ago. Things have been difficult lately at home. Harry takes up a lot of Gemma's time. He has to have constant care and she's tired all the time. We have a carer come in twice a week for the night so Gemma can get some sleep but that's all she wants to do, if you get my meaning. Stacey was a bit of fun, it was like I was free from all the worry for just a few hours. It doesn't mean I don't love my wife.'

'Donald knew about your affair with Stacey,' Edris said.

'Bloody Donald.' Rhodri rubbed his hand over his chin. 'Yeah, he was always following Stacey. She'd complain about it, but I think she liked the attention. I had no idea he was following us when we met. We tried to be discreet.'

'Did he confront you?'

'No, not at first, he put the video on Facebook and Twitter. I was terrified Gemma would see it.'

'Did you talk to Donald about it?' Edris asked.

'He talked to me. Told me he knew about the affair and that it wasn't fair on Gemma and Harry. He said he didn't blame me as he knew what Stacey was like. He told me to end it with Stacey and if I did he wouldn't tell Gemma. So I did. I met up with Stacey and told her I couldn't see her anymore.'

'Did she get angry?'

'No.'

Meadows sat forward and placed his hands on the desk. 'Rhodri, I have to be honest with you. Things don't look good. You blamed Dr Rowlands for what happened to Harry, and you don't have an alibi for the night he was killed. You were having an affair with Stacey and after you claim you broke it off she was murdered. Donald knew about your affair and now he's dead.'

'You think that I killed Donald?' Rhodri shook his head in disbelief.

'Where were you on Sunday evening?'

'At home with Gemma.'

'We will be checking with her.'

'You're not going to tell her about the affair, are you?'

Meadows thought that Rhodri looked more concerned about his wife finding out about his infidelity than he did about being arrested on the suspicion of murder.

'You're a religious man. Tell me about Leviticus,' Meadows said.

'What?'

'You must be familiar with the Bible verse "an eye for an eye."'

'I don't know what you are talking about.'

'Is this relevant?' the solicitor asked.

'Yes, it is,' Meadows said.

'How about Revelation 17.'

Rhodri looked blank.

Meadows took a photo from the file and slid it towards Rhodri.

Rhodri looked down at the photo showing the writing on Stacey's stomach and recoiled.

'Someone wrote that on Stacey's body. And this one.' Meadows took another photo from the file. 'The same writing was found on Dr Rowlands; this time, a different Bible verse.'

Rhodri turned his head away refusing to look at the image. The solicitor took a quick peek and curled his lips in disgust.

'You must have come across these verses in the Bible.'

'I don't read the Bible. Can you put them away?' Rhodri waved his hand at the photos.

Meadows wondered why Rhodri was afraid to look. Could it be that he knew what to expect from the doctor's photo, maybe it brought back the memory of brutally killing him.

Meadows returned the photos to the file. 'You go to church every Sunday.'

'Yes, for Gemma and Harry.'

'What do you mean by that?'

'When Harry was in hospital we thought he was going to die. There was a vicar there, you know a hospital chaplain. He came to sit with us. Every day he came and sat, talking in this soothing tone. He even prayed with us and it helped. I can't tell you why. Gemma and me would go to the hospital chapel, just sit there and pray. We prayed so hard for God to save our son. God answered our prayers. The more we prayed, the stronger Harry got until he was out of danger. Gemma has never forgotten that time. I figured we owed God. When we brought Harry home from hospital we started to go to church. Most of it goes over my head. For me it's simple, we go to church to give thanks, it doesn't matter that half the time I don't understand. Vicar Daniels said it's what lives in our hearts that's important, not being able to quote the Bible or read it cover to cover. When I enter the church on a Sunday morning I feel peaceful. All the anger drains away and the gnawing in my stomach disappears. For an hour or so I can be still. I don't suppose you can understand that.'

'Yes, I do understand it. Believe me, I have respect for all religions, but when those ideals and beliefs are taken to the extreme, then I have a problem with understanding. In this case, from what I can understand, some archaic form of justice has been carried out. Jesus is about love, wouldn't you agree?'

'Yes.'

'And forgiveness?'

Rhodri shrugged his shoulders.

'Did you forgive Dr Rowlands?'

'No, I could never forgive that man.'

'Some would say that's not a very Christian view. Now the doctor is dead. Do you feel that justice has been done? Do you now feel peaceful?'

'It hasn't changed anything for Harry.'

'So why kill him?' Edris asked.

'I didn't. The man had it coming. There are other people whose lives have been destroyed because he couldn't be bothered to do his job.'

'Like Sarah Kelly?'

'I suppose.'

'What is your relationship to Sarah?'

'We are friends.'

'Is that all?'

'Yes.'

'You had an affair with Stacey, perhaps you also had an affair with Sarah. She's a lonely woman, you had a lot in common. Both of you were filled with anger and hate for Dr Rowlands,' Edris said.

'No, I told you I made a mistake with Stacey. I don't make a habit of sleeping around.'

'Did you know Ryan and Jean Phillips?' Meadows asked.

Rhodri looked confused by the sudden change of question.

'No, well… I've heard of them. Mary Beynon lives next door to me. Everyone knows what happened to her granddaughter and who was to blame.'

'Yes, her daughter is in prison serving time for negligence which resulted in her daughter's death.'

'Yeah, but they were Ryan's drugs the child got hold of. He was just as guilty for her death.'

'How do you know that? You weren't there.'

'Mary told me everything.'

'Do you feel sorry for Mary?' Meadows asked.

'Yeah, I know what it feels like to almost lose a child so I imagine the pain must be unbearable.'

'Did you think that Ryan and Jean Phillips dying would bring her some peace? You figured you'd got away with killing the doctor so why not those two.'

'No, I didn't kill the doctor and I didn't kill Ryan and Jean Phillips.'

'Where were you the night of Sunday the 18th of October?'

'I already told you I'm not good with dates. It's not like I have a social life. I work and go home.'

'Do you have any evidence that links my client to any one of these murders? From what you've said so far all you have is a weak motive and possible opportunity,' the solicitor said.

No, Meadows thought. 'Your client does have a strong connection to at least three of the murders. Added to that, the injuries on the doctor are consistent with amputations on his son's hands and feet.' Meadows took a copy of the post-mortem report and handed it to the solicitor.

The solicitor read through it, the look on his face showing the disgust he must be feeling. He put the report down.

'Tell me, detective, was this writing – these Bible verses – found on all the victims?'

'Yes, apart from Ryan and Jean Phillips. A brick had been thrown through the window with the Bible reference written on it.'

'Well, it looks to me like your killer is just randomly picking out people they think have done wrong. I'm sure a lot of people know of Harry's condition. There are other injuries to the doctor that do not tie in with your theory. From what I understand the doctor had a few enemies, as did Ryan and Jean Phillips. My client has answered all your questions. He's been honest about his affair. So are you going to charge him?'

'We'll be holding your client while we await the DNA results from the samples he gave when he came into the station. We will also conduct a search of your client's home and vehicle.'

'How long will that take?' Rhodri asked.

'They can hold you for twenty-four hours,' the solicitor said.

'Given the seriousness of the crime, we will be applying to detain your client up to ninety-six hours,' Meadows said.

'I will of course oppose it,' the solicitor said. 'My client is needed at home to support his wife in the care of their child.'

'I note your concerns,' Meadows said. 'Rhodri, I would advise you to take some time to think things over. If you didn't kill Dr Rowlands but know who is responsible, you're not doing yourself any favours by keeping quiet.' Meadows ended the interview and Rhodri was taken back to the cell.

'Sorry to have kept you so late,' Meadows said.

The solicitor smiled. 'It's no problem.'

'I'll get the paperwork done for the extension and get a copy sent to you.'

'I'll come back in the morning to speak to Rhodri.'

'Good, he needs all the help he can get.'

Mike from forensics was waiting in the office. He stood up when Meadows and Edris entered.

'I've been waiting for you,' Mike said. 'I've got something for you that will solve one of your cases.'

Chapter Twenty-six

Mike placed a folder on Meadows' desk and opened it as the team gathered around. Paskin hadn't left the office and Valentine had returned, claiming she didn't want to sit around in an empty flat.

'I can now confirm that Dr Rowlands was killed in the tool shed of the graveyard. Traces of the doctor's blood were found on the floor even though some effort was made to clean it up. Here and here.' Mike pointed the markers out on the photograph. 'Blood, hair and skin were also found on the wheelbarrow.'

'So that's how the killer moved the body,' Edris said.

'Yes, but you'd still have to be fairly strong to get the body into the wheelbarrow and push it to the grave,' Meadows said.

'Yeah and Rhodri has certainly got the strength.'

'That's not all,' Mike said. He took out another photo. 'Synthetic hairs found on the doctor were a match for the ones found on Stacey Evans and also Donald Hobson. DNA samples taken from Donald were a match to the samples taken from under Stacey's fingernails.'

'What? That can't be right,' Meadows said. 'Donald was at the vicarage the night Stacey was murdered, with five other people.'

'I'm afraid there is no mistake, he was also a match to the pubic hairs found on Stacey. Looks like Donald Hobson is your killer.' Mike handed him the report.

The team around him looked as stunned as Meadows felt. He read through the report and put it down on his desk.

'I can't believe it,' Valentine said. 'The kid threw up when we went to arrest him. I can't see he'd have the stomach to kill Dr Rowlands, certainly not the way he was killed.'

'But if Donald is our killer then who killed Donald?' Paskin asked.

'Well, for a start everyone who was at the vicarage that night has lied, including the bloody vicar. The question is why would they all cover for Donald? And clearly he didn't act alone in the killings,' Meadows said.

'What if Rhodri called Stacey that night and got her to come around to the house. He holds her there and waits for Donald then they take her to the Cwm and kill her,' Paskin said.

'It wouldn't fit with the time of death and his wife would have had to be in on it,' Meadows said. 'I'm not ruling out Rhodri as an accomplice to the other murders.'

'What possible motive could Donald have for killing Dr Rowlands, and Jean and Ryan Phillips?' Edris asked.

'The same as Sarah Kelly, I guess,' Meadows said. 'Donald would have known about Erin's visit to the doctor and Sarah's complaint to the GMC. As for Ryan and Jean Phillips, the only one with a solid motive for killing them is Mary Beynon and I don't think she has the strength to be Donald's accomplice.'

'So, what do we do now?' Edris asked.

'It's late, go home and get some rest. Paskin, did uniform report on Sarah Kelly's movements?'

'Yeah, she was at home, took the dog for a walk then went into work. She is on shift all night.'

'Good, so she's not going anywhere, and neither is Rhodri. We'll come back in the morning and look at this mess with fresh eyes.'

* * *

Meadows drove home with the windscreen wipers at double speed. It was on these cold, dark, and wet nights that he was glad of his cottage. He had spent some tough winters in the commune. Endless days of rain and surrounded by mud. The cold would chill you to the bone so, no matter how many layers of clothes you wore, you never felt warm.

As he parked outside his cottage the headlights of the car picked out the broken slates laying on the ground. It reminded him that he had to ring the insurance company to get the roof fixed. It also turned his thoughts back to the night of the storm. If it hadn't been for the flooding, we wouldn't have found the doctor, he thought. Why only conceal the doctor and not the others? It had to be that the doctor's injuries would lead them to the killer which put Rhodri Lewis in the frame. He really hoped they would turn up something from the house search or forensics would come back with a match.

He jumped out of the car and made a dash for the cottage. Once inside he changed his clothes, made a cup of tea, and rolled a joint. He sat in the armchair smoking, and felt his muscles loosen and allowed his thoughts to wander. He couldn't believe that Donald was responsible or played some part in all four murders. The first time he had met him he had been afraid and the first words out of his mouth were, 'I didn't kill her.' Meadows had thought the statement odd at the time but maybe Donald hadn't been the one to put his hands around her throat. He had hated Stacey so he might have played a part in restraining her, but no, forensics showed that he was the one to sexually assault her. Did someone persuade him? Rhodri or Sarah?

Meadows took another long drag of the joint. There was something else bothering him. If Sarah killed Donald, then why take the food and blankets one day and go back to kill him the next? So far as they knew, it was only Sarah and Vicar Daniels who knew Donald was at the quarry. Vicar Daniels? Could he have killed Donald? What would be his motive?

Meadows shook his head. He was getting off track but the more he thought about it the more complicated the case became. There were too many variables and more than one suspect. Could it be that Donald had killed four people then written on himself before jumping off the quarry? Finally, tiredness overcame him, so he went up to bed and lay his head on the pillow. Sleep didn't come easily. Every time he closed his eyes he saw Donald lying at the bottom of the quarry. The limestone, his eyes snapped open. The fingerprints on the limestone and the brick thrown through Jean Phillips window didn't match Donald's fingerprints. There was someone else there, he thought. It has to be Rhodri Lewis. Meadows sighed. It didn't make a difference; he still had to go and tell Donald's parents that their son had committed a terrible crime.

* * *

The sun was fighting to break through the clouds as Meadows arrived at the office. The team was already in and were sat around the incident board awaiting instruction.

'Okay, as Donald was a match to the attack on Stacey, I think we should start there,' Meadows said. 'His alibi for that evening was watching a film with Vicar Daniels, Sarah Kelly, Tomos John, Gemma Lewis, and Mary Beynon. All gave the same story. Are they all lying to protect Donald and if so, why? Paskin, I would like you to find out all you can about Vicar Daniels and Tomos John. Valentine and Hanes, I would like you to conduct the search on Rhodri Lewis' house and vehicle. We are looking for anything that ties him to the murders, particularly a wig. I want you to tread carefully. See if you can persuade Gemma to take the child out of the house when you search. Both are vulnerable. I want phone records checked for all of these.'

Meadows pointed to the board. 'Edris and I will speak to Vicar Daniels, see what he has to say about the film evening. Until forensics come back to us matching Rhodri to the crime scene, we keep looking. Everyone on this list apart from the vicar had motive for killing the doctor. One of them threw a brick through Jean Phillips' window and hit the doctor with a piece of limestone. Gemma also has motive for killing Stacey if she had found out about her husband's affair. You need to check all the dates with her. She will protect her husband, but would she keep quiet if Rhodri killed Donald? The other thing to consider is that she may be afraid. Any questions?'

'What about Mary Beynon?' Paskin asked.

'I think it unlikely she will give you any information. She may have seen something on the night Dr Rowlands was killed. Maybe heard Rhodri coming home late. For now, let's concentrate on Rhodri Lewis and unpicking Donald's alibi. We need to find something on Rhodri and charge him by the end of the day or we are going to have to let him go. It doesn't look like we will get an extension to hold him longer.'

Chapter Twenty-seven

The sun had lost its battle against the clouds and when they arrived in Gaer Fawr a mist hung over the village, dousing it in a fine drizzle of rain. The church looked peaceful as they entered through the lychgate and took the narrow side path to the tool store. The store was built of stone and had a slate roof and wooden door. It looked as old as the church and, as Meadows pushed open the door, he wondered what its original purpose had been.

Inside there were still markers on the dirt floor where forensics had identified blood or other points of interest. Some of the tools had been removed along with the wheelbarrow.

'They must have gagged the poor sod,' Edris said. 'Anyone walking along the pavement would have heard his shouts.'

'Yes and there was also the risk of getting him in here unseen. He would have been brought here by car, that much we know. I guess they parked outside the gate. Made sure there was no one around. It would have been dark and late so chances are it was quiet, then they drag him inside and kill him.'

'Or he could have been knocked out in the car, so they grab the wheelbarrow to move him,' Edris said.

Meadows stepped out of the shed. 'So Donald and Rhodri? You would need two drivers. I'm guessing Donald at least had a provisional licence and was learning to drive. We'll have to check with his parents. One gets rid of the doctor's car, the other follows to pick him up. I would imagine it would need them both to move the doctor in the wheelbarrow to the top corner of the graveyard and dig a grave.'

'That's a lot to do in one night. How long would it take them to dig a grave?'

'It was deep,' Meadows said. 'Vicar Daniels reckoned about six hours.'

'And then they have to clean the shed and get home covered in dirt? I can't see it.'

'Maybe they dug the grave beforehand.'

'That's a horrible thought.'

'It is,' Meadows agreed. 'That part of the graveyard isn't tended to very often. The last cut of the grass would have been done for winter so they could have worked on the grave over a few nights and no one would have noticed.'

'Yeah, that works. But how did Rhodri persuade Donald to help him?'

'Or maybe it was Donald that instigated it. He knew about Rhodri's affair, so he had that over him. Donald had as much reason to hate the doctor. He would know about Sarah's complaint to the GMC. His parents said they thought he was never going to get over Erin's death and maybe he never did,' Meadows said.

'Yeah, but murder?'

'Well, I doubt Rhodri would need much persuading. Although I would say out of the two Rhodri would be more likely to be the instigator. There is also Gemma to consider. I'm sure she would have noticed Rhodri coming home late that night. His clothes would have been dirty and probably bloodstained.'

'She would likely keep quiet to protect her husband.'

'Or she could be in on it. Dr Rowlands would have got out of his car for a woman. Yet she seemed genuinely upset about Donald.'

'Maybe she didn't want Rhodri to kill him?' Edris said.

'Then what about Ryan and Jean Phillips?'

'Rhodri lives next door to Mary Beynon, she sees him come home in the early hours after he's killed the doctor so to keep her quiet he torches Ryan and Jean's house.'

'But Ryan and Jean died before the doctor was found so Mary Beynon wouldn't have made the connection; besides that's a lot of people to be involved.'

'Yeah, I guess. Maybe once they had killed the doctor and thought they got away with it they decided to kill again. Picking out victims they thought deserved to die. They did leave a three-week gap before killing Jean and Ryan Phillips.'

'We just need to find out how Donald managed to be in two places at the same time. Right, let's see the vicar,' Meadows said.

The church was locked so they took the shortcut through the graveyard to the vicarage.

Vicar Daniels looked harassed when he answered the door and was fixing his dog collar.

'Morning detectives,' he smiled. 'I'm afraid you've caught me in a bit of a hurry. I overslept this morning and I'm just about to go out to see Gemma Lewis. From what she tells me Rhodri has been arrested. Is that correct?'

'Yes,' Meadows said. 'I'm afraid we are going to have to delay you a bit longer.'

'You better come in then.'

Vicar Daniels led them to the kitchen where plates were piled up in the sink and a bread knife and tub of butter sat on the counter.

'Excuse the mess,' Vicar Daniels said. 'My parishioners come before domestic duties. I really should get a cleaner. Now, how can I help you?'

'The night of the 20th of October, you said, Donald was here watching a film.'

'Yes, that was the Tuesday night, wasn't it?'

'Yes. Are you sure about the time he arrived and left that evening?'

'He arrived around eight, he was always punctual, and left just before eleven.'

Meadows was finding it difficult to believe that the vicar could lie so easily. He showed no outward signs of deceit. He was looking Meadows in the eyes and seemed relaxed.

'What time did you start watching the film?'

'I guess it would have been before eight thirty, no later. Quarter past or twenty past, something like that.'

'And did he leave at all during the evening?'

'Not that I'm aware of. To be honest I was rather tired that evening, so I dozed off during the film. I had seen it before. He may have left the room to go to the toilet, I suppose.'

'Was he definitely in the room when the film finished?'

'Yes, because he turned the lights on.'

'We now know that Donald was responsible for the attack on Stacey Evans.'

The vicar's eyes widened in surprise. 'Donald? Surely not. I really can't see him doing anything like that. No, he was here.'

'You see our problem. If Donald attacked Stacey on the Tuesday evening how could he have been sat the whole time watching a film? You see, Stacey finished work at half eight and died sometime between nine and ten,' Edris said. 'You say you may have dozed off but there were four other people in the room. Are you certain of the times?'

'Yes, Donald came earlier than the others to help me set up the room.'

'We'd like to see the room,' Meadows said.

Vicar Daniels led them to the sitting room which was situated at the front of the house. The room had an old-fashioned feel to it with a dado rail running around the wall and landscape oil paintings hung below. Dark green curtains surrounded a bay window where the television sat on a stand. A green patterned sofa and armchair were positioned in a semicircle around a coffee table and facing the window.

'There is not enough room for six people,' Meadows said as he glanced around the room. 'Where did everyone sit?'

'I was in the armchair, my usual place. Gemma sat next to Mary on the sofa. Donald helped me move the two-seater sofa from my study and we placed it here.' Vicar Daniels indicated a space between the sofa and armchair. 'We set it back a little so everyone could see the film. Tomos and Sarah sat here. Donald had a chair from the kitchen. He switched off the lights once everyone was seated.'

'Did anyone leave during the film?'

'Not that I'm aware of.'

'Did the lights stay off the whole time?'

'Yes, Donald turned them off at the start then back on when the film finished.'

'How did Donald seem after the film?'

'He was a bit emotional. Most of us were as it's that kind of film. Mary was crying as you would expect. It brought back memories of what had happened to Ella. She said she would like to think of Ella that way, safe. Donald gave her a hug and told her that–'

'Told her what?' Meadows asked.

'That she would see Ella again one day and that God had seen to it that Ryan had been punished.'

'What do you think he meant by that?'

'Well, I assume the fire. That he meant it was God's will. You don't think that Donald had anything to do with that fire, do you?'

'How did Mary react to Donald's comments?'

'She just nodded and wiped her eyes. I don't think she said anything in particular.'

'How often do you have these film nights?' Edris asked.

'Every two weeks.'

'How many have you had?'

Vicar Daniels thought for a moment and muttered the names of films as he counted on his fingers. 'Five.'

Edris wrote in his notebook. 'So, the film night was planned in advance.'

'Yes.'

'Why were only five people invited?'

Good question, Meadows thought.

'It wasn't just five. There was a notice up in the church inviting anyone who wanted to come. I had planned to use the church hall but as there were so few of us I thought it would be cosier here.'

'You said Donald called you last Saturday night,' Meadows said.

'Yes.'

'Did he give you any indication of why he was frightened of going to the police? Tell you what he had done? I know you have a duty to keep confidences but given the circumstances it would be better if you told us everything you and Donald spoke about.'

'He said he was afraid of being arrested but he didn't say what for. He said he had done something bad. He didn't tell me what that was. I thought maybe it was something minor. Donald took the Bible very seriously and would even feel guilty if he swore. I didn't think whatever he had done would have serious consequences. He certainly didn't tell me he had attacked Stacey Evans.'

'You told us he was cold and hungry. Sarah took him a blanket and food on Saturday evening. Did she tell you?'

'No, and Donald didn't say she had been to see him, so I assumed he hadn't eaten since the Friday night. To be honest if I'd known where he was, I would have gone to him and tried to persuade him to come home. If I had–' Vicar Daniels voice broke. 'I'm sorry.' He cleared his throat. 'Maybe he would still be with us. I'm sure he would have been able to give you some explanation. I really can't see Donald killing that poor girl.'

'We don't think Donald acted alone. Who was he close to?'

'Sarah, but that was because of Erin.'

'What about Rhodri Lewis?'

'I wouldn't say they were good friends. Donald kept to himself.'

'The writing on your front door about the false prophet. You thought you may have said something during a sermon to offend someone. Could it be that the killer thinks you know something, and it was a warning to keep quiet?'

'I can't see that.'

'Is there anything you can think of that doesn't seem important? Something out of place. Someone maybe said something to you?'

Vicar Daniels shook his head. 'I can't think of anything.'

'As you know, the writing on your door wasn't the only time we came across biblical references. It was also written on the bodies of the victims. Different verses each time. Can you think of anyone in your parish that is extreme in their views?'

'No, not in the way you are implying. Bill is about the only one that probably knows the Bible better than me but I wouldn't call him extreme.'

'Do you know anyone that wears a wig?' Edris asked.

The vicar looked confused. 'No, look you are asking me to point a finger at my parishioners. I can't see any of them committing murder.'

'We have to look at everyone closely,' Meadows said. 'Even the most unlikely.' He nodded at Edris.

Edris flicked through his notebook. 'Can you tell us where you were on the evening of Monday, the 28th of September?'

'I... well... you don't think—'

'We have to check.'

'I'll look in my diary.'

They followed Vicar Daniels to his study where he pulled out a leather-bound diary.

'The 28th you said?'

'Yes.'

'I was visiting a parishioner in the hospital until 8 p.m., so I guess I would have got home about 9 p.m.'

'And after that?'

'I would have changed and sat in the sitting room reading. I usually go to bed around 10 p.m.'

'What about Sunday evening, the 18th of October?'

Vicar Daniels flicked the pages. 'Evening service at 5 p.m. then we had a wardens' meeting, we usually finish at 7.30 p.m. It's then an early night for me. After two services I'm all done in by a Sunday evening.'

'You said that last Sunday you were up until midnight waiting for Donald.'

'Yes, that's correct. I was at the church. I thought he may come. It was a long night.'

'Okay, we'll leave you to get on with your visits. We would appreciate your discretion, particularly where Donald is concerned as we have to speak to his parents.'

'Of course,' Vicar Daniels said. 'Poor souls. It will be an awful shock for them on top of losing their son.'

'I'm sure they will be grateful of your support,' Meadows said.

As they walked back through the graveyard, Edris asked, 'Do you believe him?'

'I'd like to,' Meadows said. 'If they sat down at eight twenty and turned the lights off, Donald could have slipped out and be waiting for Stacey to leave the shop. He could even have left a bit later; he watched her long enough to know she would take that route home and stop for a smoke. Most films run about two hours so it would be enough time for him to kill her and get back to the vicarage in time to switch the lights back on.'

'He would have to be very cool to carry that off,' Edris said.

'Vicar Daniels said that Donald was emotional after the film. Maybe it had nothing to do with the film. I get the impression the vicar is not telling us everything. Maybe it's out of loyalty for his parishioners, and I guess he sees the best in people and finds it hard to believe one of them could commit murder.'

'Just like someone else I know,' Edris said with a smile.

'Well, people are complex. Different shades of grey. You can find the good if you look.'

'Yeah, and you can also find the bad,' Edris said.

Meadows opened the lychgate and stepped through. 'I think we should call on Sarah Kelly. See what she has to say about the film night. Someone should have noticed Donald's absence for that length of time, and she and Tomos were sitting next to him.'

'Yeah, that one is definitely a darker grey. She's like a big fat mood cloud sucking out all the happiness.'

Meadows laughed. 'I wouldn't quite describe her like that. You have to remember she is still suffering from grief, but I think she's involved at some level. She's been obstructive since the start of the investigation.'

'Yeah and she was there the night you got attacked.'

'I can't see her hitting me over the head, but who knows, she could have been part of it. She was very persuasive about not calling anyone else out that night because of the storm.'

They had arrived at Sarah's house and Meadows gave a loud knock on the door. It took a few minutes and another knock before Sarah opened the door. She didn't look pleased to see Meadows and Edris standing on her doorstep.

'This better be important,' she said as she pulled her dressing gown tightly around her body. 'I've not long gone to bed. I was on shift last night.'

'We won't keep you long,' Meadows said as he followed her inside.

'I heard you arrested Rhodri, can't you people get anything right?' She plonked down on the sofa. 'Poor Gemma has enough to deal with. She called me last night in work. She was sobbing.'

'I can assure you we had very good reason to arrest Rhodri. So you are good friends with Gemma then?'

'Yes.'

'And with Rhodri?'

'What's that supposed to mean?'

'Are you good friends with Rhodri or is he more than a friend?'

Sarah's eyes narrowed. 'I don't make a habit of sleeping with married men. We are just friends, or rather he is the husband of a friend, that's all.'

'Would you say that Rhodri and Gemma are happy together?'

'What sort of a question is that? They have their ups and downs like any married couple but any more I couldn't tell you.'

'Has Gemma ever given you any indication that she's frightened of Rhodri?'

'No, as far as I know he is a good husband and father. Life hasn't been easy for the two of them and now you are making things more difficult. The whole village is buzzing with gossip about his arrest. There is a Halloween party at the community centre tomorrow for the little ones. Gemma feels that she can't show her face. So now Harry won't be able to go out and have some fun.'

'I have no intention of making things difficult for that family but I'm conducting an investigation into the murder of five people. I think the last thing this village needs is to dress up and scare each other,' Meadows said.

'Five?'

'Yes, we now know that Ryan and Jean Phillips' murders are connected to Stacey, Donald, and Dr Rowlands.'

'Oh, them.'

'You knew them?'

'No, but I knew what they did to Mary Beynon.'

'So you think they deserved to die in the fire?'

'A little girl is dead because of them.'

'What about Stacey Evans and Dr Rowlands, did they deserve to die?'

'You reap what you sow.'

'What about Donald?'

Sarah shook her head. 'No, Donald didn't do anything wrong. He shouldn't be dead.' Tears filled her eyes.

'Are you sure about that?'

'Yes.'

'The thing is you haven't been honest with us from the start. You have kept back information; now you need to tell us the truth, for Donald's parents' sake.' Meadows nodded to Edris.

Edris flipped open his notebook, took a glance then turned his attention to Sarah.

'Tell us about the night Stacey Evans was murdered. I suggest you think carefully because if you lie again I will arrest you for perverting the course of justice.'

Sarah raised her eyebrow but didn't appear concerned. 'What do you want to know?'

'When you watched the film, where were you sitting?'

'On the sofa next to Tomos.'

'And where was Donald sitting?'

'On a chair. He had brought one in from the kitchen as there was nowhere else to sit.'

'Who was sitting closest to Donald?'

'Me.'

'Were the lights on or off?'

'They were off.'

'Who turned them off?'

'Donald as he was closest to the switch.'

'Did Donald leave during the film?'

Sarah hesitated. 'He muttered something about going to the toilet.'

'How long was he out of the room?'

Sarah shrugged her shoulders.

'Five minutes? Half hour? Two hours?' Edris asked.

'I don't know.'

'He was sat next to you. I'm sure you would have noticed his absence if he was gone for any length of time. I'll remind you that you vouched for him the night Stacey was murdered.'

'He was gone for some time. He had been unwell recently, so I assumed he had an upset stomach.'

'And you didn't check on him?'

'No, I was engrossed in the film. What does it matter if he left the room?'

'It matters because evidence shows that Donald attacked Stacey that evening,' Edris said.

'Don't be ridiculous,' Sarah snapped. 'Donald wouldn't kill anyone. I suppose it makes things easier for you. Put the blame on Donald as he is not here to defend himself. What do you think that will do to his parents?'

'Then tell us what Donald spoke to you about up the quarry,' Meadows said. 'He wasn't just frightened about speaking to the police. Who was he afraid of? You said that Donald didn't deserve to die. Help us to find the person responsible for his murder.'

'I can't help you.'

'Can't or won't?' Meadows felt anger spike his veins. 'Haven't enough people died already? Who are you protecting?'

'I'm not protecting anyone.' Sarah stood. 'I've answered your questions now I would like you to leave.'

Meadows stood. 'Don't leave the area.' He looked around the room. 'Where's your dog?' Meadows asked.

'With Tomos. He has him when I do the night shift so he can take him out when I sleep.'

'That's nice of him. Tomos is also a good friend of yours?'

Sarah shook her head. 'Who I'm friends with is none of your business. Now I would like to get back to bed. I have another shift tonight.' She walked to the front door and opened it.

'Thank you for your time,' Meadows said as he stepped out the door.

Sarah shut the door without any further comment.

'Bloody woman,' Meadows said as he walked back to the car.

'You think she's lying?' Edris asked.

'Yes, our only hope is to turn up something in the house search or the DNA results come back positive, otherwise we are going to have to let Rhodri Lewis go. I have a bad feeling that unless we catch the killer soon someone else is going to die.'

Chapter Twenty-eight

DCI Lester was sat in the office and Meadows felt the team's unease. It wasn't that Lester was a difficult boss, he was fair and played by the rules. It was more that they wanted to make a good impression and so far they had little to show for the investigation. Meadows was sat back in his chair and listening to the conversation. He felt at ease in Lester's company. Rank and status had never impressed him, and he felt himself no better or worse than the next person.

'So, nothing at all?' Lester said.

'No, sir,' Valentine answered. 'The house search didn't turn up anything. Nothing on his computer of interest and forensics found nothing in the car.'

'I see,' Lester said. 'That and the fact that the voluntary DNA sample came back negative means that we are going to have to let him go.'

'I don't think that's wise,' Meadows said. 'Rhodri Lewis has motive and opportunity and given the injuries inflicted on the doctor—'

'You don't have any solid evidence against him. He's not the only one who has motive and given that Donald

Hobson killed the girl it could be argued that he wrote on his own body before jumping off the quarry.'

'There was morphine found in his blood, sir,' Edris said. 'And signs of a struggle and no marker pen found.'

'Yes, but those are things that could be explained. You know how it goes in court. You don't have enough for a conviction.'

'Donald Hobson didn't act alone,' Meadows said. 'If we let Rhodri Lewis go then there could be another murder.'

Lester seemed to be considering this. 'So are you saying Rhodri Lewis, Donald Hobson, and a third person committed these crimes? How many other suspects do you have?'

Meadows stood up and walked over to the incident board. 'All these have motive for the murders. Tomos John gave Donald an alibi, he also made a complaint against the doctor along with his father, Ellis John. Ellis doesn't have an alibi. Tomos' mother died of a stomach complaint and was in a lot of pain, the doctor was forced to drink bleach, I suspect to mimic the pain in the stomach of his mother. Sarah Kelly phoned Tomos the night she spoke to Donald, she claims she didn't tell anyone where Donald was hiding but she seems very close to Tomos. He even takes care of her dog when she is on night shift. Sarah Kelly has motive for killing both the doctor and Stacey Evans. She was also at Bill's farm the night I got attacked and the only person we know of that knew Donald's whereabouts.'

'Vicar Daniels also provided Donald with an alibi, he would certainly know the Bible. Although I can find no motive for him committing the murders and a Bible verse was written on the vicarage front door. Paskin, what did you manage to find out about the vicar?'

'I spoke to the bishop. Vicar Daniels took over the parish from the old vicar. It was his first post, and he has been there since. Not one single complaint. Lots of positive comments on the church website. He does a lot of good in the community. Things like giving out turkeys to all the hard-up families at Christmas. Organising fundraising for specialist equipment for Harry Lewis among other things. He's wealthy in his own right and was also left a considerable amount of money along with a house when an elderly parishioner died. He transferred it all to the church.'

'He doesn't sound a likely suspect,' Lester said. 'What about this Bible Bill character? Sounds like someone who would hold extreme views.'

'DNA and house search came back clear,' Meadows said. 'There is nothing to tie him to the murders other than he was Erin's father.'

'Well now, that's the same as Rhodri Lewis. You also have prints from a brick thrown through the Phillips' house window and the limestone found with the doctor. You have no matches on those.'

'No.'

'Then I'm afraid my decision stands. Let Rhodri Lewis go. Until you have some solid evidence, you haven't got enough to charge him, especially as there are others that have equal motive and opportunity. You already have Stacey Evans' killer. That at least will give the family some answers.'

'And what about Donald Hobson's parents? Don't they deserve answers?'

'It could be anyone. If Donald was carrying out these murders for some sort of misguided justice for Erin, Harry, and Ella Beynon, then his accomplice could even be another teenager he persuaded to join him. Donald decides to go to the police, so his accomplice kills him,' Lester said. 'I think you are going to have to cast your search wider.'

'Or it could be one of this lot.' Meadows pointed to the board.

'Not one of them has a direct link to Jean or Ryan Phillips. This investigation is a mess. This morning's headlines say we've got a serial killer in the valleys,' Lester said.

'We are doing our best,' Meadows said.

'I'm going to have to give out a press release. That statement may well be that we believe Donald Hobson was responsible for the murders and then took his own life.'

'I need to speak to his parents first,' Meadows said.

'Then don't leave it too long.' Lester stood. 'I'll ask the custody sergeant to arrange Rhodri Lewis' release.'

'On bail?'

'No, release under investigation. With his young son to care for I doubt there is a risk he will leave the area. Keep me updated.' Lester left the office.

Meadows looked around the room. The team looked dispirited.

'You think he's wrong to let Rhodri Lewis go,' Edris said.

'He's right, we don't have any more on him than we do on Bible Bill or any of the others. Right, first thing in the morning we'll go and see Donald's parents. They might be able to tell us if he had a friend we hadn't considered. Someone who called around the house. Then we better see Anthony and Cloe Evans. Valentine, I'd like you to speak to Sarah Kelly, ask her if she will come to the station to give voluntary fingerprints. See what reaction you get.'

'I have an appointment in the morning,' Valentine said. 'I should be back by 9.30 at the latest.'

'That's fine. Paskin, can you go and see Tomos and Ellis John and ask them to do the same? Tomos is a strong guy so better take Hanes with you in case there are any problems.'

'Okay,' Paskin said.

'Cool,' Hanes said.

'You can all get off home,' Meadows said with a smile.

'I'll stay a bit longer,' Edris said. 'I've got a Halloween party to go to tomorrow night. I'd rather work late tonight and get off early tomorrow to get ready.'

'A party? I thought Halloween was just for kids,' Meadows said.

'No, it's just as much fun now,' Edris said. 'It's always been one of my favourite nights of the year. Halloween was only one night when I was a kid, now they have the decorations out for a week. Out would come the pumpkins and we would dress up and scare the shit out of the neighbourhood grannies.'

Meadows laughed. 'Sounds about right for you. I'm guessing you were a wicked little sod.'

'No, it's what we all did. Didn't we, Hanes?'

'Yeah, I loved Halloween. Used to hide in the graveyard and jump out at anyone that walked by.'

'And you became policemen. I'd be surprised if anyone in the valleys has respect for you two,' Meadows said.

'Didn't you dress up?' Edris asked.

'No, I was a good boy. We celebrated Samhain. It marks the feast for the dead.'

They all stared at Meadows.

'It's not some weird ritual. It's a sort of remembrance for those who have died. Even Churches celebrate All Saints Day. It's not supposed to be about ghosts and zombies.'

Edris laughed. 'You had a very sheltered childhood. How about this year we dress up and go trick or treating?'

'I'll join in,' Hanes said.

'Nutters,' Meadows said, shaking his head. He turned to Paskin and Valentine. 'Are you two joining in with this insanity?'

'Yeah, I'm going to the party, so I'll stay on with Edris,' Paskin said.

'Me too,' Valentine said.

'You could come,' Edris said to Meadows. 'I'm sure you could make up a costume.'

'I suppose you're going to this party, Hanes?' Meadows asked.

'Erm, yeah, well it's in my flat. I would have mentioned it, but I didn't think it was your thing.'

'No worries,' Meadows said.

'If you're all staying a bit longer I want to go through everything we have. Phone records, evidence logs, and every witness statement.'

* * *

They worked late into the evening but didn't turn up anything of interest. Paskin, Valentine, and Hanes left and just as Edris was putting on his coat the phone rang. He picked it up, his face becoming serious.

'Okay thanks.' Edris put the phone down. 'A 999 call was received from the Lewis' house. Sounds like an angry crowd has gathered outside.'

'We better get over there. Come on.'

Meadows sped towards Gaer Fawr with the blue lights and siren on. Edris held tightly to the hand grab as the car rounded the corners.

'I was afraid something like this would happen after Anthony Evans' reaction when we arrested Rhodri. I wouldn't be surprised if he's rounded up a few of the farm boys.'

'Great,' Edris said. 'We're not going to stand a chance if things kick off.'

'Better make sure they've sent more than one car.'

Edris made the call for backup as the car flew over the humpback bridge and Meadows felt his stomach lurch.

'I suppose all it needed was for one person to see him come home,' Edris said.

'Yeah and half the village will be baying for his blood.'

Meadows took the turn off the main road and stopped the car where the crowd had spilt off the pavement and into the road. Two uniformed officers were trying to disperse the crowd and Vicar Daniels stood outside the Lewises' front door looking terrified.

'It's like some medieval witch hunt,' Meadows said as he got out of the car.

'Move out of the way, Vicar,' someone shouted. 'You don't want to get hurt.'

The two uniformed officers were struggling now as a scuffle broke out. One of them got punched in the face while the other discharged his taser. One man fell to the ground and the crowd turned on the officers. Edris moved quickly to help while Meadows leaned in the car and put his hand on the horn. He held it there until the attention of the crowd turned his way. He took his hand away and straightened up.

'What is wrong with you, people?' Meadows shouted. 'There is a child in that house who is terrified. Go home before we arrest you all.'

'You let that murdering bastard go,' someone shouted. The crowd joined in. 'He should be locked up, there is no justice.'

'Rhodri Lewis was taken to the station to help with our enquiries,' Meadows said. 'He has answered all our questions and he has been released without charge.'

'What about my daughter?'

Meadows looked into the crowd and saw Anthony Evans. 'Where is the justice for her? You are going to let him walk free.'

'Rhodri Lewis didn't kill your daughter. There has been a development in the case which I will discuss with you, but not here. Now unless any of you have evidence of Rhodri Lewis' guilt, then by all means step forward.' He beckoned with his hand. 'I'll be happy to take your statement right here.'

Two police cars screeched to a halt with their blue lights flashing. Meadows looked at the crowd who now looked uncertain.

'Come on, don't be shy,' Meadows said as the uniformed officers jumped out of the car.

'Go home, the lot of you,' Anthony Evans said.

There was a general murmur from the crowd, and they began to disperse, apart from a couple of men that were restrained and put into the police car. Anthony Evans walked over to Meadows.

'So what's this new development?'

'I'll call around and talk to you and your wife in the morning when you have had a chance to calm down. I don't want a repeat of what happened here tonight,' Meadows said.

'This was my idea,' Anthony said. 'I was going to come by myself, then a couple of the other boys at the farm came with me and I guess things got out of hand.'

'That may well be but taking matters into your own hands won't achieve anything. What would have happened if Rhodri had come out of the house? Would you have stopped there, or would you hurt his family to get back at him?'

'I would never have hurt Gemma or the child.'

'Maybe not but what about the rest that were here tonight? Like you said, things got out of hand. Now go home.'

Meadows walked over to Edris who was talking to one of the uniformed officers who was bleeding from the nose.

'I thought they were going to lynch you,' Edris said.

'So did I.' Meadows smiled then turned to the injured policeman. 'Are you okay?'

'Yeah, I'll be fine. Thanks for the help. If you hadn't intervened I don't know what would have happened. We didn't expect this when we responded to the call.'

'You did good. Make sure you get that seen to.' Meadows pointed to the injury.

'I will, I'm going with those two to be booked in first.'

Meadows nodded then went over to Vicar Daniels who was still stood by the door looking shaken.

'Are you okay?' Meadows asked.

'Yes,' Vicar Daniels said. 'Gemma called me. I came over straight away. I thought they might listen to me. I never expected this. They were like a pack of wild animals and there was no reasoning with them. I thought I was doing something good in this village. What would have happened if you hadn't showed up? That poor innocent child inside.' The vicar's voice wobbled.

'I think the vicar could do with a stiff drink,' Edris said.

'Let's get you inside,' Meadows said as he knocked the door. 'You can open up. It's safe now,' he shouted.

The door opened and Rhodri peered around.

'Can we come in? Vicar Daniels has had a bit of a shock.'

Rhodri frowned at Meadows but stepped back to let them inside then locked the door behind them.

In the sitting room Gemma was holding Harry and both were crying.

Rhodri turned on Meadows. 'See what you've done?'

'I had no choice but to take you in,' Meadows said. 'Now I think Vicar Daniels could do with a cup of tea.'

Rhodri looked at the vicar and nodded. 'Sit down, Vicar. I'm sorry I didn't come out to help you. I was afraid they would get inside.'

'It's probably best that you didn't attempt to go out,' Meadows said.

'What are you going to do about this?' Rhodri said. 'We will never be able to go outside again.'

'We'll get a couple of officers to keep watch overnight. I'll also talk to Anthony Evans in the morning.'

'I'm taking Gemma to stay with her mother in Bristol in the morning,' Rhodri said.

'I'm sorry, Rhodri, but you have been advised not to leave the area when the investigation is ongoing,' Meadows said.

'In that case you are going to have to arrest me again. Gemma can't drive all that way with Harry alone. What if he was to have a fit when she's on the motorway?'

'Isn't there anyone else who can drive her?'

'No, don't you think my wife and son have had enough stress? If it makes any difference, I'll call in to the station when I return.'

Meadows looked at Gemma and Harry. The child was still clinging to his mother. Maybe it would be better for them to be out of the way, he thought. If Rhodri was guilty then at least they would be safe. He nodded to Rhodri who left the room to make the tea.

'Are you okay?' Meadows asked Gemma.

'No.' She shook her head. 'Everyone thinks that my husband murdered Stacey. I have to leave my home, and everything behind.'

'It will be okay,' Vicar Daniels said. 'This darkness will soon go and there will be light again, you'll see.'

Gemma nodded and sat down in the armchair. She kissed the top of Harry's head.

'We are making progress with the investigation,' Meadows said. 'It's just a matter of elimination.'

'There you go,' Vicar Daniels said. 'It makes sense to go away now, doesn't it? The detective will soon solve the case and things will be much different.'

'Will they?' Rhodri came back into the room and handed a mug of tea to Vicar Daniels. 'The way I see it, anyone that gets questioned is going to get the same treatment. People don't see that they're much better off with the doctor gone. They soon forget what he was like now he's dead.'

'Rhodri,' Vicar Daniels said. 'That is not the attitude to have. What this village needs is peace now.'

They are not going to get that until the killer is caught, Meadows thought. 'We'll leave you now,' he said. 'I'll make sure that a police car is parked outside overnight. Vicar Daniels, would you be able to come to the station tomorrow to provide fingerprints for elimination?' He watched the vicar's reaction for signs of distress but there were none.

'I have a meeting with the bishop in Carmarthen in the morning. Will the afternoon be okay?'

'Yes, that will be fine,' Meadows said. He left the house hoping that he wasn't making a mistake by letting Rhodri leave Gaer Fawr in the morning.

Chapter Twenty-nine

There were no more incidences in Gaer Fawr overnight and as Meadows drove through the next morning all seemed quiet. Most of the houses had carved pumpkins in the windows. Some had standard triangular eyes and noses, others were more elaborately carved.

'Looks like they are going ahead with the Halloween party,' Edris said as Meadows parked the car outside the Hobsons' house.

A group of people carrying decorations were heading towards the community centre.

'I hope Hanes is doing up his flat. It adds to the atmosphere.'

Meadows didn't comment, he felt a sickness in his stomach. The last time he had been here had been bad enough, when he had to tell Anwen Hobson her son was dead. Now he was about to desecrate their son's memory.

The door was opened by Cerith Hobson. He wasn't dressed or shaved, and his eyes were bloodshot. Meadows guessed by the look and smell of him that he had been drinking all night.

'I'm sorry to intrude,' Meadows said. 'Could we come in to have a chat?'

Cerith nodded and led them to the sitting room where Anwen was sat with her eyes fixed to the television screen. She had a faraway look.

'Police, love.' Cerith picked up the remote control and turned off the television. The room fell silent.

'Have a seat,' Cerith said.

Meadows and Edris perched side by side on the sofa. It was dark in the room. Only a weak light came through the drawn curtains and Cerith made no move to put the light on and remained standing up.

'I'm sorry but I need to tell you some difficult news,' Meadows said.

'You've found the bastard that killed my boy?' Cerith asked.

'No, not yet.'

'We heard Rhodri Lewis was arrested,' Anwen said. 'We thought perhaps it was him. Cerith wanted to go around there last night.'

Meadows tried to pick his words carefully. 'We have no evidence that Rhodri Lewis was involved in Donald's murder.'

'Who then?'

'That's not what I'm here about. When someone dies in suspicious circumstances, we take all sorts of samples. Blood, hair, and DNA. The DNA sample we took from Donald as well as hair samples were a match to those found on Stacey Evans.'

'I don't understand,' Anwen said.

Meadows sat forward. 'It appears that Donald was responsible for the attack on Stacey Evans.'

'What!' Anwen jumped up from the chair. 'No, don't you dare come here accusing my son, get out,' she pointed at the door.

'Anwen, please,' Meadows said. 'I understand how distressing this is for you, but we do have evidence.'

'I don't care what evidence you think you have,' Cerith said. 'I know my son, he is not a murderer.'

'We're not saying that he murdered Stacey Evans,' Edris said. 'All we know is that he was involved in the sexual assault on her.'

Cerith was red in the face. 'My son was not a pervert!'

'You met him,' Anwen said. 'He was a shy quiet boy. How can you think he would be involved in something like that? It's not possible.'

'We don't believe that Donald acted alone,' Meadows said. 'Please sit down, Anwen. All this information will have to come out at some stage. Even if it's only at the inquest. It would be better if you tried to help us understand why Donald would have become involved in Stacey's murder. We know he was good friends with Erin Kelly. He blamed Stacey for Erin's death and we think that's why he attacked her. Maybe he didn't mean to kill her. What we don't know is who else was involved. It could have been someone close to Donald who persuaded him to act. We think Donald was going to come clean, talk to us, and that's why he was murdered. I need you to think carefully, who was Donald close to?'

Anwen sank down into the chair. 'He didn't really have any friends. No one we knew of or came back to the house. He never mentioned anyone at school. There was only Erin.'

'It's likely to be someone older than him,' Meadows said.

'Well, there were lots of people in church he spoke about. He often visited Sarah and he would do Mary Beynon's shopping for her when she wasn't well.'

'Did anyone call at the house to see Donald over the last couple of weeks?' Edris asked.

'No, not that I can think of,' Anwen said.

'What about Tomos?' Cerith said.

'Tomos John?' Edris asked.

'Oh yes,' Anwen said. 'He came around to see Donald when he wasn't well.'

'When was this?' Meadows asked.

216

'A few weeks ago.'

'Would this be just after Dr Rowlands went missing?'

'Yes, I told you that Donald wasn't well at the time.'

'I hope you're not implying that Donald had something to do with Dr Rowlands' murder,' Cerith said.

'It's possible that he was involved somehow,' Meadows said. 'He could have witnessed something or known who killed him.'

Anwen started to cry. 'Why didn't he speak to us? I asked him over and over if something was bothering him. What if he was afraid? What if whoever murdered Dr Rowlands forced Donald to attack that girl. He must have been so frightened.'

'What did Tomos and Donald talk about?' Meadows asked.

'I don't know. Donald was in his room and refused to come down. He got like that sometimes. Tomos said he would have a chat with him and say a prayer. Donald liked that. He seemed a bit better after and came downstairs. Do you think that Donald told Tomos what was bothering him?'

'I don't know,' Meadows said. 'We will speak to Tomos to find out.' Meadows stood. 'I understand that you didn't want to have a family liaison officer.'

'We would rather be on our own,' Cerith said.

'I think it would be wise from now on to accept the help. They can keep you informed of any developments. There will be a press release at some stage and even though we won't release Donald's name in connection to the attack on Stacey Evans, people in the village will probably guess. We also have to inform Stacey's family.'

Anwen put her head in her hands. 'Oh God, no.' She sobbed. 'I don't want people talking about him. Saying he did those things. He wouldn't, I just know he wouldn't.'

'I will do my very best to find out what happened that night,' Meadows said. 'Everyone has a breaking point. Donald was riddled with grief over Erin and may well have been susceptible to persuasion. Whatever happened in the last few weeks, and no matter what people say, can't diminish the love you had for your son or that he had for you. Try to hold on to that.'

Anwen nodded.

'One more thing. Did Donald drive?'

'He's had some lessons, but he hadn't taken his test,' Cerith said.

'Okay, thank you. We'll see ourselves out.'

Cerith and Anwen didn't say anything as Meadows and Edris left the room. As Meadows opened the front door, he welcomed the light. It wasn't just the darkness of the room but the heavy atmosphere that death brings to a home. Grief, he thought, casts a long shadow and it was easy for that shadow to cover you and sink into your pores.

'What now?' Edris asked after Meadows had closed the door.

'I'll give Paskin a call to see if they managed to pick up Tomos John. I think they should keep him at the station for questioning. I want to know why he visited Donald and what he said.'

'Do you think he went there to make sure Donald kept quiet?'

'Why else would he be calling around? Give Valentine a call to see how she got on with Sarah Kelly. I want this lot shaken up.'

Paskin answered on the first ring.

'Did he give you any problems?' Meadows asked.

'We haven't managed to get hold of him,' Paskin said. 'He wasn't at work. There was a man there covering for him. He said Tomos and his father went to some farmers' market in Builth Wells to pick up supplies this morning.'

'I want Tomos and Ellis brought in as soon as they get back. In the meantime go to the school and talk to Mrs Hughes, the headmistress. See who Donald hung around with in school. It doesn't sound like he had any friends his own age but better check it out if only to keep Lester happy.'

'Okay, we'll head over there now.'

'Thanks,' Meadows hung up. 'What did Valentine say?'

'Can't get hold of her. She's not answering.'

'Maybe she took Sarah Kelly to the station. She shouldn't have been that far behind us. Her car's not outside.' He indicated Sarah Kelly's house. 'Let's go and see the Evanses. Hopefully Anthony has calmed down, but I expect he will blow up again when we tell him about Donald.'

* * *

Anthony Evans was stood on the doorstep and Meadows guessed he'd been waiting and had seen the car come up the drive.

'I thought you would come earlier,' Anthony said. 'I've work to do.'

'We won't keep you long,' Meadows said.

Anthony led them into the kitchen where Cloe and Becca sat at the pine table. Cloe looked at Meadows expectantly while Becca's eyes were trained on Edris as he took a seat.

Brianna, the family liaison officer, was making tea.

'Becca wanted to stay home from school today to listen to what you have to say,' Cloe said.

'That's fine,' Meadows said as he sat down, 'but what we discuss today should go no further than this house. That means no posting on social media.'

'We can check up,' Edris said. 'You understand that it's important not to disclose confidential information.' He gave Becca a smile.

Becca nodded.

'I explained to Anthony last night that there have been some developments in the case, although it is not straightforward. We have evidence that connects Donald Hobson to the attack on Stacey.'

'Donald!' Becca shook her head. 'He's a pussy. Stacey was always teasing him, and he never once answered back. She wouldn't have let him anywhere near her.'

'You mean to tell me that that boy raped and murdered my daughter? He was just a kid, still in school,' Anthony said.

'Stacey had told a few people that Donald was following her,' Edris said. 'We also have evidence that shows that he recorded her movements.'

'But they went to school together,' Cloe said. 'They started nursery at the same time. Why would he do it?'

'Because the kid was a weirdo,' Anthony said. 'His parents must have known what he was like, what he did, and they kept quiet. They are as guilty as he is.'

'They didn't know,' Meadows said. 'I would strongly advise you not to have any contact with them. I don't want a repeat of what happened last night.'

Brianna placed a mug of tea in front of each of them and took a seat.

'So, that's it,' Anthony said. 'He kills my daughter, and nothing is done about it.'

'Donald is dead,' Meadows said.

'Yes, but his parents should be held accountable.'

'I understand you are angry, and you want justice for your daughter. The Hobsons have lost their only child, and as well as trying to come to terms with that, they also have to deal with the fact that Donald was at least in some part responsible for Stacey's murder. I think they are suffering enough,' Meadows said.

'What do you mean Donald was partly responsible?' Cloe asked.

'We don't think that Donald acted alone. Our evidence shows that someone else was present that night.'

'Who?' Anthony asked.

'We don't know.' Meadows took a sip of his tea.

'You think it's Rhodri, don't you? That's why you arrested him,' Anthony said.

'I told you last night we have no evidence to link Rhodri to Stacey's murder. What makes you think that he is responsible?'

'Well, after you took him I started to think about it. He'd look at her sometimes, you know what I mean. Give her a smile or a wink.'

'He'd flirt with her,' Cloe said. 'You know what young girls are like. She'd find some excuse to go up the fields when he was working. I didn't think that much of it at the time, only that he had a wife and son, and he shouldn't have been flirting. Then we thought what if he had taken it further? Wanted more? If Stacey refused and he wouldn't take no for an answer?'

'Then there was the night before the doctor went missing,' Anthony said.

'What happened that night?' Meadows asked.

'Stacey was babysitting that night for Harry. Rhodri and Gemma said they were going to Swansea for a night out. Stacey didn't get back until after four in the morning. I was already up.'

'Did she say why she was so late?'

'She said Rhodri's car had broken down. He'd tried to fix it himself but had to call for help.'

'Are you sure it was that night?'

'Yes,' Cloe said. 'It was a school day, and I was worried she would be too tired to go, but she went in. I had an appointment with Dr Rowlands that morning. When I got to the surgery it was bedlam as the doctor hadn't turned up and there was no one to see the patients. The papers are saying that there is a serial killer in the village. If Rhodri killed Dr Rowlands maybe Stacey knew something about it.'

'Or are you saying that Donald killed Dr Rowlands as well as Stacey?' Anthony said.

'No, at this stage we don't know if Donald had any involvement in Dr Rowlands' death, neither do we have any evidence that Rhodri was involved. Did Stacey say anything to you about that night?'

'No, other than explaining why she was so late.'

'How did she seem? Worried? Unusually quiet?'

'No, other than being tired she seemed fine,' Cloe said.

'How did she get home that morning?'

'I think Rhodri dropped her off, he usually did when she had been babysitting,' Anthony said.

'Did you hear a car?'

'I don't think so. The dogs were barking when she came in.'

'So are you going to arrest Rhodri again? You said Donald didn't act alone,' Cloe asked.

'It could well be that if Stacey walked home that morning she may have seen someone but didn't know the relevance.'

'So that's it,' Anthony said.

'We are still working on the investigation. Brianna will keep you updated.' Meadows stood. 'Please stay away from Rhodri and the Hobsons. It won't help us if we have to deal with another incident. If anything else comes to mind, let Brianna know.'

'That was interesting,' Meadows said as he started the car.

'Yeah, Rhodri didn't mention that Stacey babysat the night the doctor went missing or that they were late home.' Edris looked at his phone. 'Still nothing from Valentine. I left her a message.'

'She should have picked it up by now,' Meadows said. He dialled the station number and Sergeant Folland answered.

'Has Valentine brought in Sarah Kelly for fingerprinting?' Meadows asked.

'No, she hasn't been in.'

'At all?'

'No, I haven't seen her. She usually says hello when she comes in. Is there a problem?'

'I'm not sure. She isn't answering her phone. We'll call at Sarah Kelly's house, see if she's been there. Thanks, Folland.' Meadows hung up.

'It's not like her,' Edris said. 'She's always in on time.'

'Maybe her appointment ran over.'

'She would have called in. She knew she was supposed to see Sarah this morning.'

'Yes, you're right.'

Meadows felt uneasy as he drove back into the village and parked outside Sarah's house. There was no sign of Valentine's or Sarah's car. Meadows got out and hammered on the door. When there was no answer he got back in the car.

'You better give Valentine's parents a call. Keep it casual, I don't want to worry them. It may be that she had bad news at the hospital and called them, or even went to see them. Sarah Kelly and Tomos and Ellis John are also missing. I just hope that Valentine isn't in trouble.'

Chapter Thirty

He looked at his watch again and saw that the minute hand had barely moved. Time was crawling along, and he wasn't sure how long he could hold out. His head felt like someone was driving an ice pick into his skull over and over, and all he wanted to do was take some pills and lock himself away. He so desperately wanted it to be over.

It wasn't supposed to happen like this. It was supposed to be peaceful. His actions all along had been to make a difference. Now his plans had to be adapted and there had been little time to pull it together. The police were getting closer, it wouldn't be long now, he just had to stretch it out as long as possible. He'd seen them around the village this morning, it had been so difficult to get indoors without being seen.

If that bloody policewoman hadn't come along, it would have gone smoothly and there would have been plenty of time. He had tried to act normal, but he'd seen her looking at him. There had been a second and third look before he saw realisation dawn on her face. He thought that would be it. He had felt the heat prickle his body and sweat gather on his brow, but she didn't approach him. Maybe it would have been better if she had.

He would have been sat in a police cell now and he could have dragged it out. He didn't want it to end this way. He had a plan and she had come along to ruin it. He wondered if it was the devil's work. They say the devil is always waiting around the corner.

She had followed him alone. Why? He had no idea. She could have made a call. He had to act, he had no choice, but it still pricked at his conscience. As far as he knew she was innocent, worked against those who did wrong. She didn't deserve to die.

First, he'd had to get rid of her car. It hadn't been that difficult. The keys were in her pocket. He'd driven it into the garage and locked the door. Next he had to remove his own car. He had driven to Iris Hawkins' house. Popped in to see her then walked back. He was sure no one would see it there. If his car was missing, they wouldn't come to his house. The walk back had been difficult. He tried to stay off the main road but that meant traipsing through fields and getting wet. Now, as well as the headache, he was cold and tired and he still had to get rid of her. The police would call around, he was sure of it. He would have to wait until dark. If he could hold out that long. He looked at the shotgun on the kitchen table. It was loaded ready to use. The thought made him feel sick. He'd taken it from Iris. She'd asked him to get rid of it after her husband died. He was glad now he had kept it. He just hoped he had the strength to carry it through. He sat down at the kitchen table, he thought about eating something even if it was just to get him through the rest of the day. His stomach turned at the thought of food. Instead he picked up his bible and began to read, hoping the words would bring him some comfort.

Chapter Thirty-one

The atmosphere in the office was tense as all eyes were fixed on Meadows. Uniformed officers gathered around with the team, all keen to help with the search for Valentine. Edris was talking on the phone and Lester was stood next to Meadows.

Lester cleared his throat. 'So far we know that Valentine attended a hospital appointment at eight thirty this morning. We've spoken to security at the hospital and her car is seen arriving at eight fifteen and leaving at just after nine. The car is picked up on traffic cameras on the M4 shortly after. She would have been heading towards Bryn Mawr to the station to check in, but she didn't arrive. There are several turns she could have taken but my guess is she went to Gaer Fawr. She was due to call on Sarah Kelly this morning but why she would go without checking in is what is troubling. Sarah Kelly is missing, as is her car. There have been no sightings.' He turned to Meadows and nodded.

'Paskin, what's the status on Tomos and Ellis John?' Meadows asked.

'Builth Wells police have checked the farmer's market. There was no sign of Tomos' Land Rover. They also talked to the vendors, most of them knew both Tomos and his father from previous visits but they haven't seen them today.'

'Edris, did you have any luck getting hold of Gemma Lewis' parents?'

'Yes,' Edris said. 'Gemma and Rhodri are not there. Gemma's mother said that they weren't expecting them today or anytime soon.'

'What about the car?' Meadows asked.

'It hasn't been picked up by traffic, if they were heading for Bristol it would have been picked up on camera, besides they would have had plenty of time to get there.'

'Right.' Meadows ran his hands through his hair. 'I want as many uniforms as can be spared in Gaer Fawr. I want every door knocked. I want to know if anyone has seen Valentine or her car. Also check to see if they have seen the Lewises, Sarah Kelly, or Tomos John.'

'There are a lot of officers coming in that aren't on shift to volunteer,' Folland said. 'She's very popular and everyone wants to see her found safely.'

'Good,' Meadows said. 'Paskin and Hanes, you take the Lewis house, knock the door down if you have to.'

'Do you think that's necessary,' Lester asked. 'She could be anywhere, and you already established that Rhodri Lewis' DNA didn't match any of the crime scenes.'

'It doesn't mean that he isn't involved,' Meadows said. 'Valentine's been missing for almost four hours and so far we haven't had a single sighting. For all we know she could be being held at one of the houses. We need to search them all. Edris and I will go to Tomos John's house. That leaves Sarah Kelly.'

'I'll organise the search there,' Folland said.

'All three are suspects, she has to be with one of them,' Meadows said. 'Did Vicar Daniels come in to give fingerprints?'

'No,' Paskin said.

227

'Then we better send someone around to the vicarage. See why he didn't turn up. He may well know something or as he also had writing on his door, he could be in danger.'

'I'll organise a press release for an appeal for information on Valentine's whereabouts,' Lester said. 'I'll call personally on her parents to let them know the situation.'

'Right, let's go.' Meadows grabbed his coat.

* * *

Tomos John and his father lived in a small cottage overlooking the neighbouring farm. While Edris hammered on the door, Meadows peered through the windows. All was quiet inside.

'Let's try around the back,' Meadows said.

They hurried around the back of the cottage and saw a Land Rover parked near the back door. Meadows banged on the door then moved to the window. He could see a sink with plates and cups stacked on the side, beyond that was a bare kitchen table.

'If we smash the window I should be able to climb through,' Edris said.

Meadows moved to the door, turned the handle and the door opened.

'Tomos,' he called as he stepped inside.

The cottage was silent.

'Search this place,' Meadows said.

He ran upstairs and threw open the first door. It was a bedroom. The bed was unmade, and the wardrobe door was open. A few clothes were heaped on the bottom, the hangers were bare. He slipped his gloves on and took a quick look in the drawers then moved to the next room. It was the same as the first.

'Nothing down here,' Edris called.

Meadows checked the bathroom then joined Edris downstairs. 'It looks like they have cleared out in a hurry,' he said.

Outside they peered in the Land Rover and Edris hit his fists against the bonnet. 'Where is she?'

'They couldn't have got far without a vehicle,' Meadows said. 'If they took Valentine's car it will be picked up. We have the force out looking. Call Paskin and see if they've had any luck over at the Lewises' house.'

As Meadows was pulling away from the cottage he noticed a farmer in the field. He stopped the car and jumped out.

'Excuse me,' Meadows shouted.

The farmer looked up and started to make his way across the field. As Meadows waited he watched a knot of sparrows darting in and out of the hedgerow. They kept together as they foraged for food. They reminded him of the people he had encountered during this investigation. Alone they exuded sadness, yet they were bound together by grief. Could they have drawn strength from each other, found a common purpose and a way to alleviate their pain?'

'What can I do for you?' The farmer interrupted Meadows thoughts.

'Have you seen Ellis and Tomos John today?'

'Yeah, saw them going out at about eight this morning.'

'In the Land Rover?'

'No, Sarah picked them up.'

'Have you seen any other cars? Or maybe a woman, shoulder-length dark hair.'

'No, haven't seen anyone else today.'

'Okay, thanks for your help.'

'They're with Sarah Kelly,' Meadows said as he got back in the car. 'It was too early for Valentine, she would have been on her way to the hospital when they left. Unless she ran into them later. What did Paskin say?'

'Looks like the Lewises have cleared out and there is no answer from Mary Beynon or Vicar Daniels. House-to-house hasn't turned up any sightings of Valentine. She has to be with one of them and they have taken her out of the village. If she isn't already–'

'Don't go there,' Meadows said. 'So far the victims have been killed because they were believed to have done some wrong. Valentine hasn't done anything wrong. They left me alive that night at Bill's farm.'

'Yes, but she could be lying somewhere injured.'

'Then we do what you always do when you lose something. Retrace your steps. We'll start at the hospital. There is every chance she went to see Blackwell.'

'If Blackwell had a signal on his phone we could ring him,' Edris said. 'It would be quicker.'

'I want to go there. We can look at the footage, see who else was at the hospital at the same time. Something threw her off track and sent her chasing after someone.'

'Tomos John, his father and Sarah left early enough to go to the hospital. She could have seen one of them there,' Edris said.

'I think they have run,' Meadows said. 'They packed before they left.'

'So someone else, maybe they were supposed to pick up someone from hospital, Valentine saw someone get in the car with them and followed.'

'Could be, but where were they heading? Get someone to check the footage from the cameras this morning, see who else was on the road at the same time as Valentine.'

While Edris was on the phone, Meadows sped towards the hospital with his mind whirring. There were too many possibilities and the only way they would be able to help Valentine was to pin it down. Find which of the suspects she met with. The Lewises had gone – was it because Rhodri was involved? Was it because they knew something and were scared? The same applied to Tomos and Sarah.

'They are on it,' Edris said.

'Good, I'm thinking that Tomos John and Sarah were sat next to Donald at the film night. Maybe Tomos John followed Donald and they attacked Stacey together. He's bald so he could be the one wearing the wig.'

'Yeah, and the others may not have noticed that he left the vicarage with Donald. Sarah would have noticed.'

'But the injuries on the doctor trouble me. They are too close to Harry Lewis' amputations. Same missing digits.' Meadows thought of the sparrows he had seen in the field – where there was one, another wasn't far away. 'The only conclusion that I can come up with is that they are all in on it. Stacey was babysitting the night the doctor was killed so it would make sense to keep her quiet.'

'So, the four of them, five if you include Tomos' father.'

'Six with Donald.'

'I can't see that they all would be involved. Besides, Valentine wouldn't have tried to tackle all of them alone. If she guessed, she would have called it in.'

'Then we have to assume she learned some information and wanted to check it out first.'

Meadows pulled up outside the hospital and the two of them hurried down the corridors and up the stairs to the ward. Blackwell was sat up in bed reading.

'What's with all the visits today?' Blackwell asked.

'Have you seen Valentine today?' Edris asked.

'Yeah, I saw her this morning, what's happened?'

Meadows quickly filled him in, and Blackwell pulled back the bedsheets and swung his legs off the bed.

'Whoa,' Meadows said. 'What are you doing?'

'I'm coming with you to find her.'

'No, you're not,' Meadows said. 'You have to stay here, you're not well.'

'You can't stop me,' Blackwell said.

'No, but if you collapse again you'll only delay us. The best thing you can do for Valentine is stay here and tell us everything she said to you this morning.'

Blackwell huffed but he put his legs back onto the bed.

'I was half asleep when she came. She's been here every evening since I came in. She blamed herself for what happened to Donald Hobson and this morning she was on about putting it right.'

'In what way?'

'She said she had seen someone, but she wanted to check it out first. Something about him not wearing a wig.'

'Valentine was attending an oncology appointment,' Edris said.

'We gotta go,' Meadows said. 'We'll call you as soon as we have news.'

'Call the hospital, still no signal,' Blackwell called after them.

'Why didn't you mention this earlier?' Meadows asked. 'You just said hospital appointment.'

'Because she didn't want anyone to know, she'd found a lump in her breast so was getting it checked out. It didn't seem relevant at the time.'

'No, but it's obvious the wig the killer wears is not for a disguise. It's because of illness.'

They located the oncology department where only a few people were sat in the waiting room. Meadows approached the receptionist, showed his ID, and asked to be admitted to the office. The receptionist, a middle-aged woman with dark blonde hair, let them in. A younger woman sat at a desk and stopped typing when they entered.

'We need to have a look at your patient list from between eight and nine this morning.'

'I'm sorry, I can't show you the list. It's confidential and you of all people should know there are procedures to follow.'

'One of our officers attended this morning, Reena Valentine. She is now missing. We believe that she may have met with someone here. This person is a dangerous individual and is wanted in connection with five murders.'

'I'm sorry but I could lose my job if I handed over that information.'

Edris stepped forward. 'Do you understand what we are telling you? If this person–'

Meadows held up his hand to silence Edris. He knew Edris was about to lose his temper and it wouldn't help the situation. 'Please,' he said. 'Detective Valentine is in danger. We need to find her as quickly as we can. You are our only hope of doing that.'

The receptionist turned to her colleague. 'Della, go and find Mr Henshaw. See if he will authorise me to give the information to the detectives.'

When Della had left the office, the receptionist turned back to her computer, hit the keys, and brought up a list. 'I think it may be quicker if I help look for my boss.' She stood up and nodded to the screen.

'Thank you,' Meadows said. As soon as the receptionist left the room he leaned over, ran his fingers down the list and saw a name he recognised.

Chapter Thirty-two

Darkness had fallen while they had been in the hospital and as Meadows drove into Gaer Fawr he could see children dressed in Halloween costumes walking along the pavement. The headlights picked out their ghoulish masks and gave the village a sinister atmosphere.

'Vicar Daniels, I still can't believe it,' Edris shook his head. 'He is supposed to be a man of God.'

'Considering the Bible quotes that were left on the bodies we should have looked at him as a credible suspect.'

'We did look,' Edris said. 'There was nothing on him. His reputation is immaculate, and no one had anything bad to say about him. Then there was the writing on his door.'

'He probably did that himself to throw us off.'

'Unless he told Valentine something, and that's what sent her off looking.'

'No, she told Blackwell the person she saw wasn't wearing a wig. I think she recognised Vicar Daniels. It looks like he is sick.'

'Yeah, he's sick alright,' Edris said. 'Why would Valentine go after him alone?'

'I don't know. I imagine she wanted to be sure.'

Meadows took the turn to the vicarage and found Hanes and Paskin waiting along with two uniformed officers. Paskin approached the car as Meadows drew to a halt.

'There is no sign of the vicar or his car,' Paskin said. 'We are just about to break the door down.'

The two uniformed officers moved to the front door with a battering ram. Two swings and the door burst open.

'Vicar Daniels!' Meadows shouted as he stepped inside.

They spread out and searched the house. Meadows could hear doors opening and closing. Anxiety gnawed at his stomach as each voice reporting no sign of Valentine diminished his hopes. He returned to the front door.

'Break down the garage door,' he said to the two officers.

It took a little longer to get the garage open but when the door was finally lifted they found Valentine's car inside.

Meadows snapped on latex gloves, opened the car door, and took the keys out of the ignition. He then moved to the back of the car. He didn't want to look. A silence fell over the garage as Edris came to stand next to him. Paskin stood at the entrance. Meadows turned the key, and the boot sprang open. It was empty. He let out the breath he had been holding.

'I've put out a call for his car,' Paskin said. 'There is still no sightings of Sarah Kelly, Tomos John, Mary Beynon or the Lewises. They could all be together.'

'That would be my guess. Have you checked the church?'

'We looked when we called around earlier. It was locked.'

'You said the vicar was wealthy,' Meadows said.

'Yes, and he was left a property and money in a will, but the house was sold.'

'See if he has any other property, a holiday home or caravan in his name.'

'Okay,' Paskin said.

He turned to Edris and the two uniformed officers. 'We need to search this place. Look for any paperwork that would give us an indication of where he might go. Bank statements, old photographs, a favourite place, anything.'

Meadows started in the vicar's study. There was heaps of paperwork but nothing helpful. Paskin was going through old bank statements and Edris and Hanes were checking the rest of the house. There were several letters from the hospital with appointments for chemotherapy and some information on palliative care. It was obvious from these that Vicar Daniels was dying.

'There is a fair amount of money in his bank account but nothing that stands out,' Paskin said. 'The last statement is dated over a month ago.'

'Found this.' Edris came into the room carrying a small bottle. 'Liquid morphine.'

'There is nothing here,' Meadows said. He could feel his frustration building along with those around him. 'You said he gave the money left to him to the church. He'd have access to the accounts so there could be something there.'

'What? You think there's a property owned by the church?' Edris said.

'It's worth a look. They must have had a plan and somewhere to go. They can't use any of their bank cards or they will be picked up. Come on, there has to be paperwork in the church.'

They ran down the path to the church with the two uniformed officers behind them carrying the battering ram. Meadows tried the handle of the church door and it opened.

'It was locked earlier, honestly,' Hanes said.

'He must have come back after you came here or it's one of the wardens.' Meadows said. 'Stay here with Paskin,

Edris and I will go in. If Vicar Daniels is in there we don't want to cause him to panic.'

Meadows stepped into the porch and as he turned to walk into the auditorium, he saw Vicar Daniels standing by the altar.

'I knew it wouldn't be long until you got here.' Vicar Daniels raised a shotgun and pointed it at Meadows.

Chapter Thirty-three

Meadows raised his hands as he heard Edris take a sharp intake of breath.

'Why don't you put the gun down and we can talk,' Meadows said.

Vicar Daniels shook his head. 'I can't do that, not yet.'

'Okay, let Detective Edris leave and it will be just you and me. I won't come any closer.'

Vicar Daniels nodded.

'Go,' Meadows said.

Edris hesitated.

'I'll be fine,' Meadows said.

'I'll just be outside.' Edris moved slowly backwards.

Meadows knew that Edris would call for an armed response unit and as much as he didn't like the gun pointing at him, he knew he had to get Vicar Daniels to talk before they arrived. He needed to find Valentine.

'That gun looks heavy,' Meadows said. 'I know you don't want to hurt me, and we don't want any accidents. Why don't you lower it? I'll sit down.'

'Okay, but no sudden movements. I really don't want to hurt you.'

Meadows inched towards the pew and sat. It was only then that he realised how weak his legs felt. 'We are all so worried about Detective Valentine. Can you tell me where she is?'

Vicar Daniels glanced down at his watch. 'Not yet,' he said. He sat heavily on the steps and set the gun down keeping his hand on the barrel.

'Can you at least tell me if she is okay? I know you are a good man. I've read all the wonderful things people say about you. Not one bad word. You're not well. Valentine has a family who are worried, a lot of people care about her. She is a good hard-working woman. Is she with the others?'

'Others?'

'I know you didn't act alone. Sarah, Ellis, Tomos, Gemma, Rhodri, and Mary are all missing. They've all gone into hiding. Was that the plan? They stay away and you take the blame?'

'No, it's not like that. It wasn't supposed to happen like this.' Vicar Daniels rubbed his hand over his eyes. 'For the record, Ellis had nothing to do with it. Tomos didn't want to leave his father behind. I only wanted to make things better. I worked so hard to build a loving congregation and community, one that helps each other. When I took over the parish barely a handful of people came to church. I saw it blossom, I wanted to leave it like that but all I saw was pain. Mary Beynon looking older than her years. Her granddaughter cruelly taken and her daughter in prison. The guilt and shame making her ill, and no justice. The person responsible left to carry on hurting others.'

'We did everything we could for Ella Beynon. Her death was a tragic accident. She took pills that were left lying around the house. Her mother was negligent, and she is serving her time. We could never prove that Ryan Phillips was the one to leave the drugs in the house. It may well be that they weren't his drugs,' Meadows said.

'You don't believe that,' Vicar Daniels said. 'I know you felt guilty for what happened. You wished you never gave the child back to her mother. I also know you to be a good man. I see it in your eyes. That's why I couldn't kill you that night at Bill's farm. I just wanted to warn you. You guessed the meaning of the writing on Stacey's body and I was afraid you would figure things out before my work was done. I saw you on the bridge that night and I knew it was a sign for me to act. Everyone was busy trying to stop the flood water, so no one missed me. I asked Sarah to make sure you were okay.'

'I expect Sarah was easy to convince to help you. Another one full of grief and anger.'

'Poor woman. She has suffered so much. She needlessly lost her only child. She gave up everything for her. Her dreams of going to university and travelling. She lived through Erin. Poor child, driven to her death by a doctor who should have helped her and a spiteful girl who made her life a misery. Have you ever witnessed a mother walk behind her child's coffin? The grief so heavy they can barely put one foot in front of another. That pain never goes away. Sarah was barely living a half-life. She may appear tough, but she is as fragile as spun sugar.'

'I have seen people in pain. Seen them lose loved ones through violent crime and tragedy. You can't take that pain away. All I can hope is that the work I do goes some way towards bringing closure.'

'You and I are not so different,' Vicar Daniels said. 'We both want to see justice done.'

'No, I just find the people responsible for committing a crime. I don't decide on the punishment. I leave that to the law.'

'But the law of God is very clear.'

'And shouldn't God be the one to decide who gets punished? From my understanding it is about being able to forgive. Isn't that the way you get peace? Let go of the anger?'

'I… I tried.' Vicar Daniels bought his hand to his head and winced.

'You're not well. Please, let me help you. Just leave the gun and come with me.'

Vicar Daniels took his hand away from the gun. 'I'm tired and lost. I did do the right thing, didn't I?'

Meadows stood slowly. 'Come on, let me take you somewhere you can rest.'

'No.' Vicar Daniels grabbed the gun.

'Okay.' Meadows held his hands up and sat back down. 'Too many people have already died. Don't you think it's time to end it?'

'Yes,' Vicar Daniels said. 'That's what I intend to do but you are distracting me, all these questions. I'm trying to get you to understand.'

'I do,' Meadows said. 'What happened to Erin was tragic. She needed help and the doctor failed her on that count, but did he really deserve to die?'

'It was the only way. I had to ease their suffering.'

'And Stacey Evans? I doubt she realised that her actions would lead to Erin's death. She was just a kid herself. Who knows what guilt she carried?'

'She was never sorry.'

'I guess we will never know,' Meadows said. He noticed the vicar glance at his watch again and wondered what he was waiting for. 'This started with Dr Rowlands. Is it because you are sick? I saw the letters from the hospital.'

'This was never about me. You've seen yourself the damage that was done to Harry Lewis. Gemma and Rhodri were so thankful to God for sparing their child, but he is still suffering, all of them are. The nightly fits, the worry that the next fit will be too much for his young body. Then there was the anger that ate away at Rhodri and corroded his relationship with Gemma.'

'But you also suffered. What happened?'

'It started out as headaches, but not the normal ones you get. Then I started to feel sick. Dr Rowlands said it was cluster headaches caused by stress. So I did what he advised, cut down on caffeine, and take more exercise.' Vicar Daniels smiled. 'I guess it's my own fault. I should have known it was something more serious, but you trust a doctor, don't you? Each time I went to see him the diagnosis changed, next it was migraines and medication. By the time he referred me to a neurologist it was too late. An inoperable brain tumour. I started to forget things and think things, bad thoughts kept entering my mind. I had chemo but it was only to give me a little more time. My hair fell out, so I bought a wig. I didn't want anyone to know.' He tugged hard at his hair and the wig fell away. 'I'm dying and I didn't want to leave behind all this suffering, it was a chance to put things right.'

'By killing Dr Rowlands?'

'It came to me in a dream. You know that's the way God communicates with you. There are loads of examples in the Old Testament. I knew then my calling.' Vicar Daniels looked at his watch then picked up the gun. 'I've told you everything, it's time now.'

Chapter Thirty-four

'Wait,' Meadows said. 'You haven't told me where Detective Valentine is. She was only doing her job.'

'She was sent to stop me.'

Meadows thought that if he could keep him talking the armed response team would have time to get there. He wasn't sure what the vicar meant to do. Shoot him? And try to get away? The armed response team may have a better chance of disarming him, maybe a shot that would simply disable him, but if they thought the vicar was about to shoot him they may take a fatal shot. Meadows needed Vicar Daniels alive if he had any chance of finding Valentine.

'You didn't kill the doctor alone,' Meadows said. 'You had help from Donald.'

'Yes.'

'And Sarah, Rhodri, Gemma, and Tomos. Did Mary help you?'

'Yes?'

'How did you persuade them?'

Vicar Daniels rested the gun on the floor. 'I didn't persuade them. It wasn't like that. They were chosen.'

'How?'

'After I had my diagnosis I was feeling down so I arranged a movie night. They were the only ones to come. No one else bothered out of the whole congregation. The film had a theme of redemption. We talked about those who couldn't be redeemed, not in this life. I asked them if the hand of God was removed from them, what would they do. Sarah was the first to speak. She said she would kill Stacey and Dr Rowlands if there was no consequences. Donald agreed with Sarah. Mary of course wanted revenge for her granddaughter, Tomos for his mother, and Gemma for Harry. That's how it started.

'We planned an experiment to see how easy it would be to carry it out and if it would lighten our burdens. I bought a pay-as-you-go phone, and we placed a false call to get the doctor out of the house. It worked. Then I drove Mary to Ryan Phillips' house, and we saw that there was no one around at the dead of night.

'The more we talked about it the more it made sense. No one would miss Ryan Phillips and his mother. If he was left, he would continue to sell his drugs, until another innocent child or person died. Complaints to the GMC about the doctor had done no good, he would carry on ruining people's lives. How many more would have to suffer? We knew then that God had put us together and we needed to act.'

'What about Stacey Evans?' Meadows asked.

'Gemma knew about Stacey's affair with Rhodri, she caught a sexually transmitted disease from him, so she knew he had been unfaithful although she never let on to Rhodri that she knew. Stacey was the sticking point, we couldn't agree on her penance. So, we decided to let God decide her fate and concentrated on our plan for Dr Rowlands.'

'You called him out to Iris Hawkins' house,' Meadows said. 'Away from prying eyes, and I guess you knew information about Iris you needed.'

'Yes, I'm a regular visitor. It's also where I got the gun. It was her husband's and I said I would dispose of it for her. When the doctor arrived he found his way blocked by my car. I told him I had a puncture and didn't have a wheel brace. He didn't even look at my car. He went straight to his boot. Rhodri was hiding, he came behind the doctor, hit him over the head and we shoved him in the boot, tying his hands and feet together.

'We drove to the reservoir, transferred him to my boot then dumped his car but kept his phone. The others were waiting at the vicarage. I gave the doctor some morphine. I didn't want him to suffer too much. It wasn't easy what we did, and it was too much for Donald. He was sick. Mary kept a look out when we did what was necessary then we moved him in the wheelbarrow to the grave. I wrote on him so it would be there for all eternity. We had dug the grave over a few nights taking it in turns. No one went up that part of the graveyard in the winter; by spring the earth would have settled, and the grass grown over. If it wasn't for the storm the doctor would still be there, and Donald would still be with us.'

'You sent a text to Linda Rowlands,' Meadows said.

'Yes, it was later than planned because we were all so tired. Then I got rid of the phone, threw it in the river. Linda wasn't that bothered by her husband's absence and she's not exactly a grieving widow. We were a little worried about Donald but Tomos went to see him and convinced him that everything was okay. No one had come for us, no one was looking for the doctor, and God was on our side. I saw a lightness come over Rhodri, a release. Sarah was happier than I had seen her in a long time.

'We had to do the same for Mary. We waited a few weeks then I drove to Ryan Phillips' house alone and threw a brick through the back door window. It wasn't possible to write on their bodies but the words on the brick would burn with them. The next night I took Mary with me. We parked across the road, then when I was sure there was no one around I crept around the back of the house, removed the board from the broken window and poured in petrol. I moved to the front door and poured petrol through the letter box and soaked a rag. I gave Mary the pleasure of lighting the fire. Then she went back to the car. I couldn't let the neighbours burn, they were innocent of any crime, so I waited until the fire took hold then I hammered on the door. I saw a light come on then ran to the car and drove off.'

'Where were the others?' Meadows asked.

'They didn't come with us but would have provided an alibi if we needed one; as it was, no one came to ask questions. Mary gave a statement to the police, but it was just routine, no one guessed she played any part in the fire. That just left Stacey. It was left up to Donald. He didn't want to kill her, just humiliate her. He had been filming her for a while and he uploaded the video, but it wasn't enough. We arranged another film night and Donald left as we settled down to watch the film. I decided to follow him. I won't pretend that I wasn't shocked by what I saw. She'd tempted him and he'd succumbed.'

'Tempted him? He tied her up and raped her,' Meadows said.

'That's what she drove him to do. He left her tied up and alive. She would have known it was him, even with his silly disguise. If Donald got caught we would all be caught. So I killed her for all of us and I felt at peace. I could leave now knowing that they would be okay. There would be no more pain and suffering.'

'Stacey's family are suffering, Jean and Ryan Phillips had a family, and what about Donald's parents? They have lost their only son.'

'I know and I pray for them every day. Donald was a lovely boy, and I didn't want to kill him. That was my final test.' A tear ran down Vicar Daniels face. 'He'd got himself in a state and was convinced that he would be arrested and charged with Stacey's murder. He knew of course that one of us must have gone after him. It was too much in the end and he wanted to come clean. I went up the quarry and took him a flask of tea. I put in some morphine, I didn't want him to suffer. I told him everything he had done had been for Erin and now he could have some peace. He said the only way to have peace now was to confess. I persuaded him to go to the top of the quarry so we could say a prayer together for Erin. He guessed my intention at the last minute and he struggled but the morphine had made him weak, so it didn't take much to get him over.

'The look in his eyes will go with me to the grave. Sometimes I felt like I had been dreaming, then I would get moments of clarity and panic. I never meant for things to get out of hand. When I saw all those people at Rhodri's house last night, it scared me. They were so angry. It's not what I want to leave behind. I don't want anyone else to get hurt.' Vicar Daniels stood up and picked up the gun. 'I'm so tired now.'

'Please, just tell me where Valentine is,' Meadows said.

'She is safe with Saint Herbert.' Vicar Daniels gave Meadows a smile then put the gun under his chin and pulled the trigger.

Chapter Thirty-five

The gun shot was still ringing in Meadows' ears as the armed response team moved in. He had stood up before the vicar shot himself, he recalled shouting out but there was nothing he could do.

'Are you okay?' Edris asked.

Meadows turned his head away from the horror in front of him. 'Yeah, I'm fine.'

'For a moment I thought... we heard the gunshot.'

Meadows took a moment to gather his thoughts. 'We still need to find Valentine.'

'Did he tell you where to find her?'

'No, he said she was with Saint Herbert.'

'What? No.'

'It doesn't mean she's dead.' Meadows put his hand on Edris' shoulder. 'We need to think. Where would we find Saint Herbert?'

Edris looked blank.

'The graveyard,' Meadows said. 'A tomb, old headstone, come on.'

Paskin hurried up to Meadows as soon as he stepped outside the church. 'Rhodri Lewis and Sarah Kelly's cars have been found parked at ABS hire. It looks like they hired a minibus.'

'The vicar kept looking at his watch. He was trying to give them time. You need to alert all ports and airports. They could be leaving the country. Get a trace on the minibus and see what direction it was heading. Although I think it may be too late. Hanes, go into the village and look to see if you can find a memorial for Saint Herbert or anything connected to him, that's our only clue to Valentine's whereabouts. The rest of you' – he looked at the uniformed officers that were gathered – 'search the graveyard. Every inch.'

Meadows got a torch from the car and went to the oldest graves, his torch running over each stone and the surrounding area looking for any disturbance. All around he could see torchlights moving through the graveyard as officers spread out.

'She's not here,' Meadows called to Edris.

'What about the quarry?' Edris asked. 'It's named after him.'

'Good thinking.'

* * *

They raced up the mountain side with a stream of blue lights following behind. The barrier was still down allowing them to drive into the quarry.

'Valentine!' Edris shouted into the darkness.

'Valentine, Reena, can you hear us,' Meadows called as he ran to the kilns.

As the quarry filled with shouts and torchlight, Meadows sat down on a nearby rock. He could feel his hope of finding Valentine alive ebbing away and see it in the faces of those searching. He wished he could light a joint to clear his head. He tried to think over all that Vicar Daniels had said to him in the last moments, and all the places connected to the case. He was fairly certain now that she wasn't with the others, they wouldn't risk taking her with them if they were fleeing the country and the vicar had no cause to lie to him. Vicar Daniels must have been sure he could work out the location, Meadows thought.

'She's not here,' Edris said.

'Let's go back to the church, there may be something in the records. For all we know, Saint Herbert could be buried at another church or a memorial set up outside the village somewhere.'

As Meadows drove down the mountain the rain started. A few heavy drops at first then it fell in a great torrent so that even with the windscreen wipers at double speed visibility was poor. It reminded him of the night of the storm and the men that stood at the bridge laying sandbags.

'She could be out in this,' Edris said. 'What if she's lying in a ditch somewhere and the water is coming in. Did anyone check under the bridge? That water rises quickly.'

'You're letting your imagination run away with you,' Meadows said. 'We'll get someone to check the bridge, but I was thinking about the night of the storm and how the graveyard is sloped.'

'Yeah, and?'

'Sandbags were put along the church. The caretaker said it was to stop the water running below. Some of the old churches had crypts, didn't they?'

'They would have buried important people there,' Edris said.

Meadows put his foot down and when they reached the church, they both leapt out of the car and ran around the outside. Meadows kept his torch on the ground close to the stone of the church building as he looked for an entrance.

'There's nothing here,' Edris said.

'Then it has to be inside.' Meadows led the way in. SOCO were collecting evidence and Vicar Daniels hadn't been moved. 'Check down the side.' Meadows moved down the aisle, the sight before him made his stomach flip but he had to pass the scene.

'I need to get to the nave,' Meadows said.

Mike, the forensic officer looked up. 'Go, just try and watch where you step.'

Meadows did his best to use the pathway set out by forensics although some places he couldn't avoid stepping on as he searched the floor of the nave.

'Nothing down there,' Edris said as he picked his way to Meadows.

'Let's try the vestry.'

Meadows opened the door and was met by a smell of damp. Against the wall was an oak desk and chair, with shelves above. On the opposite wall, an old wooden cupboard.

'I'll check for a register,' Edris said and approached the cupboard.

Meadows scanned the floor. In the centre of the room was a faded oval rug. He crouched down and pulled the rug. Beneath was a wooden trap door.

'It's here.' Meadows took hold of the iron ring and yanked. The door opened easily to reveal stone steps. The smell of damp and decay grew stronger as Meadows descended the steps.

'Valentine,' he called as he shone his torch around.

There was a muffled sound. Meadows shone his torch in the direction and saw two terrified eyes looking at him.

'Reena.' Meadows rushed forward with Edris close behind.

Valentine was tied to a wooden post that held up the ceiling. Behind her sat a sarcophagus engraved with Saint Herbert's name on the side.

Meadows pulled off Valentine's gag as Edris unbound her hands and legs.

Valentine was shaking violently. Her teeth chattering.

'It's okay, you're safe now,' Meadows said. He tried to help her to her feet, but she couldn't stand.

'I've got you.' Edris scooped her up and carried her to the vestry where he draped his coat around her shoulders.

Meadows fetched a glass of water and handed it to her. 'Are you hurt?'

'No, he didn't hurt me. I'm so sorry. I saw him at the hospital and recognised him. He didn't have his wig on, and I thought about the synthetic hair found with each victim. I wanted to make sure, so I followed him. I didn't think he would realise the significance of me seeing him without a wig.'

'Well, that's my fault,' Edris said. 'I asked him if he knew if any members of his congregation wore a wig.'

'No, it's not your fault, I shouldn't have been so stupid. I thought I would ask him a couple of questions then bring him in. I thought it would make up for messing up with Donald. When I knocked the door he invited me in, said he had been expecting me. Once I was inside he pulled a gun on me. I really fucked up this time.'

'It's okay,' Meadows said. 'All that matters is that you are safe.'

'I thought I would never get out of there. He said I would be okay, that you would come for me. You know I've never prayed so much in all my life. I think I'm going to have to go to church to say thank you.'

'Church?' Edris said. 'After everything that's happened.'

'Because of everything that happened. My prayers were answered.'

'Yeah but not quick enough, while you've been hanging around with Saint Herbert we've missed the Halloween party.'

Valentine laughed. 'Well, it is All Saints' Day.'

Chapter Thirty-six

Meadows stepped into his garden, carrying a glass of wine. The chill in the air was quickly replaced by the warmth of the bonfire. He inhaled deeply and felt himself relax. He loved the smell of an outdoor fire. Edris was stood by the fire cradling a bottle of beer as he talked to Hanes and Valentine. Blackwell was sat in a chair and Paskin was tucking a blanket over his legs.

'Piss off,' Blackwell said. 'I'm not a bloody invalid.'

'Behave yourself or you won't get a sparkler,' Paskin said.

Blackwell laughed and Meadows smiled. It was good to see the team relaxing and enjoying themselves. He handed Daisy the wine and took a seat next to her.

'Thanks.' She smiled at him.

'Nice of you to throw a party for this lot,' Blackwell said.

'They missed out on the Halloween party they had planned, and I needed to clear the garden and do some burning. Bonfire night seemed like a good opportunity.'

'So, is there any news on Sarah Kelly and the others?' Daisy asked.

'The last information we have is that they landed in Belarus, I guess they chose it because there is no extradition treaty. Vicar Daniels transferred nearly all the church funds, so they'll have enough money to disappear for a while. They can't hide forever.'

'I still can't believe that a group of ordinary people got together, planned and murdered four people.'

'Five if you include Donald. They all knew the vicar had killed him,' Meadows said.

'I suppose you can understand what drove the vicar to kill them,' Blackwell said. 'A brain tumour can change your personality. It looks like it blurred his sense of reality and his faith in the end. He at least thought he was acting on God's command, but the others.' He shook his head.

'Given the right circumstances people act out of character all the time. Put them in a group and they feel anonymous. They wouldn't have felt personally responsible,' Meadows said. 'They acted as a whole. Look at the Stanford prison experiment. Those acting as prison guards acted in a sadistic way.'

'That's not the same,' Blackwell said.

'Isn't it? What about The Milgram shock experiment, look how those people acted on authority and how far they went. They were instructed to commit acts that would normally go against their morals. They had to administer electric shocks to subjects and it got to the point where the shock was increased to a level that would have been fatal. They believed the situation was real, yet a high majority still complied. There are loads of experiments that demonstrate how people act differently under authority or in a group to how they act alone. In this case they were all damaged individuals who were grief stricken and full of anger. Donald was socially awkward, no friends, and grieving for Erin. He felt safe in the group. He was impressionable. They were all given the role of judge, jury and executioner by a person they trusted and believed in.'

'So, you're saying given the right environment we could all end up being killers,' Blackwell said.

'We all like to think of ourselves as good but I reckon there is a little darkness in all of us,' Meadows said.

'I hope you are not talking shop,' Edris said as he came up to the group.

'Yeah he is,' Blackwell said.

'It's our night off and you need to have some fun,' Edris said and took a swig of his beer.

'For once I agree with him,' Blackwell smiled. 'Go on, off you go and play with some sparklers.'

Meadows stood up and held his hand out to Daisy. 'Are you coming?'

'Yeah, you too, Blackwell,' she said.

As they joined the others around the bonfire the sky lit up with a rainbow of colours as the village set off fireworks.

'Here's to Blackwell's speedy recovery,' Edris said, holding up a bottle of beer.

'I'll drink to that,' Meadows said, and raised his glass with the team.

List of Characters

Bryn Mawr police station:

Detective Inspector Winter Meadows
DC Tristan Edris
Sergeant Dyfan Folland
DS Rowena Paskin
DS Stefan Blackwell
DC Reena Valentine
PC Matthew Hanes – uniform officer
Chief Inspector Nathaniel Lester
DS Brianna Lloyd – family liaison officer

Others:

Jerome – commune elder
Daisy Moore – pathologist
Dr David Rowlands
Mike Fielding – forensic officer
Chris Harley – tech
Vicar Timothy Daniels
Gwyn Rees – church caretaker
Stacey Evans – victim

Jack Hopkins – Stacey's ex-boyfriend
Cloe Evans – Stacey's mother
Anthony Evans – Stacey's father
Becca Evans – Stacey's sister
Shannon Dugan – Stacey's friend
Alisha Morgan – Stacey's friend
Donald Hobson – victim
Anwen Hobson – Donald's mother
Cerith Hobson – Donald's father
Gemma Lewis – Rhodri's wife
Rhodri Lewis – suspect
Harry Lewis – son of Rhodri and Gemma
Erin Kelly – Sarah's daughter
Sarah Kelly – suspect
Ellis John – Tomos' father
Tomos John – suspect
William James/Bible Bill – suspect
Ryan Phillips – victim
Jean Phillips – victim
Iris Hawkins – Dr Rowlands' patient

If you enjoyed this book, please let others know by leaving a quick review on Amazon. Also, if you spot anything untoward in the paperback, get in touch. We strive for the best quality and appreciate reader feedback.

editor@thebookfolks.com

www.thebookfolks.com

Following a fall and a bang to the head, a woman's memories come flooding back about an incident that occurred twenty years ago in which her friend was murdered. As she pieces together the events and tells the police, she begins to fear repercussions. DI Winter Meadows must work out the identity of the killer before they strike again.

When the boss of a care home for mentally challenged adults is murdered, the residents are not the most reliable of witnesses. DI Winter Meadows draws on his soft nature to gain the trust of an individual he believes saw the crime. But without unravelling the mystery and finding the evidence, the case will freeze over.

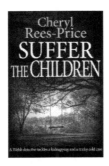

When a toddler goes missing from the family home, the
police and community come out in force to find her.
However, with few traces found after an extensive search,
DI Winter Meadows fears the child has been abducted.
But someone knows something, and when a man is found
dead, the race is on to solve the puzzle.

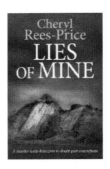

A body is found in an old mine in a secluded spot in the
Welsh hills. There are no signs of struggle so DI Winter
Meadows suspects that the victim, youth worker David
Harris, knew his killer. But when the detective discovers it
is not the first murder in the area, he must dig deep to join
up the dots.

When a family friend is murdered, a journalist begins to probe into his past. What she finds there makes her question everything about her life. Should she bury his secrets with him, or become the next victim of Blue Hollow?

All available FREE with Kindle Unlimited and in paperback.

Printed in Great Britain
by Amazon